DARK GAMBIT

THE PAWN

THE CHILDREN OF THE GODS
BOOK SIXTY-FIVE

I. T. LUCAS

Published by Evening Star Press

EveningStarPress.com

ISBN-13:978-1-957139-37-1

Also by I. T. Lucas

THE CHILDREN OF THE GODS ORIGINS
1: GODDESS'S CHOICE
2: GODDESS'S HOPE

THE CHILDREN OF THE GODS

DARK STRANGER
1: DARK STRANGER THE DREAM
2: DARK STRANGER REVEALED
3: DARK STRANGER IMMORTAL

DARK ENEMY
4: DARK ENEMY TAKEN
5: DARK ENEMY CAPTIVE
6: DARK ENEMY REDEEMED

KRI & MICHAEL'S STORY
6.5: MY DARK AMAZON

DARK WARRIOR
7: DARK WARRIOR MINE
8: DARK WARRIOR'S PROMISE
9: DARK WARRIOR'S DESTINY
10: DARK WARRIOR'S LEGACY

DARK GUARDIAN
11: DARK GUARDIAN FOUND
12: DARK GUARDIAN CRAVED
13: DARK GUARDIAN'S MATE

DARK ANGEL
14: DARK ANGEL'S OBSESSION
15: DARK ANGEL'S SEDUCTION
16: DARK ANGEL'S SURRENDER

DARK OPERATIVE
17: DARK OPERATIVE: A SHADOW OF DEATH
18: DARK OPERATIVE: A GLIMMER OF HOPE
19: DARK OPERATIVE: THE DAWN OF LOVE

PERFECT MATCH

PERFECT MATCH 2: KING'S CHOSEN
PERFECT MATCH 3: CAPTAIN'S CONQUEST

THE CHILDREN OF THE GODS SERIES SETS

BOOKS 1-3: DARK STRANGER TRILOGY—INCLUDES A BONUS SHORT STORY: **THE FATES TAKE A VACATION**

BOOKS 4-6: DARK ENEMY TRILOGY —INCLUDES A BONUS SHORT STORY—**THE FATES' POST-WEDDING CELEBRATION**

BOOKS 7-10: DARK WARRIOR TETRALOGY

BOOKS 11-13: DARK GUARDIAN TRILOGY

BOOKS 14-16: DARK ANGEL TRILOGY

BOOKS 17-19: DARK OPERATIVE TRILOGY

BOOKS 20-22: DARK SURVIVOR TRILOGY

BOOKS 23-25: DARK WIDOW TRILOGY

BOOKS 26-28: DARK DREAM TRILOGY

BOOKS 29-31: DARK PRINCE TRILOGY

BOOKS 32-34: DARK QUEEN TRILOGY

BOOKS 35-37: DARK SPY TRILOGY

BOOKS 38-40: DARK OVERLORD TRILOGY

BOOKS 41-43: DARK CHOICES TRILOGY

BOOKS 44-46: DARK SECRETS TRILOGY

BOOKS 47-49: DARK HAVEN TRILOGY

BOOKS 50-52: DARK POWER TRILOGY

BOOKS 53-55: DARK MEMORIES TRILOGY

BOOKS 56-58: DARK HUNTER TRILOGY

BOOKS 59-61: DARK GOD TRILOGY

BOOKS 62-64: DARK WHISPERS TRILOGY

MEGA SETS
INCLUDE CHARACTER LISTS

SOFIA

"You know who I am." Sofia handed the guard her identification card. "Why do you stop me every time I come home?"

"It's the protocol." Pioter smiled apologetically as he scanned her card and handed it back to her. "Are you here just for the weekend? Or are you going to stay longer this time?"

"I don't know. It's up to Igor."

Everything was up to Igor, but she shouldn't complain. At least she was allowed to leave the compound and attend university. Most of his subjects weren't as fortunate.

The founding group of pureblooded Kra-ell males were the elite of the compound and had more freedom and privileges than anyone else, but they couldn't come and go as they pleased either. Igor was a control freak who kept even his nearest and dearest on a tight leash.

Not that anyone was dear to him.

The male was cold and calculating, and if he were human, he probably would be classified as a sociopath. The Kra-ell might have a similar opinion of him, but no one was stupid enough to voice it.

He was ruthless and cruel to the purebloods and the hybrids, but surprisingly, he wasn't a monster to the human inhabitants of his compound. Perhaps he thought of them as pets, or maybe he pitied them for their short lifespans.

Supposedly, the pureblooded Kra-ell could live for a thousand years, but no one knew how long the hybrids would live. The oldest one was in his eighties, and he looked like he was in his twenties, so they might live just as long as the purebloods.

It was frustrating how little she knew.

Igor and his cohort of close pureblooded males didn't share what they knew with anyone. Not even their children and grandchildren.

One would think that being related to Igor's second-in-command would allow Sofia access to more information or get her preferential treatment, but it didn't. It might have elevated her status just a little over the humans with no Kra-ell blood in them, but most importantly, it provided her with a little more protection from unwanted advances.

Valstar might barely acknowledge her existence, but she was thankful for whatever advantage having him as a grand-father provided her.

Her relation to a high-ranking Kra-ell was most likely the reason she'd been selected to pursue higher education in the human world. Like the other fortunate young humans who'd been granted the opportunity, Sofia was under Igor's heavy-handed compulsion to keep the compound and the existence of the Kra-ell people on Earth a secret. She had to call once a week and report her progress to him, and she also had to make the long drive from the university to the compound for a monthly face-to-face meeting with her dear leader to rein-force the compulsion. But all of that was a small price to pay for her slice of freedom.

What was Igor afraid of, though? That she or one of the other students would reveal that they were the human descendants of aliens who drank blood? Or that their leader was most likely conspiring to take over the human world?

First of all, no one would believe them, and they would be subjected to a mental health evaluation. Secondly, none of them would do that willingly and endanger their families.

Well, she wouldn't, but in truth, she couldn't speak for the others.

Her mother was a piece-of-work Kra-ell hybrid who resented her human daughter, but she wasn't horrible enough for Sofia to want her dead, and her human father was great. Sofia loved him and her two aunts. She also had friends who were dear to her. Most were human, but there were a couple of Kra-ell hybrids who she considered friends as well.

Both were males who were interested in her as more than a friend, but Sofia had no intentions of hooking up with anyone from the compound, human, hybrid, or pureblooded Kra-ell.

She might never escape Igor's rule and live a normal life in the human world, but she could stretch out her studies for many more years and enjoy her freedom. He wanted her to learn foreign languages and master them, and that took time. Thankfully, the linguistics department of the University of Helsinki offered enough variety to keep her studying for many years to come.

After parking her ten-year-old Honda in the underground garage of the administrative building, Sofia climbed the stairs to the first floor, where she was stopped by a guard and her backpack was searched, and when she reached the second floor, she was stopped again by one of Igor's personal guards.

"Good evening, Gordi." She handed him her backpack for inspection. "Do you need to search me?"

She was wearing leggings and a form-fitting long-sleeved shirt that clung to her slim frame like a second skin. She couldn't hide a pin under that outfit, which was why she'd chosen to put it on. She'd hoped it would spare her a pat down.

"You know that I do." He motioned for her to lift her arms.

"Where do you think I can hide anything?" She did as he asked.

"Your hair." He motioned for her to release her tresses from the bun she had it gathered in. "You could hide a small firearm in that thing."

She rolled her eyes. "As if I would do something as stupid as that." She pulled out the pins holding the bun up, shook her long hair out, and let it cascade down her back. "Better?" She handed him the pins for inspection.

Gordi's eyes lit up with arousal. "You have such beautiful hair. Why do you always put it on top of your head like that?" He returned the pins to her.

It wasn't a style any of the Kra-ell pureblooded or hybrid females would ever adopt, which was precisely why she had.

It pissed her mother off.

"That's how I like it." She pretended not to notice the gleam in his eyes as she gathered her hair, twisted it on top of her head, and secured it with the pins. "Can I go now?"

Regrettably, the hybrids found her attractive for some reason.

Her dark hair, her height, and her slimness were traits she'd inherited from her Kra-ell grandfather, and her blue eyes and her gentle nature came from her Finn father. She was too thin to be considered attractive by human standards, and wasn't exotic enough to be attractive to the purebloods, but the hybrids found her features pleasing.

"Wait here." Gordi returned the backpack to her. "I'll check if Igor is ready to see you."

Slinging a strap over her shoulder, Sofia let out a silent breath and thanked the Mother that she was Valstar's granddaughter. If she were any other female, human or hybrid, Gordi could have commanded her into his bed, and there would have been very little she could have done to refuse him without courting severe retaliation.

Technically, it wasn't regarded as a command but as an invitation, and technically she could refuse, but in reality, no one dared to. To refuse a hybrid or pureblooded Kra-ell was to offend him, and since they held all the power in the compound, they could and would make her life and the lives of her family hell.

Gordi came out of Igor's office. "You can go in now."

"Thank you." She ducked into the room and immediately bowed her head. "Good evening, sir."

"Good evening, Sofia." Igor regarded her with his cold, calculating eyes. "How are your studies progressing?"

"Very well, sir. I receive top grades in all my classes."

It was the same exchange they had every month, and she often wondered whether Igor checked her grades by having them emailed to him.

Perhaps he had done it in the beginning, when he hadn't been sure she was up to the task, but after eight years of proven success, it would have been a waste of his time to keep checking on her.

Sofia was fluent in six languages and could converse in seven more, and she had no intentions of stopping unless Igor commanded her to quit.

He nodded. "I am satisfied with your progress. Keep up the good work."

She bowed again. "Yes, sir."

"Let's take care of your compliance with the compound's security rules, shall we?"

Sofia swallowed. Despite having gone through that once-a-month process for years, she still hated how it felt to have her will re-squashed with a ten-ton anvil.

"Yes, sir."

5

EMMETT

"*H*ere are all the contest entries." Riley dropped a pile of printed papers on Emmett's desk. "I'm surprised that we only got forty-two." She glanced at the stack. "Are you sure you don't want me to read through them first? I can rate them and save you some time."

"Thank you for the offer." He smiled at her. "But I will enjoy reading them myself. I'm curious to find out what we caught in our net."

It wasn't a writing competition, and Emmett didn't care how well or how badly the essays were written. All he cared about was whether they hinted at the author's paranormal talent.

The contest had been Eleanor's idea. Those who couldn't afford to participate in a paranormal retreat could submit an essay to win a free subscription to Safe Haven's newsletter. They would also get unlimited access to its extensive library of self-improvement seminars and motivational materials. It was a good way to collect the names and email addresses of potential paranormal talents. Later, they could invite those who showed promise to participate for free and continue testing their abilities.

"As you wish." Riley cast another disapproving look at the stack. "It's such a waste of paper to have them printed. You could've read the emails on your computer screen."

"You know that I'm old-fashioned." Emmett lifted the first page. "I don't like staring at screens."

Shrugging, his office manager turned on her short, sensible heel and walked out the door.

Riley, who had taken over the management of the community and the retreats in his absence, was still adjusting to his return and her perceived demotion. She didn't like it, but she needed to get over it, or he would have to replace her with someone with a more subservient attitude.

Safe Haven was Emmett's baby, his creation, and even though he was sharing it now with Kian and the clan, he had close to full autonomy to do with it as he pleased.

Eleanor was running the paranormal enclave with the government talents that she'd recruited in her former job. Marcel had replaced William at the lab the clan had built on the premises and was temporarily supervising a team of scientists. Leon was in charge of security for the entire complex, and Anastasia was helping create content for the new paranormal retreats. That left Emmett to do what he did best, which was promoting the spiritual and paranormal retreats with his guru persona and giving the place its spiritual spin.

Leaning back in his chair, he got comfortable and started reading the first essay. He found nothing of interest and put it in the *no* pile. The next five landed on top of it, and the next two formed the *maybe* pile.

The tenth one was titled: *How the Lions and the Rats became allies. A fable.*

That should be interesting.

Emmett leaned back in his executive chair, lifted his feet onto the desk, and began reading.

A long time ago, in a far, faraway land, there lived a ferocious lioness named Viva who led a very large pride. Many different animals lived in that land, some big, some small, but the lions ruled over them all.

Viva was a proud female, and she paid little regard to the animals living in her territory who were too small for a lioness to eat. But there was one rat named Crafty, whose shenanigans were so outrageous that they had reached even Viva's ears. As his name implied, Crafty was cunning and smart, and he got away with mischief that other animals would never dare to try.

Emmett's heart thundered in his chest.

His father had named him Veskar after an animal from their home world that was similar to a rat and was known for being crafty. Only members of Jade's tribe knew him as Veskar, and Emmett knew of only two who were still alive and free, both residing in the immortals' village. The rest of their tribe had been either murdered or captured, so if this was written by one of them, it must have been submitted from captivity. Given that the first part of the fable was written from the pride leader's perspective, Jade must be the author.

The next part was written from the rat's perspective.

Crafty had a healthy respect for the lions, and he stayed away from them whenever he could. Those big cats normally didn't eat rats, but they might eat a rat who was prone to mischief.

Wishing to find a place where there were no lions and where rats were treated with respect, Crafty left the lions' territory and never looked back.

He traveled across the lake to where the humans lived, and he found a community of village rats who were all very well fed.

With his cunning and his smarts, it didn't take Crafty long to take over as the leader of the pack. Those spoiled village rats who never had to work hard for their scraps were now his to command.

He was the king of the rats.

Happy and contented, Crafty basked in his success, and the only thing missing from his perfect life was the satisfaction of showing his fellow wilderness rats how well he had done for himself. From time to time, he thought about swimming back across the lake to tell his family and friends about his wonderful new life in the human village, but it was too risky.

What if, while he was gone, another rat took over as the leader of the pack?

What if, on the way, Crafty encountered one of those ferocious cats and got eaten?

He stayed where he was and forgot all about those he had left behind.

This part did not give Emmett any new clues, and he was starting to doubt that the email had been sent by Jade. There were probably many fables featuring rats and other animals. If he searched the internet, he would probably find many more that had nothing to do with him.

The next part reverted to the lioness.

One day, when the big cats were all asleep, a massive earthquake shook the ground, collapsing the pride's home, killing some, and trapping the rest under a pile of stone.

Not just the lions suffered. Many of the small cave dwellers were squashed under the avalanche of rocks. Those who survived fled through passages and openings that were too small for the big cats to fit through. The lions' size, the foundation of their superiority, was now a hindrance.

They were doomed.

"How many survived?" Viva asked once the count was done.
"Thirty adults and sixty cubs," answered the lion who had counted the live ones.
Viva's heart sank. "How many died?"
"One adult female and her four cubs," the one who'd counted the dead said mournfully. "And if we don't find a way out of the collapsed caves soon, we will all die here as well."
"Who could save us?" a lioness cried out. "Does anyone even know that we are trapped?"
"Maybe the little critters who escaped through the nooks and crannies will tell someone who will be willing to help us," another lion said.
The only ones who could help were the humans, and they didn't understand animal language.
Despondent, Viva did not say a thing. She lay down and put her head on her paws.

Emmett was done with only the first one out of the three printed pages when he straightened in his chair, snatched the phone off his desk, and called Eleanor. "Come to my office right away. It's urgent."

"On my way." She ended the call.

3

MARCEL

*M*arcel didn't appreciate being called mid-morning by Eleanor and asked to come immediately to Emmett's office. If it were anyone else, he would have demanded explanations before rushing over, but Eleanor wasn't the type to get worked up over nothing.

The door to Emmett's office opened before he had a chance to knock. "Thanks for coming." Eleanor smiled apologetically. "I would have come to you, but I'm not allowed in the lab."

Normally, she would have been correct, but he would have allowed her in if she'd called and explained her problem. As long as he was there with her and made sure that she didn't see what he and the team were working on, it would have been okay.

"What's the emergency?" Marcel closed the door behind him.

"This." Emmett waved a stack of papers. "The email arrived two days ago, but I only read it today." He handed him a three-page document. "I need Kian to see it, but I don't want to send it from here in case it's encoded, and someone can follow the email to the village. I don't know the protocol for sending secure emails, but I assume that you have a safe channel of communication in your lab, and I need you to send it to him along with a note from me explaining what's going on."

Marcel read the title. "How the Lions and the Rats become allies. A fable." He lifted a brow. "It's a children's tale. Why does it need encryption, and what does it have to do with Kian?"

"It's from Jade," Eleanor said, cutting straight to the chase. "She wrote it in such a way that only Emmett would know it's from her. It's a call for help."

"Did you read it?"

Emmett might have seen in the story what wasn't there, but Eleanor was not prone to flights of fancy.

"I did. Without Emmett's explanation, I would have thought nothing of it, but with his input, the fable becomes a coded cry for help."

"How do you know it's from her?" Marcel asked Emmett.

The guy grimaced. "My Kra-ell name is Veskar. My father wasn't happy about the birth of a hybrid son who looked too human for his taste, so he gave me an insulting name. Veskar can be loosely translated as a crafty rat." Emmett pointed to the pages in Marcel's hands. "The fable's hero is called Crafty, and he's a rat."

"I see."

Marcel sat down and read the first page. "Do those numbers mean anything to you?"

Emmett shook his head. "They don't, but I'm sure that they are not random. I just don't know what she's trying to communicate."

"How many members did her tribe have?"

"None of those numbers add up to anything that makes sense," Eleanor said. "Emmett and I already tried to figure it out, but the numbers don't match the total number of the tribe's population, not the number of males or females, and not the number of humans. Not during Emmett's time in the tribe, and not right before the attack."

Marcel nodded. "That's what I thought. The sixty-four and thirty-one or the sixty and thirty could be latitude and longitude coordinates." He read the passage. "Thirty adults and sixty cubs lived. One female and her four cubs died." He lifted his head and looked at Emmet. "Longitude is also called meridian, and the synonyms for meridian are the greatest, the uppermost, and so on. Therefore, the number of adults could represent longitude. Latitude lines are also called parallels, and some of the synonyms for parallels are secondary and kin, which means that the number of cubs could represent the number for latitude."

"Oh, that's so clever of her." Eleanor crossed her arms over her chest. "And it's even cleverer of you to figure it out."

Marcel wasn't sure that it was. If Jade was trying to communicate a secret message in an email that she knew was monitored, that wasn't clever at all. He wasn't the only one who could figure out that those numbers were coordinates. Not that he was convinced that they were. It was just a hypothesis.

"Let's check those coordinates." Marcel pulled out his phone, opened the map application, and typed in the numbers. "Sixty longitude and thirty latitude point to St. Petersburg. Let's check sixty-four and thirty-one." His brows lifted. "Interesting. It's probably a coincidence, but this set of coordinates is smack in the middle of a place called Karelia, which sounds a lot like Kra-ell. The area straddles northwest Russia and the eastern portion of Finland. The coordinates fall on the Russian side."

Eleanor turned to Emmett. "Mey said that the enemy Kra-ell male's echo she'd heard had a Russian accent."

They could be reading into the fable things that weren't there, and combining mismatched pieces of a puzzle, but Marcel was willing to suspend disbelief.

"Let's see if there are any more clues hiding in the story." He continued reading.

One day as Crafty was sitting on his throne and conducting pack business, a rabbit he had known from the wilderness hopped over. "Crafty, how good it is to see you. Did you hear what happened to the lions' pride?"
"I did not."
After the rabbit told Crafty about the earthquake that had trapped all the big cats underground, he sighed. "Even the cubs are too big to fit through the crevices that my family and I used to escape. They will all die in there." The rabbit shook his head. "I wish I could help, but I'm just a small rabbit, and all I can do is run."
Crafty might have disliked the lions' haughty attitudes, but they had never been his enemy, and he did not wish to see them all dead. He wouldn't leave the cubs to die of starvation.
The rabbit might be helpless, but a smart rat with a large pack could do what even the powerful lions could not. He could dig an escape tunnel and prove the real value of rats. They weren't just parasites who lived off human scraps. They could be powerful and respected allies. Crafty summoned his followers and told them his plan. "The pride will forever be in our debt, and we will never hunger for meat again." He stretched to his full height and lifted his paws. "We will prove to everyone that rats are not at the bottom of the food chain and that we deserve as much respect as the lions. With our smarts, determination, and cooperation, we can do what none of the other animals can."
One of the bigger rats lifted his paw. "How do we know that they won't eat us once we get to them? Lions don't usually eat rats, but they will be hungry, and they have cubs that they will be desperate to feed."
"I will tunnel through the last couple of feet alone and talk

to their leader. If she swears not to let anyone of her subjects eat us, I will come back, and we will enlarge the tunnel so they will be able to get out."

"She might promise you that and then eat us after we free her," a female said. "Or she might just eat you before giving you a chance to explain."

Crafty laughed. "I would not be much of a meal, and the pride's leader is too smart to eat her only hope of survival. She's a mother, and she'll do anything to save the cubs, even if it means making an alliance with rats. She's also proud, and if she gives me her word, she will stand by it."

"What about the other cats?" the big male asked. "They will eat us for sure."

It was possible. The leader might have lost her hold on the pride, or she might be injured and weakened, and they might not listen to her, but Crafty couldn't just do nothing and let them all die.

"She won't let them. Let's go!" He singsonged that special tune that would ensure the pack's compliance. "We will prove to the world that rats are not to be sneered at."

It took the pack three days to swim through the lake and then another seven days to burrow underground, and when Crafty smelled the lions, the live ones and the dead, he made the signal for his pack to stop. "I shall continue alone from here."

As he dug through the last three feet, he didn't bother to make the tunnel more than two inches wide, compressing his body and squeezing through.

When he emerged from the tunnel the lions were asleep, and as he scurried as fast as his paws could carry him to the largest lioness, the others lifted their massive heads and bared their teeth.

He slid between her outstretched paws. "Don't eat me! I came to save you!"

Her big feline eyes widened. "How?"

He stood up and stretched to his full height of seven and a half inches. "My name is Crafty, and I am the leader of a big rat pack. I promised my subjects that you and yours would forever be in our debt if we dug a tunnel and got you out. But you and your subjects must swear alliance to me and mine. You also need to swear that you will not eat any members of my pack and that once you are free, you will share your kills with us."

Hope surging in her heart, the leader nodded her massive head.

To save her family, she would kiss the rat on his little whiskers if that was what he demanded in payment, but all he was asking for was assurance for the safety of his pack and future scraps. It was a very small price to pay to save the weakening cubs.

They wouldn't last much longer.

"I have heard of you, Crafty, and I know that you are a very smart rat. I swear it on my life and the lives of everyone in my pride that if you and your pack save us, you will never go hungry for meat for as long as we live. My pride and I will share our kills with you and yours, and we will never eat any of your subjects or any other rats." She grimaced. "Rats were never a food source for us and never will be." Weakened from hunger, she lifted herself with effort and turned to the others. "Swear it, and let's get out of here."

After the lions repeated the vow that their leader had made, Crafty returned through the tiny tunnel he had dug for himself and told the others what was promised.

When the rats had finished digging the rest of the tunnel and freed all the lions, the leader of the pride and her subjects kept their promise. From that day on, the pride of lions and the pack of rats lived in harmony and mutual respect, and no one in that part of the world dared to look down their noses or whiskers at Crafty or any other rat.

16

Marcel shifted his gaze to Emmett. "Does seven or three mean anything to you or seven and a half inches?"

Emmett shook his head. "They don't. The only thing I got from the fable was that Jade and the other females were trapped, that they had children with them, and that they needed me to save them in a stealthy manner, maybe literally by digging a tunnel. Without your input, I would have never suspected that the numbers of the adults and cubs could represent coordinates."

4

KIAN

*A*fter Kian had read the fable, Emmett's explanations, and Marcel's interpretation of the numbers, he read it again and groaned.

The last thing he needed to add to the long list of things he had to worry about was damned Jade. He didn't want to get involved, and he hated getting dragged into a conflict that didn't concern him. Not directly anyway.

Then again, perhaps Jade and the Kra-ell were part of the complicated tapestry the Fates were weaving, and the clan had to get involved.

He needed to talk to someone about it, and that someone was Syssi.

Turner was a great strategist, and Kian planned on consulting him next, but the guy lacked vision. He was excellent at analyzing what was but not as good at imagining what could be.

Syssi, on the other hand, was excellent at it without allowing herself to get carried away, and he needed his wife's level-headed perspective before getting back to Emmett.

He picked up the phone and called her.

"Hello, my love," she answered with a smile in her voice. "Did you miss me since we talked this morning?"

"Terribly. Are you on your way back?"

It wasn't even noon yet, but on Fridays, Syssi and Amanda ended their day early to avoid the weekend traffic, and sometimes they cut it even shorter and headed home before lunch.

"We are. Do you want to meet for lunch at the café?"

"I'd love to. But first, I need your opinion on something. Amanda's too."

"Of course."

"Emmett got an email that he thinks is from Jade. It was written as a fable and contained a hidden message that only Emmett would get. It was submitted to a contest Safe Haven was running. I would like to read it to you."

"I'm curious to hear it," Amanda said. "I remember Vrog and Aliyah talking about Jade's storytelling skills."

After Kian had read the fable to them and then Emmett and Marcel's take on it, Amanda asked, "Did Jade have children before getting captured? I don't remember Emmett or Vrog mentioning it."

"I don't know, but I assume that she did. Like us, the Kraell welcomed children and did everything they could to have more, especially purebooded ones. I doubt that Jade would have failed to conceive during the time since her arrival on Earth."

"Then if she had sons, they were murdered along with the other males." Amanda sighed. "I can't imagine the horror of being the captive of the murderers of her children, and then having more kids with them. From all we've learned about her, she's a powerful and ruthless female who's also a strong compeller. If she could, she would have killed them and escaped. Given that she didn't, her captor or captors must either be keeping her locked up in a dungeon and chained to a wall, or they are more powerful compellers than her."

"The other possibility is that they took her children and

threatened to harm them if she didn't cooperate," Syssi said. "In the fable, she said that a mother would do anything to save her family. It might have been a clue."

As Kian had expected, Syssi and Amanda were looking at the fable from a completely different angle. Marcel had focused on the coordinates, Emmett had focused on what Jade was expecting of him, and Eleanor, well, she was probably focused on the threat that Jade posed to her personally and to the clan.

"Fables are usually full of clues," Syssi said. "And we know that Jade is smart. She might have hidden more information in there than is apparent at first glance."

Kian groaned. "Did either of you deduce how many enemy warriors we would be facing and what safeguards they employ? That would be very helpful."

For a moment, neither one said anything, and he could imagine Syssi and Amanda exchanging looks and shrugging.

"We probably need to read it again," Amanda said. "The only thing that comes to mind is the caves where the pride lived. Can you check in the satellite footage if there are any caves in the area of those coordinates?"

"The resolution is not that good, and in a heavily wooded terrain like Karelia, the visibility will be minimal. That's probably the main reason they chose it for their base."

"I wonder if the name Karelia has any significance," Syssi said. "It's phonetically almost the same as Kra-ellia. If you switch the third and second letter around, you get the land of the Kra-ell."

"It's probably a coincidence."

"I'll research it later," Amanda said. "If it's older than the estimated year of the Kra-ell's arrival, then it has nothing to do with them."

"Not necessarily," Syssi said. "Remember what Aliyah said about the scouting team? Kra-ell scouts might have arrived many centuries before Jade and her cohorts."

As Syssi and Amanda continued discussing the name, Kian leaned back in his chair and closed his eyes. There were too many variables to the story, and he wasn't ready to risk his people to rescue Kra-ell, who could potentially become his clan's enemies.

On the other hand, the three who had joined his clan seemed fairly loyal, but that was because it was in their best interest. They were alone among an ocean of humans, with no tribe to call their own, and the clan offered them protection and a community that accepted them.

Things might change when they got reunited with the other survivors of their tribe.

But that was a secondary worry. First, he needed to figure out whether attacking Jade's captors or finding a way to smuggle Jade and the others out would benefit the clan in the long run or harm it.

Opening his eyes, Kian leaned forward. "Can you both stop by my office when you get here? I will get lunch delivered and arrange for a conference call with Emmett, Eleanor, and Leon. Maybe Marcel as well. We can all brainstorm it together."

"I would love to brainstorm with you." Amanda sighed. "We used to do it all the time, and then you fell in love with Syssi and forgot all about your baby sister."

"You introduced us."

"True. So, it's my fault." She laughed. "Oh well. I can't say that I'm sorry. Anyhoo, we will need to drop the girls at Mother's first. We promised to visit her after lunch, but she won't mind if we leave. She's more interested in spending time with her granddaughters than with Syssi and me."

"That's not true." Syssi chuckled, probably because Amanda was making a face. "Okay. It's somewhat true. But even so, we need to explain why we can't stay and apologize. It would be rude to just drop the girls at her place and leave."

5

MARCEL

*M*arcel had hoped that sending the email and notes to Kian would be the end of his part in the Jade saga, but the call he'd just gotten from the boss dispelled his illusions.

Kian wanted him, Emmett, and Eleanor to assemble in Leon's office and participate in a video conference meeting with him, Syssi, and Amanda.

Did Kian hope Syssi would get a vision about Jade? And why did he need Amanda?

Hell, what did Kian need him for?

Marcel was a computer engineer, talented, but nowhere near William's caliber, and he wasn't a Guardian or a strategist either. He'd been a Guardian back in the day, but that was a long time ago, and his military career had been short.

He hadn't been well suited for the role.

It required a certain level of emotional detachment that he'd struggled to achieve. Some of the things he'd seen and experienced still haunted him. Ironically, what had finally helped him achieve detachment had happened after he'd left the force, but he refused to let his mind go to that dark time in his life.

He'd left it all behind and had chosen a very different path.

Marcel had realized that using his brain appealed to him much more than using his brawn, and dealing with numbers was much less stressful and gut-wrenching than dealing with death and misery.

He'd chosen the field of engineering, mechanical at first, then electrical, and recently computer science, but even though he'd left active duty, Marcel had never regretted the long years of training and the time he'd served. The skills he'd learned were useful, and he was part of the reserve force, training a couple weekends a year to maintain his skills.

If the clan needed him, he was ready and able to defend his people, but the Kra-ell were a different story. Jade and her plight tugged at his heartstrings, but so did many other misfortunes.

The world had many maladies that needed fixing, but even the gods had failed at that task, and that was when the world had been a much smaller and simpler place.

As a male ruled by logic, Marcel didn't dwell on the impossible. Jade was not his problem, and he didn't think she was the clan's problem either. In fact, he regretted deciphering the fable and figuring out that the numbers of adults and cubs could potentially represent coordinates.

Without that piece of knowledge, Kian wouldn't have even considered a rescue attempt that could cost the lives of Guardians.

As Marcel entered Leon's office, Emmett and Eleanor were already there, and the big screen behind Leon's desk was on, displaying an aerial video of downtown Los Angeles.

"I brought us coffee." Eleanor motioned to the lone paper cup on the round conference table.

The others held theirs in their hands.

"Thank you." He took the lid off and sat down. "Were you waiting just for me?"

"We are waiting for Kian," Eleanor said. "He will call as soon as Syssi and Amanda get to his office."

Marcel leaned back with the cup in hand. "Did Kian say why he wants Syssi and Amanda to attend the meeting?"

"He didn't." Emmett crossed his arms over his chest. "He should have included Vrog and Aliyah instead." He cast a glare at Leon and then shifted his dark gaze back to Marcel. "I wanted to call them to let them know about Jade, but your buddy Leon said that I needed to ask Kian's permission first. I would have ignored him and called them anyway, but I didn't want to antagonize Kian. I can't rescue Jade and the other members of my tribe with only two other hybrids to help me. I need the clan's Guardians, and I need Turner to come up with a plan."

It was on the tip of Marcel's tongue to say that Emmett might have to make do with his two former tribe members and perhaps advice from Turner. The clan shouldn't get involved in the Kra-ell mess, and Turner would no doubt advise Kian to stay out of it. Marcel was still trying to come up with a diplomatic way to say it without quashing the guy's hope, when Leon's phone rang.

"Yes, boss," Leon said. "Everyone is here. I'm switching to video."

As they all faced the camera mounted on top of Leon's laptop, half of the screen behind the desk showed the four of them crowding the small round table in Leon's office, while the other half showed Kian, Syssi, and Amanda in a similar setup, only larger.

"Hello, everyone." Syssi waved. "This is such exciting news. Kian read the fable to me and Amanda, and we are both sure that there are many more hints hidden between its words. We will make copies and take them home with us."

Amanda waved as well. "I have a question for Emmett.

Did Jade have children while you were still a member of her tribe?"

Emmett nodded. "She had a son, and Vrog told me that she had another one after I left. They were both massacred along with the other males."

6

KIAN

Syssi sucked in a breath. "That's horrible. I can't imagine the suffering, the rage, the need for revenge."

Surprised by her vehemence, Kian looked at Syssi with new eyes. She was usually so gentle, so mellow, but perhaps becoming immortal had changed her, or maybe it was motherhood.

Her eyes blazed, and if she had fangs, he suspected that they would have been fully elongated by now.

"If she hasn't killed them all, it means she can't," Emmett said. "Jade is a force to be reckoned with. She's a powerful compeller, and she has no qualms about killing. Whoever is holding her must be even more powerful than her."

"That's what Amanda and I figured," Syssi said. "She has access to the internet, so she's not rotting in some dungeon, but they must have something that they are holding over her. Maybe she had more children in captivity, and she's not striking against her captors because she is protecting her kids."

Amanda shook her head. "They must have kept her in a dungeon until they got her pregnant and then used the child

6

or children to control her. Otherwise, she would have retaliated before getting with child. They probably used drugs as well. That's what the traffickers do, and it works." She shivered. "I know that Jade is not a clan member, and we don't owe her anything, but she and the other females are basically sex trafficking victims, and rescuing them is what we do."

"It's not the same." Kian let out a breath. "The local dens that we raid to free the victims are not fortified compounds with super-strong Kra-ell guarding them."

Leon nodded. "I bet Jade's tribe wasn't the only one those Kra-ell have raided, killed the males, and abducted the females. Their goal is obviously to breed more pureblooded Kra-ell, so by now, they might have a large number of warriors."

"Jade didn't know that other Kra-ell survived the crash, but her captors did," Kian said. "They also knew how to locate them."

"Maybe they managed to save some of their advanced technological gear," Leon said. "The original Kra-ell settlers could have been implanted with locator devices that only their technology could detect. We know that Navuh tried to implant his warriors with trackers, so it's not such a far-fetched scenario."

It was possible, but thankfully, the Kra-ell who had been born on Earth and the hybrids didn't have them. If they had, Jade's captors would have found Emmett a long time ago, and since he'd spent months in the village, that would have been a catastrophe. The same went for Vrog and Aliyah.

Just to be safe, though, he would ask Julian to run scans on them again.

"We still don't know how they got scattered in the first place." Kian crossed his arms over his chest. "We assume that their arrival had something to do with the Tunguska event, and the assumption that their ship was sabotaged is based on what Aliyah overheard as a small girl. The explanation might be completely different. Jade and her original group of pure-bloods might be the bad guys, and her captors might be law enforcers who brought them to justice. Maybe there was a mutiny, and the commanders executed the deserters but spared the females because of their value as breeders. Or maybe tribal wars are part of their culture, and maybe executing the males and capturing the females is a common tactic."

Syssi gaped at him. "Including their young children? The Kra-ell are ruthless, but they value children. They wouldn't do that."

Amanda winced. "The Japanese used to do that. If someone was deemed a traitor, their entire family was killed. They weren't the only ones either. I can start listing all the known offenders, but the list is long and depressing."

Shaking her head, Syssi slumped in her chair. "I have no words. Is there no limit to cruelty?"

Not knowing how to comfort her, Kian put a hand on her shoulder. "Let's focus on Jade's fable. If it even came from her."

"It did," Emmett said. "I recognize her style of storytelling. If I show Vrog and Aliyah the fable, they'll probably confirm my assessment."

Kian could understand Emmett's eagerness to share the news with his fellow tribe members, but it was premature.

"I don't want them to know yet. We need to figure out what to do about it first."

"Jade needs help," Emmett said. "She wouldn't have reached out to me if she could find a way out of captivity herself. She and the other females must be suffering terribly." He rubbed a hand over his long beard. "I'm surprised that she recognized me from my picture, and I'm also curious about how she stumbled upon Safe Haven's advertising. We ran ads on Facebook, but mainly in the US. We did very little

28

international advertising and then only in the English-speaking markets."

The same had occurred to Kian, and the answers he'd come up with were worrisome. The least bothersome and the most likely was that Jade had been searching for something that had led her to Safe Haven's website. She'd recognized Emmett, and if she could see the male behind the long hair and beard, so could others from her tribe, and someone might have alerted their captors to the Kra-ell male disguising himself as a human spiritual leader.

"Maybe she searched for something related to self-improvement or free love," Syssi offered. "The system Emmett implemented and the rules of conduct mimic traditional Kra-ell sexual exchanges. The men must wait for an invitation from the women, and they are not allowed to initiate. That might have caught her interest, and she dug deeper. She could've also searched for information about paranormal talents. Did she know that you could compel?" she asked Emmett.

"I thought that she didn't, but given what she wrote in that fable, she did. Crafty had a special sing-song voice that ensured his pack's cooperation. That's a good way to hint at my ability to compel."

"I agree." Syssi turned to Kian. "She probably wanted to butter Emmett up. She described Crafty in a very flattering light."

Emmett chuckled. "Jade is incapable of buttering anyone up. It's not part of her makeup."

"Twenty-some years in captivity can change a person," Eleanor said. "She has children, and so do the other females. Viva the proud lioness was willing to do anything to save the cubs, and so is Jade."

Both Syssi and Amanda nodded their heads.

"So, what do we do next?" Emmett looked at Kian. "Do I answer her fable with one of my own?"

"A fable is a good idea, but not as an answer email," Marcel said. "The contest winners will have access to the Safe Haven library. You can hide your fable somewhere among the other stuff."

"Don't do anything yet." Kian pushed his chair back. "I'll collect satellite footage from the area those coordinates point to, but given how densely wooded Karelia is, I don't expect to glean much information from that. I also need to discuss the situation with Turner. He's an expert on hostage retrieval, which is what we are dealing with. If anyone can get Jade out of there without a war, it's him."

"I think war is inevitable." Eleanor put a hand on Emmett's shoulder. "It's not just about getting Jade out. They have many Kra-ell females and their children trapped there as well. Besides, they pose a threat to the clan that needs to be eliminated."

"That's the part I'm not sure about," Kian said. "They don't know about our clan's existence, and I want to keep it that way. If they ever find out that our females can provide them with long-lived offspring, they will do everything in their power to hunt us down."

"They can try," Leon said. "Navuh has been trying to find us for centuries, and he has thousands of warriors at his disposal. One small group of Kra-ell is irrelevant to us."

Kian took a deep breath. "I think that if Navuh really wanted to find us, he would have by now. We are good at hiding, but we are not that good. He needs an enemy to keep his people united and motivated, and humans are deemed irrelevant. They are the sheep, and we are the lions protecting them. We are the real threat. The moment we are out of the picture, he will lose the glue that holds the Brotherhood together, and he knows that."

7

SYSSI

*S*o that was why Kian had been less paranoid about security lately.

Syssi had been wondering about that. A couple of years ago, he wouldn't have allowed prospective Dormants to come and go as they pleased, and he'd been much more careful about who he allowed into the village and when.

She'd heard Kalugal voice the same argument about Navuh and his lack of effort to locate the clan, and it seemed that Kian had bought it.

Was it smart, though?

It sounded logical, and maybe it was even true, but despots did not always act logically, especially when their followers became restless. When that happened, the dictators became desperate to distract them from whatever they were unhappy about, which was a lot given that they served a ruler who didn't give a hoot about them.

The easiest way to distract people and unite them behind a cause was to stir up trouble and rile them up. The violent emotion of hate overshadowed the grievances they had with their leaders, and suddenly the vilified enemy became the focus, and not their crappy living conditions and lack of freedom.

Navuh's warriors hadn't seen a battlefield in several years, and Syssi had no doubt that they were getting restless. They couldn't be satisfied with the Brotherhood's weapons, drugs, and prostitution activities. They were trained to fight, and lately, Navuh had trouble finding hot spots he deemed relevant for them where they could spread their particular brand of terror.

Then again, the world was changing, and the most vicious battles took place in the political arena. Perhaps Navuh had decided to limit his efforts to influence policies, and since that required a lot of money, he utilized his warriors to make it.

The days of well-paid mercenary armies were apparently over, or maybe he'd just realized that there was more money in the business of war than in the war itself.

"I will have to announce the contest winners by next Friday," Emmett said. "But I want to do it earlier and open a channel of communication with Jade. I like the idea of hiding my response among the seminars and motivational material, but I need a couple of days to figure out how to do it so only Jade will find it and not her captors."

He was such a vain male. Jade was an experienced storyteller, and it still had probably taken her weeks to come up with the fable that would convey all she wanted to tell Emmett. It would take him just as long.

"I won't have an answer for you that quickly," Kian said. "I also want you to show Turner and me what you've written before you post it on the website. This is a new enemy we are facing, and I don't know what their capabilities are and what kind of risk they pose. I refuse to be rushed." He gave Emmett a hard look. "Jade has waited for twenty-some years. She can wait a couple more weeks."

Emmett shook his head. "I need to announce the winners

no later than next Friday, and she will have to be one of them. That's the limiting factor."

"I might decide that not answering her is the best option," Kian said. "If her captors suspect something, they will be monitoring her web browsing activity, and if there is nothing for her to find, they won't either, and they will let it go."

"Turner will tell you to do just that," Leon said. "The compound is located on the Russian side of Karelia, and Turner doesn't like working on their turf. The best he can offer you is hiring a local operator."

Kian nodded. "That might be good enough to assess the situation. As I mentioned before, satellite footage is likely to give us very little information, and flying drones in a remote area where no one else does it will raise the captors' suspicions. We need boots on the ground, and it's better if they are locals who know the language and customs and can play the part of innocent passers-by."

"Jade might be out of time." Emmett's eyes turned pleading. "The Mother only knows what she's being subjected to. The least I can do is acknowledge her."

"I know that you're impatient," Kian said softly. "But Safe Haven is a strategic location for us, and if your message is discovered, you will lead Jade's captors straight there. Even if we could manage to evacuate our people in time, we would lose our new base and the investment that went into it, and you would lose Safe Haven. Are you willing to sacrifice it for Jade and the other females? I was under the impression that you didn't care for them much."

"I didn't, and I still don't. They were stuck-up elitists who looked down their noses at me because I was a hybrid. It didn't matter that I was smarter and craftier than all the pureblooded males put together. I still didn't get to breed with one of the pureblooded females. But I have a feeling that the years in captivity have taught Jade a valuable lesson." He smiled. "She now appreciates Crafty, the smart rat."

From the corner of her eye, Syssi could see Eleanor bristling.

"If you hope to breed with a pureblooded female, tell me now." Eleanor pushed to her feet. "I will have no problem finding immortal males to breed with me."

Smiling, Emmett pulled on her hand. "I love it when you get jealous, but you have nothing to fear. I was talking about the past before I knew you even existed. You are the only female for me, and I will never look upon another with desire in my eyes. Only you stir my heart, my love."

8

SOFIA

*S*ofia's heart was racing as she made her way to Igor's office. What could he possibly want with her this late in the evening?

He wasn't interested in humans for his sexual needs, so that wasn't it, and she hadn't broken any rules. She'd been an obedient little human, doing everything by the book.

Was he going to inform her that her days at the university were over?

As usual, she was searched as she entered the administrative building and then again when she got to his floor.

"What did you do?" Gordi asked, adding fuel to the fear gnawing a hole through her stomach.

"Nothing. I don't know why he wants to see me. Is he angry?"

Gordi chuckled. "Igor doesn't show emotions. He looks the same when he's happy and when he's mad."

She knew that. Igor never raised his voice, never sighed or groaned, and he never smiled or scowled, either. If not for his alien looks, the male could have been a world champion poker player.

"Wait here." Gordi left her standing by his station and knocked on Igor's door. "Sofia is here," he told the boss.

"Let her in," Igor said in an even, unhurried tone.

With a pitying look, Gordi motioned for her to go in.

She crossed the threshold with her eyes cast down and bowed. "Good evening, sir."

"Good evening, Sofia. Please take a seat."

That was surprising.

Igor hardly ever told her to sit down during their once-a-month meetings. Usually, she would remain standing for the entire ten-minute or less ordeal, with her legs shaking and her knees about to give out.

"Thank you, sir." She lowered herself to the edge of the chair and lifted her eyes to her ruler.

"You are going on a trip." He pushed a brown envelope toward her. "All the information is inside, including your passport."

She reached for the envelope with shaking hands. "Where am I going?"

"The United States. I enrolled you in a paranormal talent retreat. It starts in a week and will last two weeks. I want you to snoop around and collect information for me."

Her head snapped up. "What kind of information?"

"Anything that's noteworthy. A member of my staff showed a great interest in that place, and I'm curious whether there was more to it than she claims."

Igor didn't have females on his staff. The only one he could be referring to was Jade, the prime female and the mother of his only daughter. She wasn't officially part of his staff, but she held an elevated position.

Ugh. Why me?

The last thing Sofia needed was to make an enemy out of Jade. The female might be under Igor's compulsion, but she could still do a lot of damage to a human and call it an accident. Igor might punish her, but he wouldn't execute her. She was the most powerful female in the compound, and she produced the most powerful offspring for him.

"Fall semester starts in two weeks," Sofia tried feebly.

"You can lose a week or two of language studies. It's not rocket science."

Desperate for another excuse, she tried to play on Igor's patriarchal philosophy. Perhaps it would work in her favor for once.

"Maybe someone else is better suited for a spying job? A male perhaps?"

"Females are better for undercover work. Humans don't expect trouble from their women, and the only attention you will attract will be carnal in nature, which you can use to your advantage. Human males are easily manipulated when they are sexually interested in a good-looking female like you."

Sofia's hands became clammy.

Igor expected her to have sex with men to get information out of them, and if she refused, even her grandfather couldn't protect her.

Not that he would try.

She was a dispensable human, and he would demand of her to be a good little soldier and do exactly what she was told.

"Human males don't find me attractive," she tried, not expecting it to work. "I'm too skinny and too tall."

Igor regarded her with his expressionless eyes. "You are a pretty girl, and you're soft and submissive, which is what they prefer. You'll do just fine."

He was wrong about that. She might be considered soft and submissive by Kra-ell standards, but she was just an average human female who enjoyed sex that didn't involve a fight for dominance and was a natural extension of a loving and respectful relationship, or at least friendship. She had nothing against others enjoying casual hookups, but it wasn't for her.

During her years in the university, Sofia had dated many guys, and she'd had two serious boyfriends. One relationship had lasted for over a year, and the other four months, and both had been about more than sex, but they hadn't been the all-consuming love she'd read about and yearned for. It had been difficult to get close to a guy when she couldn't tell him anything about herself or bring him home to meet her parents.

Her preferences didn't matter to Igor, though, and she couldn't afford to keep arguing. He'd been patient with her so far, but she knew that she'd reached the limit of what he was willing to allow.

Bowing her head, she said, "I will do my best not to disappoint you."

"Make sure that you don't," he said without changing his tone, but the threat was palpable.

"What should I tell them when they ask me personal questions? I mean, what's my cover?"

"When lying, it is always best to stay as close to the truth as possible. You are a linguistics student from Finland who has a paranormal talent that she wants to explore. Valstar will explain the rest." Igor motioned for her to get up. "Wait outside by the guard station. He will see you when he's ready."

Pushing to her feet, Sofia bowed. "Thank you, sir. Goodnight."

9

KIAN

*S*aturday mornings were usually reserved for playtime with Allegra, but it wasn't unusual for emergencies to eat into that special time. The best way to handle it was to combine business with pleasure, which was what Kian had done by inviting his mother to share breakfast with him, Syssi, and Allegra and inviting Turner and Bridget to join them a little later for cappuccinos and Okidu's latest baking masterpiece—a chocolate cake with raspberry topping.

He needed to give his mother an update about the latest developments with Jade, and he needed to get Turner's advice.

Sitting on the couch and sipping on a cup of tea, Annani regarded him from under her long, red eyelashes. "You are not inclined to assist Jade, are you?"

"I'm not." He handed Allegra another piece to try to fit into the cube. "I don't want to poke that sleeping bear."

"So why did you invite Turner? Are you worried that at some point Jade's captors might pose a threat to the clan?"

Kian nodded. "She might have led them to Safe Haven with that email. I've told Leon to raise the alert level, and I'm considering taking the paranormals out of there and dismissing the bioinformaticians. If Jade's captors come to investigate, they will find nothing of interest."

Annani cradled the teacup between her palms. "Except for an underground lab with the latest innovations in computing."

"After Marcel locks it up, they won't be able to get in, and if they do, it's not what they are looking for."

"What will they be looking for?"

"Emmett or other Kra-ell."

Syssi walked into the living room and sat on the floor next to Kian. "You need to get Emmett out of there as well."

"I do. But he will not leave willingly."

As the doorbell rang, Okidu opened the door and then escorted Bridget and Turner into the living room.

Turner bowed to Annani. "Good morning, Clan Mother."

"Good morning to you too, Victor, and please, call me Annani."

He smiled. "As you wish."

She'd asked him to call her by her given name several times in the past, and he did, but then he'd reverted to calling her Clan Mother.

"Good morning." Bridget walked over to her and leaned to kiss her cheek.

"Cappuccinos, anyone?" Syssi asked. "They are a must with Okidu's chocolate raspberry cake."

"I will have one." Bridget sat next to Annani. "I stopped by the clinic to check up on Eric. He's doing exceptionally well for someone who has been unconscious for so long. I really don't understand why he hasn't woken up already."

Annani's lips twitched with a suppressed smile. "He must be dreaming very pleasant dreams and does not wish to wake up."

So far, Eric had received transfusions only from Toven

and none from Annani. Toven's blood seemed to be working just as well. Annani and Toven had decided not to risk mixing their blood donations unless Eric took a turn for the worse.

"Is Hildegard watching Eric?" Syssi walked over to her cappuccino station.

"She is." Bridget sighed. "I wish we had one more nurse. With Gertrude setting up shop in Safe Haven, Hildegard has to do double shifts. She's not happy about it."

"What about Julian?" Annani asked. "What is he doing with his time?"

"He has his hands full with the halfway house and the sanctuary, but we are considering hiring a human doctor for that and having Julian work more hours in the clinic. Until now, we haven't needed a doctor full-time in the village, and I was able to make do with Hildegard and Gertrude shouldering most of the care. But now that we are expecting several Dormants to attempt transition at the same time, and with Gertrude gone, we need him here."

"You could ask Merlin to fill in temporarily," Kian suggested.

"Julian has been apprenticing with me for a while, and he knows how to handle transitioning Dormants. Merlin doesn't have the same experience."

Annani sighed. "I wish for your clinic to be so busy that you, Julian, and Merlin have your hands full with transitioning Dormants."

Bridget smiled. "I wish it too, but then someone will need to take over managing the rescue missions."

"About that." Kian rose to his feet and sat on one of the armchairs. "I think you should train someone to take your place, or at least take over the day-to-day management. I know that this project is your baby, but your medical expertise is wasted on administrative tasks that a less qualified person can do. Now that we have a gifted bioinformatician in the village, you should go back to research and find out what makes us immortal."

Bridget let out a long breath. "I've been thinking a lot about that lately, and the truth is that I'm afraid to discover the secret. What will we do with it? Can we share it with humanity? The consequences could be disastrous."

Syssi walked over with a tray loaded with five cappuccino cups. "That won't be that bad if their immortality comes with reduced fertility like it does for us."

Bridget took one of the cups. "It's not something I want to be responsible for." She shuddered. "I would feel like the inventor of the atomic bomb. Was he aware of what he was unleashing upon the world?"

"He was," Turner said. "But his team wasn't the only one developing a nuclear weapon. The Nazis were also developing their own bomb, and so were the Japanese. It was a macabre race with the highest of stakes. The champion got to win the war and protect their own people, but at a terrible cost. In a later interview, the head of the American team of scientists quoted a line from the *Bhagavad Gita*; 'Now I am become Death, the destroyer of worlds.'"

ANNANI

A loaded moment of silence followed Turner's historical reference.

Annani doubted that Turner or Syssi were aware of the clan's part in helping the United States win that race. Bridget knew, and so did Kian, but they chose not to mention it.

It was a sad reality that a technology that could provide clean, inexpensive energy to the world could also be used for such mass destruction. And it was an even sadder reality that sometimes the only choice was to either become the destroyer or be destroyed.

Kian was the one to break the silence. "Let's move to the subject of Jade and what to do about her."

As he read aloud Jade's fable and then added Emmett and Marcel's explanations, Annani's heart went out to the female. How terrible it was for her to be captured and used for breeding by the murderers of her children and her mates.

Annani did not believe that the Kra-ell did not feel love for their mates and their offspring. Their society might be rigid and militant, but they came from the same stock as the gods and the humans, and therefore must feel love.

Hopefully, Turner would convince Kian that it was essential to the clan's security to eliminate the threat Jade's captors posed and rescue her and the other females.

However, Annani was not going to pressure Kian into going to war with those Kra-ell. If he and Turner decided that the risks of an attack outweighed the future risks of not addressing the problem now, she was not going to intervene.

"Can you send me a copy of the fable?" Turner asked. "I would like to read it again and pay attention to the details. Maybe I will discover more clues."

"I'll do it right now." Kian pulled out his phone and searched for the document. "I'll send you a copy as well," he told Bridget.

"I want to take another look at it, too," Annani said. "Maybe I will notice something that no one else did."

"Of course." Kian typed on his phone, and a moment later, Annani's device pinged with an incoming message.

Knowing that it was from him, she did not bother retrieving it from the hidden pocket in her gown.

Turner did not look at his phone either. "If you want my opinion, I can tell you right now that I don't think you should get involved. There is a slight risk of those Kra-ell coming to sniff around Safe Haven, and you should make sure that there is nothing for them to find. The paranormals can stay, but Eleanor and Emmett and all the other immortals should either make themselves scarce or return to the village. Safe Haven managed without them for many months, and it can do it for many more."

"That was my gut instinct as well, but it's not as simple as that. The first ever paranormal retreat is about to begin, and I need Emmett and Eleanor to monitor the incoming talents. You know how robust the security in Safe Haven is. It should be fine."

Turner's expression was smug. "The place is a fortress,

and it could easily withstand a Doomer attack, but we don't know what kinds of weapons and tricks the Kra-ell have."

"That's my next point," Kian said. "I want to collect intel on the potential threat these Kra-ell represent. I want to know how many of them there are and what kind of weapons and technology they have."

Turner nodded. "I agree. Start with collecting satellite footage, and we will take it from there."

"What about people on the ground?" Kian asked. "Do you have a local contact you can employ?"

"I do, but only for collecting intel. If you decide to launch a rescue mission, I wouldn't use humans for that. Unless I can assemble an army, which I can't do in Russia, a team of humans doesn't stand a chance against the Kra-ell." He rubbed his chin. "Maybe they do if we equip them with earpieces and your exoskeleton battle suits."

Kian shook his head. "The suits are built with immortals in mind. Humans won't be able to move fast enough in them. They are too heavy."

"That's what I thought," Turner said. "But the earpieces will be necessary for the human recon team as well as for the immortal assault team. My hunch is that the leader of Jade's captors is a powerful compeller. We know that Jade is one, and yet she didn't manage to get free in over two decades. Also, since he's going against Kra-ell tradition and committing what is no doubt considered sacrilege for them, he must have a way to exert his will over them."

"Maybe the leader is a she?" Syssi suggested. "Since they are murdering Kra-ell males and taking the females captive, it makes more sense to us that the leader is a male, but as the saying goes, assumption is the mother of all failures. Kian speculated that Jade's tribe might have been considered rogue. If so, the female in charge of their expedition might have punished them for their act of treason. Males are expendable in their society, so they were executed, but females are rare and precious, so they were taken prisoner."

Turner's pale blue eyes did not reveal any emotion, but in their depths, Annani could see the wheels of his brain spinning.

"It's possible," he said after a long moment of contemplation. "If that's the case, she would not be breaking away from tradition, and she would have her people's loyalty. It would also explain why the humans and their children were allowed to leave unharmed. Females are more merciful. Still, my hunch is that the leader is a male who got tired of the matriarchal world order of the Kra-ell and decided to make a change. A powerful compeller can make his people do whatever he or she pleases." His lips twisted in a grimace. "History is full of such examples, which I don't wish to repeat. You all know what I'm talking about."

"You are assuming that the leader is a he who got tired of the matriarchal rule based on human history," Bridget said. "That's why it makes more sense to you. It doesn't mean that it is so. The Kra-ell have a different tradition, a different belief system, and a different morality."

"Well said." Turner smiled at his mate. "We won't know until we get more information."

Kian let out a breath. "I don't have any Guardians who are compellers, Emmett has no military training, and Kalugal, who is our strongest compeller, hasn't seen combat since WWII. He's also a new father who is obsessed with keeping his son away from exposure to germs. He would not want to go out on a rescue mission."

Annani knew better than to offer herself. Kian would never agree to risk her, and although she had confidence in her ability and was willing to go, even she knew it would not be a smart move.

"I need to talk to him," Bridget said. "The child needs to be exposed to human germs so he can develop immunity.

Kalugal can't keep him in a bubble until he's thirteen and ready to transition."

Syssi chuckled. "I think that's what he plans."

Kian took a sip from his cappuccino and put the cup down on the coffee table. "I like having Kalugal staying in the village. It adds another layer of security that I've grown accustomed to, even depended on. So much so that I didn't like it when he left for more than a day until Toven arrived. And before anyone suggests Toven, there is no way the guy would agree to go on a mission, and I wouldn't risk him either. He's too valuable."

"Is that why you relaxed the security?" Syssi asked. "Because we have powerful compellers in the village now? Or is it because you believe Navuh is not really making an effort to find us?"

He arched a brow. "The only thing I allow now that I didn't before is letting more people into the village, and that's definitely because I have powerful compellers to keep them from telling anyone about us. Navuh is a threat that I would be a fool to take lightly, but having Lokan watching his father's moves enables me to sleep better at night."

Turner leaned back against the couch cushions and crossed his legs. "That only works as long as the other side doesn't have an even stronger compeller. If any of these people fall into Navuh' s grasp, he can get them to talk. And if Jade's captor is of the same caliber as Navuh, he can get anything he wants out of them, including from immortals. But that's only a problem if either of those compellers captures a head Guardian or a council member. No one else knows how to get into the village."

"You do," Kian smiled at him. "But even if a civilian is caught and questioned, he or she knows enough to point our enemies in the right direction. We can withstand most attacks, including from above, but I don't want us to be in a position where we have to defend ourselves. That being said,

I need to balance the two critical components necessary for the clan's survival. One is security, and the other is new blood. The lack of either one would have the same end result, just in different time frames. If we isolate ourselves, we will be safer, but we will eventually die out."

SOFIA

*T*he wait next to Gordi's station was even worse than the meeting with Igor.

There was no extra chair, which meant that Sofia was forced to stand and suffer the covetous looks from the guard. She could've opened the envelope and read the instructions, but maybe Gordi hadn't been informed about her new mission, and she was supposed to keep it a secret?

Igor hadn't compelled her to keep it quiet. Was it an oversight? Or was it just temporary so she could discuss it with her grandfather, and she would have to see Igor again after the briefing?

It was her first mission, so she didn't know what to expect.

Damn. It was also her first trip abroad, outside of Russia and Finland, and she should be excited. Instead of focusing on the negatives and what Igor expected her to do, she should focus on the positives.

She was about to fly on an airplane for the first time, and she was about to visit the great United States. Would she get a budget to buy new clothes?

"I found one of your pins." Gordi held it out to her. "You must have dropped it when you were fixing your hair."

"Thanks." She took it from him and stuck it in her bun.

How come Gordi was always there when she was summoned?

Was he Igor's only guard?

Would he answer her if she asked?

"It's always you when I come here. Doesn't Igor have any other guards?"

He crossed his arms over his chest. "Why do you ask? Do you want to come visit me?"

"I was just curious. I never see anyone else outside Igor's door."

"I'm his daytime guard. When he retires for the night, someone else takes over."

Leaning against the wall, she mirrored Gordi's pose and crossed her arms over her chest. "I don't know why he bothers with guards. The entire compound is under his complete control, and no one from the outside can get to him." She chuckled. "Even a helpless human like me is under compulsion to defend Igor if he's attacked."

Gordi gave her a once-over that had goosebumps rise on her arms, and not the good kind. He gave her the creeps.

"A pretty female like you has other weapons at her disposal."

Sofia rolled her eyes. So, he was in on Igor's plans for her and her mighty vagina.

Males were so stupid. How the hell did they get to be in charge? Brawn was no longer a prerequisite for leadership. In the twenty-first century, brains ruled.

Besides, if what her cousin Helmi had told her was true then the Kra-ell were supposed to be ruled by females.

Helmi had learned that from her hybrid boyfriend, who'd learned it from one of the fables Jade taught the kids. According to the fable, the Kra-ell society was supposed to

50

be ruled by females. They were like a pride of lions, but instead of one male lion and four lionesses, it was the other way around, and a Kra-ell female had a harem of several males. It was such an absurd notion that Sofia would have dismissed it completely if not for the fear in Helmi's eyes when she'd told her what she'd learned.

Her cousin feared for her boyfriend's life and what would be done to him if Igor realized that he had figured it out. Helmi believed that the Kra-ell who knew about the traditional ways were compelled to never mention it. Jade was powerful, so it was possible that she'd somehow managed to circumvent the compulsion with her stories, and only a smart hybrid like Tomos could uncover the hidden message.

It was true that the pureblooded females were as vicious and ruthless as the males, but the males were obviously stronger. Also, many more boys were born to them than girls, but somehow, the number of adult pureblooded males and females was more or less even. She had her suspicions about how that was achieved, but they were too terrible to even think about.

What if they did what the Chinese had done when the one child per family policy had been in effect? They had supposedly killed newborn baby girls because the parents wanted a boy to inherit the family's name and assets. Did the Kra-ell dispose of the boys?

As a door down the hallway opened, and her grandfather stepped out, Sofia pushed away from the wall and dipped her head. "Good evening, sir."

He would have beaten her up if she called him Grandfather.

"Come." He ducked back into his office, leaving the door open for her.

Sofia followed him inside and closed the door behind her.

"Sit down." He pointed to the chair across from his desk.

"Thank you, sir."

"Do you have any questions about your mission?"

"I have many." She lifted the envelope and put it on his desk. "I didn't have a chance to read through it yet, and I don't want to ask questions that are already answered."

He waved a hand in dismissal. "We will meet every day until it's time for you to leave, so you'll have many more opportunities to ask questions. The more prepared you are, the better. Ask away."

Letting out a breath, Sofia allowed her shoulders to slump a little.

Valstar might be gruffer and less polite than Igor, but he was easier to deal with. There was emotion in his dark eyes, and he was less terrifying.

"I asked Igor about my backstory, and he said to stay close to the truth. I'm supposed to be a linguistics student who is interested in exploring her paranormal talent. First of all, what paranormal talent? And secondly, what do I tell people when they ask me where I'm from?"

He regarded her with puzzlement in his eyes. "Your mother told me that you have an eerie ability to tell whether a person is telling the truth when you look at their reflection in a mirror while they talk. That's a good enough paranormal ability to get you into the retreat."

She chuckled. "It's a parlor trick. I entertain my friends with it."

Sometimes the image in the mirror twisted, showing her an expression that the person looking in the mirror didn't wear. But it was probably just in her mind, and even if it wasn't, it didn't tell her whether they were telling the truth or lying. All the mirror revealed was what they were really feeling at the moment.

"It doesn't matter if it's real or bogus as long as you have something you can talk about at the retreat."

Valstar opened one of his desk drawers and pulled out a small box. "You are not there to actually explore your talent.

You are there to snoop around and report back home." He opened the box, pulled out a pendant, and let it dangle on its chain from his fingers.

"What is that?"

"It's a communication device. At the retreat, they ask the guests to leave their phones in the office. We need you to be able to communicate with us at all times." He opened the locket and showed her the small picture they had put inside.

It was of her, her father, and one of her aunts.

"This is your family. You are an only child, and your aunt is your mother." He chuckled. "You can explain the familial resemblance by saying that your parents are second cousins."

She took the locket from him. "Or I can say that my mother died when I was little, and I was raised by my aunt. Igor said to stay close to the truth."

Valstar looked at her with appraising eyes. "You don't look like your father or your aunt, so a dead mother could explain that. But on the other hand, you don't want people to remember your story too clearly, so it needs to be as mundane as possible. A dead mother will stick in their memory."

"You are right, sir."

"I'm always right."

JADE

"What's wrong with you?" Drova offered Jade a hand up. "Are you feeling okay?"

"I'm not in my best form today." Jade took her daughter's hand and let her pull her up. "I should go hunting."

"Yeah, you should. You look pale."

The concern in her daughter's tone was surprising. Drova was usually too self-centered and full of herself to notice, and even when she did, she didn't care.

"Do you want to come with me?" Jade offered.

Drova arched a brow. "Don't you prefer your trusty side-kick to hunt with? You always say that I'm too slow and cramp your style."

Jade offered her a tight smile. "You bested me today and proved yourself. Maybe you will manage to keep up."

Drova grinned. "Let's go. Just you and me."

Her excitement over a simple thing like going on a hunt with her mother made Jade pause.

Perhaps she'd been too hard on the girl. Maybe if she had pretended to lose before and complimented Drova on her win, the girl would have grown more confident in her ability and would have strived to do better to impress her.

They stopped by the security office, got their badges, and headed out the gate.

"What's been going on with you lately?" Drova asked once they were away from earshot. "Are you going into your fertile cycle?"

"Yeah. That must be it. I hate it."

That wasn't it at all. Jade's nerves had been frayed since she'd sent the email to Veskar three days ago.

So far, Igor hadn't said a thing or indicated in any other way that he was onto her, but that didn't mean much. The guy had the best poker face in the known universe.

Drova nodded. "I get it. I would hate it too."

Would she?

Igor's compulsion prevented Jade, and the other captured females, from telling those who were born in the compound about how they'd gotten there and what happened to the males of their tribes.

There hadn't been any new captures in over a decade, and when the last group of females had arrived, Drova had been too young to question where they had come from.

Had Igor found all the remaining survivors? Or had he just exhausted those he could find?

There had been many more people on the ship, and if they'd survived, they would have had children, and there would have been many more females for him to capture.

She hoped the others weren't dead and that they were just better at hiding than she had been.

"I'm not looking forward to my first fertile cycle," Drova said quietly. "Going into heat is a bitch."

"It's not that bad when you have a choice of partners." That was the most Jade could say on the subject, and even that had been difficult to get out.

"I have a choice." Drova regarded her with puzzlement. "Don't you?"

How little she knew.

"It's considered a great affront to refuse a summons. I wouldn't dare say no to your father."

When things were the way they should be, and females controlled reproduction, refusing an invitation had been considered an insult to the female who'd issued it, but no male had been raped or whipped for refusing.

He just hadn't been invited again.

It was very different in Igor's camp, and especially for her. Igor was worse than most of his lieutenants. He felt entitled to all the females in the compound, including the mothers whose sons he'd slaughtered.

But of course, she couldn't tell Drova any of that.

"I know that you can't stand him," Drova said quietly. "You don't even try to hide it. And I also know that you can't refuse him. Perhaps if you weren't as ferocious, he would choose someone else. He wants the strongest female in the compound, and that's you."

Drova seemed to be more astute than Jade had given her credit for. She was right about that, of course, but she didn't understand Jade's motives. Being the prime female allowed her access to things that the other captured pureblooded and hybrid females didn't get.

The humans in the compound had the most freedom, but Igor made sure they couldn't be used to get information in or out of the compound.

The guy was evil incarnate and just as smart as the humans' devil. He was very precise in phrasing his compulsion. He didn't leave any wiggle room.

"What can I say? I'm a proud female, and I like the position of Prime too much to give it up."

It was a total lie, but that was what she let everyone believe. No one was under the illusion that she enjoyed Igor's company. They all knew that she despised him, but they also knew her to be vain and power-hungry, and that was explanation enough for them as to why she was willing to tolerate him.

No one other than Kagra knew that she was doing it in the service of her fellow captured females, tirelessly looking for a way out and risking her life. It wasn't a selfless quest. Jade wanted revenge, and if she got to avenge her family, she would gladly die for it.

Her daughter smiled smugly. "I'm the daughter of the two most powerful purebloods in the compound. It was only a matter of time before I overpowered you."

Jade clapped Drova on her back. "Only because I was distracted and malnourished. It won't happen again."

"We shall see about that." The girl sprinted ahead.

13

DARLENE

"Five days." Darlene sighed. "And still no change."

Geraldine put her hand on her arm. "Bridget says Eric is doing great, and five days is not that long."

"I know. That's what everyone keeps telling me, but he's unconscious, and I can't just shake it off and think it's fine because his vitals are strong, and his fever has gone down."

The truth was that it was becoming her new routine, and that worried her as well.

Darlene slept on a cot in Eric's room, showered in his bathroom, and ate breakfast, lunch, and dinner at the café, usually accompanied by members of her family or Max.

Shai, Cassandra, and Onegus didn't work on Saturdays, so they'd joined her and Geraldine for breakfast today, and William and Kaia had promised to stop by later.

Those two were a match made in heaven. They loved their work nearly as much as they loved each other and didn't take breaks even on the weekend. Heck, they were so enamored with the secret project they were working on that it was like their honeymoon.

Nevertheless, they made time to keep her company nearly every day.

It wasn't only her family and Max, though.

People stopped by their table and asked about Eric, offering their support and promising to pray for him, which was really nice.

The sense of community in the village was amazing, and even though she was worried and stressed, or maybe because of that, she appreciated it greatly.

How had she lived without it for so many years?

Living with Leo hadn't been a life. They'd traveled, and they'd gone out to nice restaurants, but they had been mostly alone, and given that they hadn't gotten along, it had been miserable.

"Hello." Cassandra waved and smiled, pulling Darlene out of her reverie.

When she turned around to see who her sister was waving at, she saw Mia, Toven, and Mia's grandparents heading their way.

"Good morning." Mia's grandmother smiled. "How is Eric doing?"

"As well as can be expected," Cassandra answered for Darlene. "Come join us."

"We are heading out to Arcadia," Mia's grandfather said. "But we can stay for a few minutes."

Shai and Onegus got up and brought another table and more chairs to make room for everyone.

"Can I get you something to drink?" Onegus asked.

"No, thank you." Mia smiled up at him. "We are meeting Margo and Frankie for brunch."

"When are they moving into the village?" Cassandra asked.

Mia had been talking nonstop about her friends moving to the village and about matching them up with immortals. Darlene had never met them, but she felt as if she already knew them.

"The additional Perfect Match machines are not ready

yet," Toven said. "I don't want them to quit their jobs before I can provide them with new ones in the village."

"Are they not ready yet because William is busy with other things?" Geraldine asked.

Darlene shook her head. "Some of the components are delayed. I'm sure you heard about the chip shortage. Those machines need thousands of them."

Geraldine turned to her father. "Can't you do anything about it? Money talks and your compulsion ability talks even louder."

"I wanted to, but William said that it's not a good idea. We don't want to draw attention, and it's better to let things progress at their natural pace. They will get here when they get here. There is no rush."

Geraldine scrunched her nose. "I don't like it. We have two potential Dormants that could make two clan males very happy. Why waste time? When you go back to your home in Arcadia, you should invite some of the eligible bachelors to come over and meet your friends. Maybe they can find their truelove matches even before they get here."

"That's a wonderful idea." Mia's grandmother said. "I had my eyes on a couple of gentlemen. The next time I see them, I'll invite them to dinner in our house to meet Margo and Frankie."

"We should go." Toven rose to his feet. "I don't want us to be late."

"Of course, dear." Mia's grandmother followed him up and so did her husband.

As the four headed toward the pavilion, Darlene smiled and waved, but her mind wandered back to Eric. All that talk about matchmaking and truelove mates made her restless. She should go back and sit by his side, but as she shifted her gaze to the clinic door, she saw William and Kaia walking out.

"Eric is fine." William pulled out a chair for Kaia. "I took a peek while Bridget tested Kaia's healing progress."

"How is it going?" Geraldine asked.

Kaia sighed. "The healing time shortens by a few seconds every day. It's frustrating how slow the progress is."

"I can imagine." Geraldine patted her arm. "Your family must be very far from the source."

"Yeah. That's what Bridget suspects. I'm young, so my transition was easy but slow. Syssi and Andrew are also far from the source, but they are older, so their transition was more difficult and longer than mine, but once they woke up, their healing time was much faster than mine. Bridget is worried that future generations of Dormants will have their immortal genes so diluted that transition will no longer be possible."

14

PARKER

"What's taking that girl so long?" Lisa gave the swing a mighty push. "She was supposed to meet us here more than half an hour ago."

Parker swung slowly, patting Scarlett's head on every downswing. "Are you in a hurry to go somewhere?"

Lisa huffed. "I'm not, but I don't like being stood up. My mother told us to be here at ten to meet Cheryl, and we were here right on time."

Parker had seen the girl only once when he'd passed by the café and she was entering the clinic, but other than her long dark hair, he hadn't seen much of her because she'd had her nose glued to her phone.

"Oh boy," Lisa exclaimed. "I take it all back." She jumped off the swing and rushed toward a girl who was pushing a double stroller with two crying babies inside and a little girl with an angry face stomping beside her. "What happened?"

The babies were covered in snot, and their puffy cheeks were streaked with tears, the little girl was glaring daggers at them, and Cheryl was pretty.

She was short and a little chubby, but in a cute way, and she had smart eyes.

"They are stupid." The little girl clutched a doll to her chest. "They want Sylvia, but she isn't theirs." She stuck her chin up and headed toward the swing Lisa had vacated.

Realizing that it was too tall for her to reach, she looked at Parker. "Can you help me get on the swing?"

"Sure." He hopped down and lifted her into the seat. "Do you need me to hold you?"

"No. I'm a big girl. Just give me a push. Not too hard."

"Yes, ma'am."

Cheryl rolled her eyes. "I'm never going to have kids."

"Can I take one of them out of the stroller?" Lisa waited as Cheryl wiped their noses and faces with a bunch of tissues.

"Yeah." Cheryl crumpled the tissues and put them on the shelf under the double stroller. "Let's put them in the sand-box. I brought toys for them to play with."

As soon as Cheryl dumped the plastic buckets and shovels in front of the twins, the babies forgot all about the doll they'd wanted so badly and got busy digging.

"I'm sorry for getting here late." Cheryl sat down on the edge of the sandbox. "I wasn't supposed to babysit today, but my mom looked exhausted, and I saw an opportunity to make a quick buck, so I offered to take the little ones to the playground with me. Usually, they are not that difficult. I don't know why the boys got so upset over the stupid doll. They never wanted to play with it before."

"Maybe something else is bothering them." Parker sat down next to her. "It's all new to them."

"Or they might be coming down with something." Lisa sat on Cheryl's other side. "By the way, I'm Lisa, and I'm still human." She offered Cheryl her hand. "Welcome to the village. I'm so glad to have another human girl here." She smiled at Parker. "No offense, but you are no good at applying nail polish."

She'd never asked him to do that, so how would she know that he was no good at it?

Maybe he was a natural?

"Thanks." Cheryl shook Lisa's hand and then shifted her eyes to Parker. "What about you? Are you still human?"

He puffed out his chest. "I'm immortal."

"Awesome." She smiled tightly. "My mother wanted me to talk to you about your school."

"What do you want to know?" Lisa asked.

Cheryl shrugged. "The usual stuff. Is Instatock popular here?"

So that's why she'd had her nose glued to her phone.

Lisa nodded. "It's the new craze, but Parker and I decided to stay away from it. It's way too addictive."

"For a good reason." Cheryl pulled out her phone. "Most kids might watch the funny videos and take part in the challenges, but did you know that you can make tons of money from it?"

Parker's interest got piqued. "How?"

"Becoming an influencer. Brands will pay you to put up videos wearing their clothes or shoes or applying their makeup. I didn't know that until I started getting offers. I'll show you."

Her videos were very subtle, and if he hadn't known that she'd been paid to promote the product, he wouldn't have noticed anything promotional about the video. Cheryl explained that was what the people paying her wanted. They didn't want it to look like an advertisement.

An hour later, Parker's head was spinning with the possibilities. How come he hadn't known about the money that could be made on Instatock?

"I don't get it," Lisa said. "If you make so much money from the app, why do you need to babysit?"

Cheryl narrowed her eyes at her. "I don't make a lot of money yet. My channel is not big enough. But when I get more followers, I'll get paid more. It's a lot of work, but it's worth it."

"I don't know about that." Parker helped one of the twins retrieve a lost shovel. "It sounds like too much work for too little money to me. How long have you been putting videos on the platform?"

"Almost a year, but I'm still building an audience, and the potential is there. It just takes time."

"When you actually start making money, I will consider giving it a try, but I don't think I can come up with enough things to talk about."

"When I started, I didn't know what to do either, and my first videos sucked, so no one watched them. You learn as you go, and you build a following. It all takes time." Cheryl smiled conspiratorially. "It's a golden opportunity. The app is new, and not many people know how to produce the kind of content that attracts an audience. By the time the big influencers figure it out, I will be way ahead of the crowd."

Parker liked the girl's entrepreneurial spirit. Lisa was great, and she was smart, but it was book smarts. One day she would probably become a doctor like her brother. He was also a good student, but he wanted to be a businessman and make a lot of money, and apparently, he and Cheryl had that in common.

15

SYSSI

*S*yssi hurried after Amanda, trying to catch up to her leggy sister-in-law. Even in four-inch heels and pushing a double stroller Amanda walked faster than her.

"Slow down." Syssi jogged through the ten-foot gap Amanda had created. "Do you need to pee, is that why you're rushing?"

Amanda huffed out a laugh. "That only happened when I was pregnant. I'm just excited about our good news."

"I still think we should let her know that we are coming. What if the house is a mess?"

"So? I don't mind a messy house, and I want to surprise her."

Spoken like a woman who'd had a butler clean after her, her entire life.

"If she looks embarrassed, we stay on the front porch and don't go inside. I'll tell her that we are in a hurry to get home."

"Da-da," Allegra said in a demanding tone.

"We are going to see Daddy in a little bit, sweetheart."

"Da-da." Allegra's tone changed, indicating frustration.

"I don't think she means Kian." Amanda leaned down and smiled at Allegra. "What are you trying to say, sweetie?"

"Da-da. Da-da."

Syssi shook her head. "She wants to talk so badly, and she gets annoyed when we don't understand what she wants to say with her da-das and her ni-nis and all the other sounds she makes."

Allegra's bottom lip quivered, and a moment later, a tear slid down her little cheek, tugging on Syssi's heartstrings.

"Come to Mommy, baby girl." She unbuckled the straps and lifted Allegra from the stroller.

Her daughter heaved a sigh and put her head on her shoulder.

"Maybe she's tired," Amanda suggested.

"She napped in the car on the way to the village, and she was fine until I couldn't decipher her meaning."

On her shoulder, Allegra heaved another dramatic sigh and sniffled.

Syssi had a feeling that her daughter had inherited her auntie's and grandmother's penchant for drama. Given that she also seemed to have Kian's temper and assertiveness, they would have their hands full with her.

As they reached Amanda and Dalhu's former home, Amanda lifted the double stroller over the three steps and walked up to the front door.

"It feels strange to knock on my own door." She looked at Syssi over her shoulder.

"It's no longer your home. It's now Karen and Gilbert's."

Given the cooking smells, Karen was home, but she must have not heard the knock. Amanda knocked again, louder this time.

When the door opened a moment later, Karen looked surprised but not put off by the unexpected visit.

"Hello, ladies. What a nice surprise." She pulled the door open all the way. "Please, come in."

Syssi smiled apologetically. "I wanted to call ahead, but Amanda wanted to surprise you. I hope we are not inconveniencing you."

"Not at all. I've gotten used to visitors dropping by throughout the day. It's actually quite nice." She led them to the living room, where the twins were playing on a mat on the floor. "My only interaction with my neighbors back in the Bay Area was the occasional hello."

"Da-da!" Allegra chirped happily.

Syssi laughed. "This time I have no problem understanding what she wants." She put her down on the mat next to the boys.

Evie was sleeping in the stroller, so Amanda left her there but kept an eye on her.

"Can I get you something to drink?" Karen asked. "I can't offer you cappuccinos, but I can make Turkish coffee."

"That sounds lovely," Syssi said. "But we are not going to stay long. I just wanted to deliver the good news. The university will need a new system administrator in a couple of months. The current sysadmin is pregnant, and she's taking maternity leave in seven weeks. She wants to stay home with her baby for a year and come back to work part-time after that. She was very happy to hear that you are looking for a position and wouldn't mind switching to part-time when she returns. Not that I think she will. I think she will decide to stay home for longer than that."

Karen sat down on one of the armchairs. "That's very serendipitous. Are you sure you didn't use mind tricks to make the current sysadmin take such a long maternity leave?"

Syssi put her hand over her heart. "I would never do that even if I could, but I can't thrall. Amanda can, of course, but she wouldn't do it either. We spoke to Nikki together. She said that the job is yours, but you still need to come in for an interview and fill out all the necessary paperwork."

"That's not a problem. Thank you for arranging the job for me."

She didn't ask about the pay, but Syssi doubted it mattered. Gilbert was making more than enough to support the family, and Karen didn't need to work if she didn't want to.

"How is Gilbert doing with managing his projects remotely?" Syssi asked.

"It's a learning process, and he will have to go back from time to time until he has all the systems in place." Karen pulled up her almost black hair and twisted it into a bun on top of her head. "The transition can't happen overnight even with Kian's tutoring." She chuckled. "I've never used the word transition so many times in a day. I need to find some synonyms."

"Change, transformation, evolution," Amanda offered. "Progression."

"When is Gilbert going to do it?" Syssi asked.

"He's waiting for Eric to wake up. He's not going to do it until Eric is back on his feet." Karen swallowed. "Gilbert wants to make sure that his brother is there for us in case he doesn't make it."

Gilbert was several years older than Eric, and he was slightly overweight, but he seemed to be in decent shape and didn't have any medical problems. "Gilbert is going to be just fine," Syssi said with conviction in her voice.

"I hope so," Karen said with much less conviction.

"Do you think your boss will give you a letter of recommendation?" Amanda asked, probably just to change the subject.

"I know she will. Surprisingly, she was very accommodating. When I told her that I need to be here for my daughter, and I don't know when I'll be able to go back, she said that she understood. She's also a mother. I told her that I would make an effort to be available to train the new person over the phone and through video calls."

"Excellent." Amanda clapped her hands. "Now she has the motivation to give you a stellar recommendation letter. Not that I think you'll need it for this job, but it's always good to have."

"Certainly. I told a similar story to Cheryl's principal. She wants to finish this year online and join Parker and Lisa at the school next year, but I hope to change her mind about that. The year has just started, and there is no reason for her to be cooped up at home the entire time. She needs the company of other kids her age."

"You should take her to visit the school," Amanda said. "It's a beautiful campus, and she can hitch a ride with Lisa and Parker."

Karen winced. "Is Lisa driving?"

"She is, but you don't need to worry." Amanda pushed to her feet and walked over to Evie, who was starting to wake up. "The car can practically drive itself, and it's very safe. It won't let her get into an accident."

"I heard. Shai ordered cars for us and explained the features. The clan should market and sell them. I think they will make a lot of money."

"Speaking of money," Syssi said. "The pay is probably less than what you were making at your previous job, but the position comes with benefits." She smiled. "Daycare is included, and your babies will be a five-minute walk away. For a mother, it doesn't get any better than that."

"I agree." Karen smiled at the children playing on the carpet. "That alone is worth the move here." She winked. "The immortality is just an added bonus."

16

SOFIA

"*T*his is for you." Helmi handed Sofia a package wrapped in brown paper.

It was soft, so it was probably a shirt or a dress. "You didn't have to get me anything. I will be back in two weeks."

Helmi didn't get to leave the compound, and her ability to purchase clothing and other small luxuries was limited to mail orders that arrived twice a month, together with the other supplies.

A lot could be said about Igor's ruthless hold over his people, but he wasn't stingy, and in some ways, he treated the humans living on his compound better than the purebloods and the hybrids.

They earned wages that corresponded to the jobs they held and how well they performed them, their living quarters were adequate, and once a woman delivered at least one hybrid child or reached the ripe age of thirty-five without conceiving, she was allowed to get married and have human children with one of the human males living in the compound. They were also free to choose a hybrid, but hybrids didn't usually commit to one woman. Tomos was the exception rather than the norm, but there was no future for him and Helmi. To survive among the other hybrids, he had to pretend that he only used her for sex and had no feelings for her.

Hybrids were supposed to emulate the purebloods and be all about honor and duty. To the Kra-ell, feelings were considered a weakness.

Still, Igor knew that duty and honor as well as fear and compulsion were not enough to motivate people to do a good job. He was never going to be loved or admired, but it was much easier to control humans as well as hybrids and purebloods when they had something to lose other than their lives and the lives of their loved ones.

"I got you a nice dress." Helmi smiled sheepishly. "Well, I got it for me, but it's way too small, and returning it is too much hassle."

That made more sense.

Except Sofia didn't wear dresses or skirts. She was too tall and too skinny to look good in them.

"Try it on." Helmi waved a hand at the package. "I want to see how you look in it."

Checking the time, Sofia shook her head. "Igor expects me in fifteen minutes, and it's a ten-minute walk to his office."

Helmi shuddered. "You are so brave. I feel like peeing myself every time I see him. Thankfully, as far as he's concerned, I don't exist, so I just dip my head and wait until he goes away."

Since Helmi didn't leave the compound, she didn't need private meetings with Igor to reinforce her compulsion. The once-a-week speeches he delivered were good enough to keep her and the other humans under control. The purebloods and hybrids were a much smaller group, and they were treated to separate sessions.

Sofia had no idea what went on in those, but she

suspected it was more or less the same sermon-like lectures, just more of them.

"I felt like peeing myself as well the first few times." She chuckled. "He still scares me, but I can handle it better now."

She tore open the wrapping paper and unfurled the black dress. "It's beautiful."

The bodice was made from a stretchy fabric and looked slim. The double skirt was wide and long enough to cover her knees, the outer lace layer a little longer than the slip underneath. It also had a narrow patent-leather belt to cinch the waist.

"I'll try it on when I get back."

"Knock on my door when you return. I want to see it on you." Helmi rose to her feet and kissed Sofia's cheek. "Good luck with Igor."

She flinched. "Thanks. I need it."

Sofia hadn't seen Igor since he'd assigned her to the mission last Saturday. During the week, Valstar had trained her on using the communication device discreetly, and he coached her on the cover story they had prepared together.

Igor probably wanted to see her to reinforce his compulsion. He would ensure that she did what she was supposed to and kept her mouth shut about the Kra-ell and the compound and everything that was even remotely connected to it. He was very precise in his wording, ensuring that he didn't leave any loopholes.

After she'd passed both inspection points, Gordi announced her, and a moment later, he let her into Igor's office.

She bowed. "Good evening, sir."

"Please, sit down." He motioned to the chair.

For some reason, his politeness made him even more terrifying. Sofia would have preferred to remain standing and be done with the meeting faster.

"Thank you, sir." She sat on the edge of the chair and put her clammy palms on her leggings.

"Valstar tells me that you are ready," Igor said.

"I hope I am. I'm still not sure what I'm looking for."

"Report to Valstar anything that catches your attention, and he will tell you what to do next." His voice was imbued with compulsion.

"Yes, sir."

He pinned her with his intense, dark eyes. "You will keep the existence of Kra-ell and anything that pertains to us a secret. You will not tell anyone about us in any form—oral, written, mimed, or implied."

The oily sensation his compulsion always evoked in her slithered over her skin, coating her in a filthy film that felt suffocating.

"Yes, sir."

"You will keep the location of this compound a secret."

Wasn't that part of the previous prohibition?

"Yes, sir."

"You will not tell anyone who you really are, and you will stick to the story Valstar composed for you."

"Yes, sir."

When he was done with his list of compulsive orders, Sofia thought that they were done and started to push to her feet.

"Sit down."

"Yes, sir."

"I want you to be clear on your duties. As long as you report once a day to Valstar, tell him everything you found out, and follow his instructions, I'll consider it a job well done."

"Yes, sir." She closed her hand over the pendant.

His eyes followed her hand. "That pendant stays on you at all times. You don't take it off for any reason other than to shower or to swim in the ocean. If anything happens to it, find a phone and call the emergency number Valstar made you memorize."

"Yes, sir."

His eyes bored into hers. "If you fail to do any of those things, your family and friends will pay. Am I clear?"

She was under such a heavy compulsion to obey his every word that the threat was redundant, but it still filled her with dread and made her gut clench painfully.

"Yes, sir."

17

MARCEL

*K*ylie Baldwin poked her head into Marcel's office. "I'm making myself a coffee. Would you like some?"

There wasn't a drop left in his mug, and he would have loved a fresh one, but letting Kylie make it for him would mean her planting her butt in his office and flirting with him, which he preferred to avoid.

"Thank you, but I'm good."

She eyed his empty mug. "I'll put it in the sink." She snatched it off his desk before he had a chance to refuse.

He let out a resigned sigh.

She would be back with the coffee. She'd done that before.

He hated manipulative people, and he was especially wary of manipulative females. It was a mistake to underestimate them just because they were less aggressive and more subtle in their dealings. What they lacked in brawn, they compensated for with brains and an innate ability to make men do stupid things to gain their favor.

He'd been a victim of female manipulation once, but he was a quick study, and it wasn't going to happen again.

The surest way to avoid it was to disengage when a female was showing too much interest in him.

He knew that Kylie's interest wasn't because he was such a charming fellow or a good conversationalist, and he wasn't handsome enough to justify her persistence either. He was good-looking in the same way that most immortals who were not too far removed from the source were, and it was usually sufficient to get hookups but not enough to incite such intense pursuit.

Even if he allowed a woman to remember him after the sex, chances were that she wouldn't want a relationship with a guy who barely talked, rarely smiled, and was more interested in machines than people.

As he'd expected, Kylie returned with two mugs of coffee and put one on his desk. "You're not being a chauvinistic boss if you accept my offer to get you coffee." She sat across from his desk. "It only counts if you expect me to get it for you."

"Thank you." He took the mug. "It didn't occur to me even for a moment that accepting your offer might be misconstrued as chauvinism. I just wasn't in the mood for coffee five minutes ago." He lifted the mug to his lips and took a sip.

"Right." She eyed him from under lowered lashes. "How are William and Kaia doing? Is her mother getting better?"

Despite his opposition, Kaia's mother's health had been the excuse they had ended up telling the crew. Evidently, Kaia and her family were not superstitious. Besides, it was true to some extent.

Kaia's step-uncle was still unconscious, and her stepfather was just waiting for his brother to wake up from the coma to attempt transition himself. Kaia's mother would probably wait for her partner to grow fangs and develop venom to activate her dormant genes, but her life would be in peril at some point.

"Her mother's condition is stable but not improved." That wasn't a lie, either. Karen's health had not changed in any way since her arrival at the village. "Kaia and William will most likely not be back by the time the project is done." He forced half a smile. "You are stuck with old, boring me."

"You're not boring. Compared to William, you are fascinating." She looked at him from under lowered lashes, her lips curving in a suggestive smile.

Marcel stifled a groan. Kylie was getting bolder with her flirtation attempts.

She was pretty and smart, and if Marcel had met her in a bar, he probably would have hooked up with her. But she was too pushy for his taste, and there was something unpleasant about her that he couldn't put his finger on. She wasn't a bad person, but she wasn't kind either. He wasn't attracted to her, and on top of that, she was his employee.

"I assure you that there is nothing fascinating about me. What you see is what you get." He waved a hand over his outfit. "Every single day."

To save time in the mornings, he didn't bother with a variety of clothing. Instead, he had several identical sets of turtlenecks and slacks. It was casual yet elegant and suitable both for work and for club hunting.

Boring but efficient.

Her eyes sparkled. "What I see is a handsome, well-dressed, well-spoken, and well-educated man. You found what looks best on you and stuck with it. There is nothing wrong with that."

Should he be blunt and just tell her to back off?

The contract the bioinformaticians had been hired for would reach its term in several weeks, and he wouldn't have to see Kylie or the other two ever again. The problem was that the project was not nearly finished, and if Kaia and William decided that they wanted to keep the team until they were done deciphering the journals, the contracts would have to be renewed for at least another year.

Smiling tightly, he picked up his mug and took a sip.

It was time for a white lie. "You are a fine woman, Kylie, and if you weren't my employee and I was single, I would have very much liked to get to know you better. Regrettably, it's not in the cards."

Kylie's face fell. "Are you married?"

"I am not, but I am involved with someone."

"Then why isn't she here?"

"What makes you think it's a she?"

He wasn't gay, but Kylie deserved some payback.

"You are not into men, Marcel. Don't insult my intelligence."

Busted.

"How can you tell?"

She rolled her eyes. "I watch you in the dining room. Your eyes follow the pretty ladies, not the pretty lads."

"I'm an aficionado of female beauty. But you are right. My significant other is a lady, and she's currently working on a project abroad."

"That's a shame." She rose to her feet. "If things don't work out between you and your lady, or you get tired of waiting for her to return, you know where to find me." She walked out the door and slammed it behind her.

Marcel let out a breath.

Kylie wasn't stupid, and she'd figured out he'd been lying, but so be it. At least she wouldn't bother him again.

Or so he hoped.

18

SOFIA

*S*ofia boarded the bus with a fake smile on her face, nervous butterflies in her belly, and a new friend.

Roxana, or Roxie as she preferred to be called, had started talking to her as soon as she'd walked into the Safe Haven designated meeting place at the train station, and she hadn't stopped chattering since.

The woman was the perfect companion, exactly the type Valstar had told her to befriend.

Roxie was in her late thirties or early forties, she wasn't too smart or too pretty, but she was bubbly, kind, and funny. Everyone liked her, but people quickly tired of her never-ending prattle and drifted away.

Sofia smiled and nodded and kept close to her. As Valstar had coached her, a talkative person attracted attention at first, but then they became invisible because people wanted to avoid her, and being inside that invisibility bubble with Roxie was great for a wannabe spy.

If only Sofia knew what she was supposed to spy on.

Clutching the pendant, she walked to the back of the bus with Roxie trailing behind her and introducing herself and Sofia to every person they passed.

"That knockout is my new friend Sofia. She's a ballet dancer from Finland, but she didn't get a spot in the Finnish national ballet because she was too tall."

Sofia rolled her eyes but didn't comment. Roxie had asked her if she was a ballet dancer, probably because she was so slim and flat-chested, but Sofia had told her that she'd never been to a ballet class in her life.

Evidently, Roxie thought that she'd been lying and was inventing a whole backstory for her.

Sofia didn't mind.

On the contrary, she was going to encourage Roxie's stories. The more outrageous they were, the more unlikely it was that anyone would dig deeper to find out the truth.

"Can you imagine that?" Roxie stood with her hand on her hip next to two women sitting a couple of rows over. "They are so discriminatory in those ballet troupes. Someone should do something about it. I want to see fat girls and tall girls and every body type in between getting equal time on the stage."

"You are absolutely right," one of the women said. "Who said that all ballerinas need to be skinny and flat like boys? I hate those outdated standards."

"I agree with you completely," the other woman said. "I'm so happy to see Victoria's Secret finally showcasing full-bodied models wearing their lingerie. Those are their real customers, not some starved, stick-insect with legs." She turned to look at Sofia. "No offense, but you would fit right in with those emaciated models."

Right, no offense. Did they think that only overweight people had issues with their body image? Sofia would have loved to have cleavage and hips.

"That's the way I am, and it's not because I'm starving. I can eat cheesecake all day long and not gain any weight."

"Poor baby," the woman said in a mocking tone. "If I even look at a cheesecake, I immediately gain five pounds."

As Roxie and the other women laughed and commiserated, Sofia pulled out the book she'd gotten at the airport and started reading.

When everyone was on board, Roxie sat down next to her. "Lydia and Felicity are so nice. I'll ask if we can be put in adjacent rooms so we can party together." She winked.

What kind of partying did she have in mind?

Sofia had read everything she could find about the Safe Haven resort. They offered spiritual retreats and had only recently added a paranormal one to their portfolio. They promoted free love, but thankfully they left all the power in the females' hands. The males were not allowed to even issue an invitation, but they were allowed to try to impress the ladies.

Hopefully, they wouldn't pester her. If she had to hook up with someone to get information for Igor, she would reluctantly do it, but not for any other reason.

After the bus driver checked everyone's names, verifying that all the guests were accounted for and no one who wasn't supposed to be there had boarded the bus, they were on their way.

As the two guys sitting in the row in front of them started discussing their paranormal talents, Roxie gasped. "I can't believe that I didn't ask you what's your paranormal talent yet." She tilted her head. "Or did I forget, and you told me already?"

"You didn't forget." Roxie had been too busy telling Sofia about her dream interpretations. "My talent is catoptromancy."

Roxie made a face. "What's that?"

"It's also called enoptromancy, and it is divination using a mirror."

Sofia had never heard those terms either. She'd looked them up so she could talk about her so-called talent as if it was a real thing.

"What's divination?" asked the guy sitting across from them. "Is it like fortune-telling?"

"It is, but mine has a twist. I can see a person's true nature when I see their reflection in the mirror. If they are pretending to be nice but are evil, they will look ugly to me. And if they are not very attractive but have a pure soul, they will look beautiful to me."

No one was purely good or bad, not even Igor, so that was a bogus claim, but it was a simple way to explain it.

"Does any mirror work?" Lydia or Felicity asked. Sofia didn't know which name belonged to which lady.

"It has to be either round or oval."

It was another fake claim, but that was the mirror she'd brought with her, and she intended to keep it in her room so no one could ask her to actually demonstrate her ability.

Lydia or Felicity nodded. "When you get settled in and get your mirror unpacked, I want to take a look. Maybe your mirror will show me that I'm an angel." She batted her eyelashes.

"You will just see your own reflection. I'm the only one who might see something else."

19

MARCEL

*M*arcel chose a seat in the back of the dining hall. It wasn't the best spot if he wanted to sneak out before Emmett's performance ended, but it was good for observing the crop harvested for the first paranormal retreat.

Emmett was excited to welcome his guests, and according to Eleanor, he'd been rehearsing his speech in front of the mirror in his full prophet regalia, but with how preoccupied he was with Jade's communication attempt, his performance might not be one of his best.

The guy was bristling with impatience as he waited for Kian to get back to him about a response to Jade's email.

Marcel could understand Emmett's frustration. But unlike Emmett, he believed that Kian would tell him to forget that he'd ever received the email.

If left alone, those militant Kra-ell posed a remote risk to the clan. If provoked, they would pose an immediate threat. Besides, Jade and her people were not the clan's problem.

The dining hall was filling up slowly, and as several people sat at his table, Marcel nodded in greeting and then pretended to read on his phone so they would leave him alone.

He was there as a spectator, not a participant.

"Why are you sitting all the way back here?" Eleanor loomed over him. "Come sit with me at the front."

"I prefer it back here if you don't mind. I'm tall, and people always complain about me blocking their view."

Eleanor put a hand on her hip and struck a pose. "You're not that tall. What are you? Six two? Six three?"

"Six feet and three inches."

Eleanor huffed out a breath. "I'll tell Emmett that you are all the way in the back. He's upset enough as it is, and he doesn't need the added aggravation of thinking that you didn't come." She turned around and strode purposefully to the front of the room.

The two people sitting across the table from him avoided his eyes, probably thinking that he'd been offended by Eleanor's harsh tone.

He wasn't. In fact, he admired how protective she was of her mate. Some found Eleanor abrasive and unpleasant, but he liked her. She was direct, assertive, and devoted to those she cared about. He'd heard that it hadn't always been the case, but he didn't hold her past against her. Fates knew that his own past was far from perfect and that he had changed significantly, perhaps not for the better.

He'd turned disillusioned and mistrustful.

If he ever found his truelove mate, which he probably wouldn't, she would hopefully be an honest, strong woman like Eleanor, but perhaps a little softer around the edges.

The problem was that he was attracted to the exact opposite. Fragile damsels in distress were his Achilles' heel and the type he had to fight the hardest to resist. As his experience had taught him, in most cases it was just an act.

Luckily, Kylie Baldwin hadn't figured out his weakness yet, and she was pretending to be tough and assertive like

Kaia, thinking that she could snag her own happily ever after with William's replacement.

He couldn't fault the woman for wanting that, but he could fault her for being obtuse and not giving up when he had done everything he could do to discourage her. Even after the lie he'd told her about his supposed lady friend, Kylie was still making him coffee and giving him suggestive looks.

"Do you know Emmett Haderech?" the woman sitting across from him asked. "I couldn't help overhearing your conversation with the lady, and it sounded like you were friends with him." She sounded like a teenager talking about her celebrity crush.

Marcel nodded. "I know him." He shifted his eyes away from her, indicating that the conversation was over.

He and Emmett were not pals, and Marcel had nothing to do with the paranormal program and shouldn't have been invited to the opening luncheon. But ever since he'd found the coordinates hidden in Jade's fable, Emmett had regarded him as a confidant, and he'd insisted on Marcel watching him deliver his speech to the attendees of the first paranormal retreat.

As a new group entered the dining hall, a willowy young woman caught Marcel's eye. She looked like a ballerina, very slim and seemingly fragile, but her posture and the way she walked indicated otherwise.

There was coiled strength in her, and her gait was fluid, like a dancer's.

Her shoulders were squared, her head held high, and her dark hair was gathered in a neat bun. Not even a wisp escaped the carefully done coif.

She was too tall to be a ballet dancer, but she looked the part.

Perhaps she was a yoga enthusiast, but she lacked the calm that yoga was supposed to provide its practitioners.

Even from across the room, Marcel could see that she was tense and uncomfortable, which made his protective instincts flare.

He forcefully doused the flames as soon as they had ignited.

The woman wasn't in any danger at Safe Haven. After the village, it was probably the best guarded civilian complex.

Perhaps she wasn't used to being among so many people, or maybe she wasn't used to talking about her paranormal talent. Some flaunted their abilities, real or imagined, while others tried to hide them, afraid of being ridiculed or called freaks.

As she scanned the room looking for a place to sit, her eyes met his for a brief moment, and her lips parted as if she was surprised.

Marcel tried to smile, but he was too slow. By the time he commanded his lips to curve up, she had shifted her eyes away, and the connection was lost.

Still, even though the entire thing hadn't lasted more than a second, her face remained etched in his memory. The blue eyes, so big and intense, the incredibly smooth olive-toned skin, the pronounced cheekbones, and the lush, red lips.

Was she wearing lipstick? Or was it the natural color of her lips?

For some reason, Marcel felt compelled to find out.

20

SOFIA

*T*he blond man in the back was gorgeous, and shifting her gaze away from him had required effort.

He looked about her age, maybe a year or two older, but his bearing was of someone who was in charge, someone who shouldered a lot of responsibility.

Sofia was willing to bet that he wasn't one of the retreat's attendees. He just didn't look the part of someone with a paranormal talent.

He dressed like an executive, with slacks, not jeans, and a black turtleneck, Steve Jobs style. His hair was perfectly groomed, he wore a severe expression on his handsome face, and he was too good-looking.

What was he doing in the retreat?

Maybe he was a news reporter?

Or maybe a biographer?

Emmett Haderech was a colorful character, and the free-love community he'd built was fascinating. Without a doubt, there was plenty to write about, but when she'd researched Safe Haven, she hadn't found any books about it, and what she'd found on the internet wasn't much either.

Apparently, Emmett Haderech enjoyed being steeped in mystery. It added to his mystical and spiritual guru appeal.

After she and Roxie found a place to sit, she dared to peek at him again. His eyes were still on her, and she quickly looked away, pretending that she was looking for someone or something else.

Roxana elbowed her. "Sofia darling, you are not paying attention." She leaned closer to whisper in her ear. "If you keep looking at the young man in the back of the room, he will expect an invitation. I'm sure that you've read about the free-love philosophy of Safe Haven."

"I've read about it," Sofia whispered back. "But I'm here to explore my paranormal talent. Not to hook up with anyone."

Roxie giggled. "Yeah, I can see that you are so uninterested that you keep gazing at the back wall," she said loudly.

"Please, keep it down," Sofia murmured. "You're embarrassing me."

"Oh, sweetheart." Roxie patted her arm. "You need to loosen up. We are here to have fun." She made a suggestive gesture that didn't leave room for misinterpretation.

As several of the people at their table started chuckling and laughing, Sofia wanted to slide down her chair and hide under the tablecloth, but thankfully, Safe Haven's spiritual leader chose that moment to walk into the dining hall.

All eyes turned to him, and the laughter stopped, replaced by clapping.

Emmett Haderech cut an impressive figure in his flowing white robe, his rich dark beard, and shoulder-length hair. Based on a simple calculation of how many years the resort had been operating under his leadership, he had to be at least in his mid-fifties, but he didn't have a single white hair.

Maybe he was coloring it or wearing a wig?

That made more sense. His hair was way too thick and shiny to belong to a middle-aged human.

"Good afternoon." Emmett Haderech lifted his arms, the

sleeves of his white robe flowing down his sides like two sails, or maybe wings. "I'm overjoyed to have so many paranormally talented people attend this first-of-its-kind retreat. Before I begin, I would like to reward you all for being the pioneering group. Since the paranormal program is a perfect complement to our regular personal growth and spiritual offerings, and the benefit of participating in both is astounding, I invite everyone who completes this retreat to enroll in an additional one at a fifty percent discount. Also, everyone who enrolls today will be entered into a lottery for three free spots on our upcoming retreat." He smiled. "From past experience, I can assure you that you will experience such monumental personal growth that you will want to extend your stay at Safe Haven."

He was an excellent salesman, but it was too soon to make a sales pitch. He should have made the offer at the end of the retreat, and not before he even delivered his welcome speech.

Then again, what did she know about sales? Maybe now was the best time, before the actual classes began and people got disappointed.

After the clapping subsided, Emmett Haderech continued. "I would like to welcome you all to explore your paranormal talents and share your experiences with each other. I know that it is not easy to be different in a world of conformity. It's difficult enough to think critically and independently and express your opinions in this harsh and judgmental world, let alone have abilities that others do not understand. Leave that world outside of Safe Haven's walls. You are safe within them."

As clapping and cheers erupted, Emmett Haderech smiled, his very white teeth gleaming against his olive-toned skin and dark beard.

He let the audience clap and cheer, only lifting his arms when the cheers started to taper off.

After a long moment, everyone hushed, and he lowered his arms, "I want you to know that within these walls, you are all precious, you are all appreciated for who you are, and you are free to be the best version of yourselves, whatever that might be. In the first few days, most of you will still carry the weight of that oppressive outside world on your shoulders, and many will fear to open up their minds and hearts, but when you realize that you are safe, that you are loved for who you are, and that you are not judged, you will start to thrive. Hopefully, the seed planted in this safe haven will continue to grow and blossom long after you go home, and if we've done our job right, you will spread the light to those you care about and who care about you." He paused and lifted his arms again. "Welcome to the rest of your lives."

As the clapping resumed with even more enthusiasm than before, Sofia wiped tears from her eyes, and she wasn't the only one. Next to her, Roxie was crying unabashedly, and Lydia was blowing her nose into a napkin.

During the speech, Sofia had felt as if Emmett Haderech had been talking directly to her, but everyone else in the audience had probably felt the same. Except, their oppression was all in their minds, while hers was very real. His words didn't apply to them as directly as they applied to her.

These people didn't know what real oppression was like. They could speak their minds, and the worst that could happen to them was a heated argument with those who didn't agree with them. She lived in a place where dissent was impossible because Igor ruled them with his power of compulsion. Those who had strong minds and could somewhat resist knew that they would be severely punished, and their disobedience would result in pain or even death, not just to them but to their loved ones.

"Oh, my God." Roxie sniffled. "I want to move in here. I never felt like I belonged anywhere before. I was always the odd bird that didn't fit in. It would be so nice to just be me and not worry about what anyone thinks of me. I'm so tired of subduing my spirit to appease others."

"I hear you, sister," the woman sitting next to her said.

Sofia stifled a chuckle.

If that was Roxie subdued, she didn't want to be around the woman when she wasn't.

21

MARCEL

*M*arcel hadn't intended to stay for the luncheon, but he couldn't leave without at least learning his mystery lady's name.

He'd watched her during Emmett's speech, which had been surprisingly shorter than he'd expected and quite good. It had been somewhat moving, but not enough to be a tear-jerker, and yet many in the audience were shedding tears, including his mystery woman.

He hadn't seen the tears, but he'd seen her wiping them off with her thumbs.

Perhaps paranormals were more emotional or just more open with their emotions, or maybe Emmett had imbued his voice with a little compulsion to amplify the effect of his words.

Marcel hadn't felt it, but if the compulsion had been subtle enough, he wouldn't have.

As people lined up for the buffet, he rose to his feet and walked over but didn't join the line until his dancer arrived with her friend.

Standing right behind them, he waited for the other woman to stop talking so he could introduce himself, but as she kept going on and on, he was reduced to discreetly sniffing his mystery lady's hair.

It wasn't a scent that he recognized. She didn't wear a commercially made perfume, and it wasn't a soap fragrance he was familiar with either. To him, she smelled like pine trees and sunshine.

Poetic much?

Marcel shook his head. It had been many years since a woman had captured his interest so strongly and even longer since he'd felt poetic.

Finally, the talkative one noticed him and turned around. "Well, hello, handsome fellow. I'm Roxana." She offered him her hand. "And you are?"

"Marcel." He brought her pudgy hand to his lips and feathered them over her skin.

"Oh, my." She fanned herself with her other hand. "Are you French?"

"I'm originally from Scotland." He let go of Roxana's hand and shifted his gaze to the object of his fascination, offering her his. "Hello."

"Nice to meet you." Hesitantly, she put her long-fingered hand in his palm but didn't give him her name.

"I detect a slight accent." He forced a small smile. "Where are you from?"

"Sofia is from Finland," Roxana said. "She's a ballerina."

Finally, he knew her name, and his suspicion as to her occupation had been confirmed.

"Then I guessed correctly. When I first saw you enter the dining hall, I thought that you were a dancer."

"I'm not." Sofia found her voice. "I can dance as well as the next person, but I've never studied ballet or received any other formal dance lessons."

"You didn't?" Roxana tilted her head. "So why did you tell me that you were a ballerina?"

"I didn't. You said I was, and I didn't want to correct you in front of your friends and cause you embarrassment."

Roxana rubbed a hand over her forehead. "Maybe one day you will be a dancer. Sometimes my precognition plays tricks on me, and I confuse the future with the present." She smiled brightly. "I'm a dream interpreter and a seer."

"That's lovely." Marcel was still looking at Sofia.

She smiled. "I'm twenty-seven years old, so it's probably too late for me to pursue a career in ballet."

"If you're not a dancer, then what do you do?" Marcel asked.

"I'm a linguist."

He'd expected her to say that she was a yoga instructor or maybe even a self-defense teacher, but he hadn't expected something as mundane as a linguist.

"Do you teach languages?"

She nodded. "I assist several of my professors with under-grad classes while I keep expanding my repertoire."

So, she was a perpetual student like Sylvia. Some people enjoyed the lifestyle of academia, and if they could afford it, why not. Perhaps Sofia came from a wealthy family who didn't mind supporting her academic endeavors.

As their turn at the buffet arrived, they loaded their plates, and when they were done, Roxana turned to him. "Join us at our table."

He would have preferred for Sofia to extend the invitation, but she seemed remote. If not for the look they had exchanged when she'd entered the dining hall, he would have thought that she was uninterested, but that one unguarded moment gave him hope.

"Is there room for one more?" he asked.

"Of course." Roxana gripped his forearm as if she was afraid he would run off if she didn't hold on to him. "People are mingling. I'm sure some of our companions have moved to other tables."

Sofia still didn't look enthused about him joining them, but she didn't object either.

In contrast, Roxana's exuberant friendliness was endearing, and he was grateful to her for inviting him to join them. She didn't seem to be interested in him for herself, probably assuming that he was too young for her, so she must be doing it for Sofia.

That was sweet.

Some might think her pushy and loud, but Marcel saw the good heart underneath. Not that he was such a good judge of character, but as long as she had nothing to gain from being friendly toward him, he had no reason to suspect her of not being genuine.

As they sat down, he prepared to ask Sofia a thousand questions, but since she looked tense, he switched to Roxana. "Did you know Sofia from before, or did you two meet here?"

"We met at the train station," Roxana said. "Did you arrive at one of the other collection points?"

"I'm not a retreat attendee. I work here."

"Oh, how fascinating." Roxana's eyes sparkled with mischief while Sofia lowered hers to her plate. "I'm so excited to meet a member of the free-love community. I have so many questions about how the community works and the rules of engagement, so to speak." She waggled her brows.

"I'm not a member. I'm here temporarily to work on a project. I'm a computer engineer." He shifted his gaze to Sofia. "Where are you from?"

She paused with her fork midway to her mouth. "Roxie already told you that I'm from Finland."

"Originally. I meant, where are you from in the United States?"

"I don't live here. I live in Helsinki." She hesitated. "I came for the retreat, and then I'm going to tour the country for several months and absorb the language. I'm fluent in English, but there are so many idioms and phrases that I still

96

need to learn. I figured that the best way to do that was to travel and talk to people, so I took a semester off to learn firsthand."

Something was off about that speech.

Sofia didn't seem like the talkative type, and yet she'd just given him a long explanation that had been delivered so fast that it seemed rehearsed.

"Your English is flawless, and you have only a very slight accent. What other languages do you speak?"

"I'm fluent in German, French, Russian, Swedish, Norwegian…" She was much more relaxed when she spoke about the various languages she'd studied and her level of proficiency in each. It also seemed less rehearsed.

Sofia was hiding something, but it was probably as mundane as her visa status. She'd probably entered the United States on an ESTA, which was valid for only ninety days, and she planned on staying longer or maybe even finding a job.

Lunch went by with Roxana monopolizing the conversation, which seemed to suit Sofia just fine, and Marcel wasn't complaining either. He wasn't a great conversationalist, and with Roxana doing all the talking, he could relax and focus on watching Sofia.

When lunch was over, and the retreat attendees were summoned to proceed to their next activity, Sofia gave him a shy smile. "It was nice meeting you."

"The pleasure was all mine. I would like to see you again."

Grinning, Roxana gave him a discreet thumbs up and then turned to join the throng of people leaving the dining hall. She'd deliberately left them alone.

He made a mental note to thank her later.

Clutching her pendant, Sofia gave him a tight smile. "I'm sure we will bump into each other again. Safe Haven is not a big place."

Nice try, but he wasn't as easily deterred. "How about coffee later today after your activities are over?"

"I don't know when that will be, and I still need to unpack. Perhaps we could meet tomorrow?"

"Tomorrow it is. I'll meet you in the dining hall after lunch."

"I might have a class right after."

"Then we will make plans for the evening. I know that you had to surrender your phone when you came here, so I have no way of contacting you." He took her hand. "It's like in the old days when people had no phones. If a gentleman wanted to pursue a lady, he had to show up in person. I think it was better that way." He kissed the back of her hand. "Until we meet again, Sofia." He dipped his head. "Farewell."

22

SOFIA

"*L*et's try it again." The instructor, a chubby woman called Barbara, held up a pen. "Close your eyes, imagine an object as vividly as you can, including how the light is reflected off it, its smell, if it has any, its shadow, and hold the image in your mind. Partners, do your best to guess what the object is."

"Shoes," Roxie said. "Elegant men's dress shoes."

Sofia shook her head. "Wrong again."

"Damn it." Roxie let out a breath. "I was so sure that you were thinking about Marcel, and he did wear very nice dress shoes. I remember thinking that he could check his hair in their reflection because they were so clean and shiny. That man knows how to dress, and he is meticulous about his appearance, which can be a warning sign. It's never good to get involved with a perfectionist. It's not good to get involved with a schlump either, but someone that's in between is a good choice."

As Roxie kept going on about the qualities of the perfect man, Sofia tuned her out.

It was the last introductory class of the day, and after that, all she had to do was find a secluded spot so she could report what she'd observed so far to Valstar and be done with her duties for the day.

A shower, a comfortable bed, and the Spanish romance she'd gotten at the airport seemed like the perfect ending to a stressful day. And since the novel was meant to help her with Spanish reading comprehension, it wouldn't be a frivolous activity either.

The introductory classes had been interesting, especially Dr. Eleanor Takala's presentation, but it had been difficult to concentrate, with Roxie's constant blabbering and muttering. She never ended a comment with just one sentence. One idea flowed into the next in a never-ending stream of consciousness. But that wasn't the only thing distracting her. Her thoughts kept wandering back to Marcel, his handsome face and his shy smile popping into her mind's eye.

When she finally managed to banish him from her thoughts, Roxie would make a comment about him, and he would once again occupy her mind.

There was something about Marcel that called to her, and it wasn't just his good looks or his smooth, cultured voice. She wasn't a young girl anymore, and she wasn't foolish enough to get infatuated with a guy only because he was handsome, well-dressed, soft-spoken, eloquent, and intelligent.

Oh, well. Those qualities were plenty enough to deserve infatuation, but she wasn't attending the retreat to find a boyfriend.

She was on a mission, and so far, she hadn't observed anything important enough to report unless Igor was interested in learning about paranormal abilities.

Most of the purebloods could compel humans, and some could compel hybrids, but none of them were as powerful as Igor. Maybe he wanted to find out why?

Dr. Takala explained the various paranormal abilities and the scale she used to evaluate their strength. It was a simple one-to-ten scale, with one being intuition and ten being able to read thoughts or affect objects with one's mind, which none of the attendees could do. But she hadn't explained why some people's abilities were stronger than the abilities of others.

It was probably genetic.

That was why Igor tolerated Jade's disdain for him and kept her as his main breeder. He wanted his children to be powerful compellers like him, and none of the other pure-blooded females were as strong as her.

Unsurprisingly, Dr. Takala had never heard of mirror divining, and she'd been rightfully skeptical of Sofia's supposed talent, but she hadn't seemed suspicious. Many of the other purported talents seemed just as bogus as Sofia's.

Some people claimed to be able to retrieve memories stored in objects or remote view what was happening in a specific location without ever visiting it before, just from seeing a photograph. There were telepaths, seers, fortune tellers of different kinds, and a host of other paranormal terms that Sofia didn't remember offhand but had written down in her notebook.

She could recite what she'd written to Valstar, but she doubted Igor would find it useful. Most of that stuff could be found on the internet, and Igor didn't need her to attend a retreat thousands of miles away from the compound to learn the terms of various paranormal abilities.

"Earth calling Sofia." Roxie waved a hand in front of her eyes. "The class is over." She put her hands on her hips. "Were you daydreaming about tall, blond, and handsome?"

"I was not." Sofia collected her things and put them in her backpack.

As they followed the string of people leaving the class, Roxie fell in step with her. "Do you want to grab a coffee before dinner?" she asked. "Or are you meeting *Marrrcel...*" she rolled the r's. "Even his name is sexy."

"I'm not meeting him today."

"Oh, yeah?" Mirth danced in Roxie's eyes. "Are you meeting him tomorrow?" She threaded her arm through Sofia's.

"Maybe. He said that he would wait for me outside the dining hall after lunch, but I'm not sure it's a good idea."

Roxie regarded her with incredulous eyes. "Why the hell not?"

"I don't enjoy casual sex, and I don't want to lead him on. The retreat ends in two weeks. It's better not to get involved with anyone while I'm here."

Perhaps it was a mistake to say that. If Valstar commanded her to seduce some guy, she would have to explain to Roxie why she'd changed her mind.

Roxie shrugged. "Suit yourself, but I'm going to partake in the free-love community, and since we share a room, you might have to make yourself scarce for a couple of hours each night." Roxie winked. "So maybe going out with Marcel could fill in the time pleasantly."

Roxie hadn't left her side since they'd met earlier that morning, so she couldn't have met anyone yet. Maybe she'd seen someone she liked?

Was it possible that she was asking to find out whether Sofia was interested in Marcel because she was interested in him herself?

He was way too young for her, but Roxie didn't seem like the type who would be bothered by a thing like that. The woman was unconventional in every way, wearing outrageously colorful clothes and a wild multi-colored hairdo, so there was no reason to think she would follow convention regarding the appropriate age of her lovers.

"Did you see someone you liked?" Sofia asked

"Not yet, but I'm going to during tonight's social."

"What social?"

Roxie rolled her eyes. "Didn't you look at the schedule?"

"I didn't," she admitted. "I planned to go over it later."

"Well, there is some kind of social activity each night." She grinned. "Maybe you can invite Marcel to join. The community members are going to be there."

"He's not a community member. He's here temporarily."

"So? I'm sure he can attend the social."

"Maybe tomorrow." Sofia pulled her arm free. "I'm going to drop my backpack in our room and then go for a run on the beach. I'll meet you in the dining hall for dinner."

Roxie didn't look like she engaged in athletic activities, so hopefully, she wouldn't offer to join her. Sofia needed to find a secluded spot and report to Valstar.

"Isn't it too late for running on the beach?"

"I love running at night. The moon is out, and it's so peaceful."

Roxie shrugged. "Have fun. I'm going to find Lydia and Felicity. See you later, alligator."

Sofia smiled and waved.

Should she tell Valstar about Marcel?

The only thing interesting about him was that he worked at Safe Haven, so if Igor wanted to find out things about the people who lived and worked there, Marcel could be a good source. But then Valstar might tell her to get close to him.

It wouldn't be a hardship.

Marcel wasn't a charmer, but there was a quality about him that Sofia found attractive. He was reserved and refined, like a gentleman in one of the historical romances she liked or a prince from a fairytale. But most importantly, he liked her, and seducing him would be easy.

23

DARLENE

"Good morning, sunshine." Max walked into Eric's room with two cups of cappuccino and two wrapped pastries.

"Thank you." Darlene took the cup from him and patted the spot next to her on the cot. "Come sit with me and tell me about your mission last night."

They'd gotten into a routine during the two weeks since Eric had lost consciousness. Early each morning, Max showed up with coffee and pastries or sandwiches from the vending machines. They sat on her cot and used the chair as their table. He told her about his missions, and she listened, hoping that Eric was listening too.

Bridget had said that it was important to talk around him, and maybe that was why she pretended not to notice that Max was with her in the room. As long as they stayed out of the waiting area, it seemed to be fine with her.

The thing Darlene loved the most about Max was that he wasn't treating her as the poor woman who was anxiously waiting for her mate to wake up. He was treating her like a fellow soldier who was keeping a vigil over an injured comrade.

His visits cheered her up.

The question was why he was doing that. Was it just out of friendship? Was he doing it for Eric's sake or for hers?

Max glanced at the monitors instead of asking her whether there was any change, which was another thing she appreciated about him. He knew that if there was anything to report, she would tell him without being asked.

"We freed four girls and one boy, and we left two of the scumbags for the police to find. The other two didn't make it." He smiled evilly. "Oops."

"I'm glad." She took the lid off the cappuccino and took a sip. "It would have been even better if all four were an oops."

He shook his head. "We need to leave some behind to feed the authorities a story about a rival trafficking gang. Otherwise, the police will start looking for the missing victims and the vigilantes who are cleaning up the scum for them."

"It's sad and shameful." Darlene unwrapped the Danish. "The authorities don't do anything when they think the victims were taken by other traffickers, but they would have if they thought someone saved them."

Max nodded. "It was easier in the old days when there was a sheriff in town with a deputy or two. Most of the time, he didn't mind getting help from citizens ridding his community of filth."

She eyed him with a frown. "Have you been watching Westerns lately? When have you ever lived in a frontier town? From what I was told, the clan always resided in the city."

"Not back in Scotland. I'm talking about the old, old days. But you are right. They weren't called sheriffs. I just thought that the term would be more familiar to you."

"Oh." She shook her head. "I can't wrap my mind around how old you and the others are."

He grinned. "But we don't look it."

"No, you don't." She gave him an appreciative look. "Can I ask you something?"

"Anything."

"Why are you being so nice to Eric and me? I appreciate it, but it also makes me uncomfortable not knowing what your expectations are."

Eric hadn't had a chance to tell Max about his outrageous threesome idea, so it couldn't be about that.

Max looked away and then sighed. "Eric reminds me of someone I cared a lot about."

Oh, boy. So, Eric had been right, and Max was gay. Had he been in love with a human who resembled Eric? But if that was the case, why had he flirted with her? Had it been for show?

Maybe his macho Guardian friends weren't as tolerant of his sexual preferences? After all, they'd been born and raised in a different era, and they might have retained those awful attitudes toward gay people.

"Who was it? Was he a human?"

He shook his head. "Din is an immortal, and thankfully very much alive."

Perhaps the taboo on mating within the clan didn't apply to same-sex couples? They wouldn't produce a child together, so it made sense that the rules were laxer for them. Still, it had probably been frowned upon.

"Do you want to talk about it?"

"It's not a story I'm proud of. I was a bastard to my best friend. Din was like a brother to me, and I ruined our friendship over a girl." He sighed. "I'm still a bastard, but at least now I'm aware of it and strive to do better. I'm competitive and aggressive, and my empathic ability is almost nonexistent. I often don't realize that I'm being a jerk until it is too late. Like I didn't realize that Din had fallen in love with the girl and was taking it slow because he cared for her. I thought that he was just failing to seduce her, and since I always had to win, I seduced her instead and bragged to him about it."

Darlene grimaced. "Ouch. That's really douchey. I hope he beat you up."

"I wish he had. I would have taken the beating and pretended to lose so we could still be friends. But all he did was give me a look that said he was never going to forgive me and walked away. It happened nearly fifty years ago, and he still doesn't talk to me. It was one of the reasons I answered Bridget's call and moved here. The castle wasn't big enough for the two of us not to bump into each other, and the hatred in his eyes slew me each time anew."

"Did you try to talk to him?"

Max chuckled sadly. "Numerous times. I even asked Sari to intervene. He's never going to forgive me, and I can't really blame him. I deserve his eternal contempt."

Darlene shook her head. "Fifty years is a long time to hold a grudge. He should have gotten over it by now."

"First of all, fifty years is not long for an immortal. Your perspective on time will change once you transition. And secondly, he probably decided that I'm too rotten to deserve his friendship, and he's not wrong."

Putting herself in Din's shoes, she might have thought the same thing. Max had considered the guy his best friend, and yet he'd failed to realize that Din's feelings for the girl had run deeper than usual and that he hadn't thought of her as a hookup. On the other hand, Max had saved Din a lot of heartache down the line. The girl was human, so there had been no future for them anyway, and secondly, if she'd let Max seduce her while she was seeing Din, she hadn't deserved those deep feelings.

"Is she still alive?"

"I didn't keep tabs on her, but I hope she is. She would be in her seventies now."

"I bet she's been married a couple of times. In the long run, you did Din a favor."

"Maybe. But it was still a rotten thing to do, and I'm ashamed of myself."

"You've learned from your mistake, and you're striving to become a better man. You should forgive yourself."

"I thought that I did and that I moved on, but then I met Eric, and he reminded me of the friend I lost."

"Does Din look like Eric?"

"It's not so much the looks that are similar as it is the temperament and the attitude." Max sighed again. "Din and I used to have so much fun together, swapping silly banter and pretending to be more than friends to confuse the girls. Eric exudes a similar vibe. He embraces life and doesn't take himself too seriously. Din used to be like that until I betrayed him. After that, he became bitter." He sighed. "I have a confession to make."

Guessing where he was going with that, Darlene tensed. "You felt the same urge to compete with Eric. That's why you pursued me. And now you are trying to compensate for it."

"It's not as straightforward as that. I liked Eric from the moment I met him, but I didn't think of him as competition because he was human, and I knew that you would have to move on and find an immortal male to induce your transition. I stayed close to you so when you realized that you needed to let him go and choose an immortal, I would be the obvious choice. I offered to induce Eric because I was impatient to find out whether he was going to turn immortal or not."

Suddenly feeling suspicious again, she narrowed her eyes at him. "Did you botch his induction on purpose?"

His brows dipped low. "I'm not that rotten, and even if I were, I'm not stupid. I knew that if I failed to induce him, someone else would step in and give him another shot. I did my best and left the rest to the Fates."

She believed him about that but was still mad as hell. "Did you hang around hoping that Eric wouldn't make it?"

He put his hand over his chest. "Fates forbid. I hung around because I realized that you and Eric were truelove mates, and there was no room for me in your life as a lover or a mate. But I still want to be part of your and Eric's life as a friend."

She was still not convinced that he didn't have ulterior motives. "What about your attraction to me? Did it just disappear?"

He chuckled. "Not at all. I still think you are sexy as sin. But once Eric's fangs come online and he starts pumping you with his venom, the attraction will go away." He lifted his hand to his chest. "Just so there is no confusion, I didn't hang around to try to seduce you. I wasn't going to repeat that mistake and lose your and Eric's friendship. I promise you. I've learned my lesson."

24

SOFIA

*S*ofia must have jogged three miles along the rocky shore before she felt that she was far enough from the resort to stop and initiate the communication with Valstar.

The last person she'd met was so far away by now that even if he were a pureblooded Kra-ell he couldn't hear her, but she was worried about him nonetheless, checking every couple of minutes if he was following her.

He'd stopped her, asked her a few friendly questions, warned her to not get too far away, and even given her a once-over, but it hadn't been sexual. If it were, she would have been much less worried. There was nothing unusual about a guy talking to a girl he found attractive, but his interest had been more professional in nature and indicated that despite his civilian clothes, he was a guard.

Why would the resort's security wear civilian clothing? Were they working undercover?

After that encounter, Sofia had decided to put even more distance between herself and Safe Haven than she'd originally planned.

A rock formation that stretched from the shore inland

looked like a good place to hide. She didn't need much space, and even a crevice would do.

She found one that was shallow, not deep enough to shield her completely, but enough for her to press her back against and blend into the rock. With the dwindling light and her dark coloring, she would be nearly invisible from afar, so even if someone decided to venture as far as she did, she would see them long before they saw her.

Pulling the miniature earpiece out of the locket, she put it in her ear and pressed on the picture side of the pendant to activate the device.

"Sofia." Her grandfather came online right away.

He was also wearing a device like hers. Only his was stored inside a pocket watch. It wasn't necessary for him to hide the communication device, but he'd explained that the spy gear was sold in pairs of either two pendants, two pocket watches, or a pendant and a watch.

It was most likely manufactured in China, like everything else.

"I'm ready to submit my daily report," she said.

"First, tell me, how are you fitting in with the paranormal crowd?"

Since when had Valstar become chatty or cared about how she was doing? Their interactions had never been personal. Preparing for the mission was the most time she'd ever spent with her grandfather, and it had been as impersonal as if they weren't related.

"I followed your instructions and found a talkative friend. She is a great cover for me. As I was afraid, my supposed mirror divining was so unusual that I was the only one the instructors had ever encountered, and it raised a few eyebrows, but there were others with all kinds of strange talents that I'd never heard about, so I didn't stand out. Do you want me to tell you about what the others claimed they could do?"

"Igor is not interested in humans with paranormal abilities."

For a moment there, she'd thought that was why Valstar had asked how she fitted in, but apparently, he was inquiring whether anyone suspected that she was a spy.

"If someone could tell me what Igor is interested in, I would know what to look for. As it is, I'm flying blind."

"Find out more about the organization and the people who run it. I've researched the founder on the internet, but there isn't much about him. See if you can get an audience with him."

Why was Igor interested in Emmett Haderech?

The guy could deliver good speeches, but his theatrics were ridiculous. Was anyone impressed by his white robe and shiny wigs?

"I'll try. I need to settle in first. It will be suspicious if I ask for an audience right away."

Valstar growled. "You have all of two weeks to find out everything there is about those people. Don't waste time. You know what's at stake."

Sofia swallowed.

Valstar would most likely suffer for her incompetence, but that didn't bother her as much as what Igor might do to other members of her family who were not as important.

Should she mention Marcel?

She didn't have anything else to report, and she needed to buy herself and her family time. Marcel knew Emmett Haderech, so maybe he could help her get an audience.

"I might have an in," she said quietly. "One of the guys working here showed interest in me. I thought that getting involved with him would waste precious time, but he might know things about Emmett Haderech and the other people working here. What do you think I should do?"

"Take advantage of him, of course. Pump him for information."

Sofia stifled a groan. "He said that he's here only temporarily and that he's working on some project, but he didn't say what that project was. What if he doesn't know anything? Given what's at stake, I really don't want to waste time."

"It's not going to be a waste," Valstar said. "In fact, that's great news. I'll report to Igor that you've already found a source. That will dispose him more favorably toward you, and he might grant you an extension to complete your mission. Seduce the guy and make him fall for you, so he will invite you to stay with him after the retreat is over. It will give you access to the management and more time to collect information."

Right. She could seduce Marcel easily, but to make him fall in love with her? How was she supposed to do that?

It either happened, or it didn't.

She had very limited experience with men, and neither of her two boyfriends had fallen head-over-heels in love with her.

She wasn't the type to evoke extreme emotions in a guy.

Sofia closed her eyes and let her head drop against the rock behind her. "I'm meeting him tomorrow for coffee. He seems interested, and I'm going to encourage him, but I'm afraid of botching it. I'm not a great seductress."

"You'd better be."

"I know." She let out a breath. "I'll try to contact you tomorrow, but if I'm successful and I end up in his bed, I might not be able to."

"Find the time. Igor wants to hear from you daily."

"Yes, sir."

As Valstar ended the communication on his end, Sofia slid down the monolithic stone and sat on the rocky sand, oblivious to the discomfort. What was a little physical pain when her soul was shriveling from what she was forced to do?

She wasn't a spy. Her heart wasn't in it, and yet she had no choice but to manipulate and deceive an innocent man. The worst part was that she didn't even know to what end.

What was Igor going to do with the information? Attack Safe Haven? He hadn't asked her to find out about its defenses, so it didn't seem like that was his plan.

He was right to suspect Jade's interest in the place, though.

The only reason Sofia could think of for Jade to show interest in Safe Haven and its paranormal program was to find a way to circumvent Igor's compulsion.

Heck, everyone living under Igor's thumb, including her grandfather, would have loved to find a way to do that. But if that was what Igor suspected, he should be interested in the various paranormal abilities, especially anything that had to do with nullifying compulsion. Except, that was not what he wanted her to investigate.

How the hell did he expect her to succeed when he wasn't telling her enough to point her in the right direction?

Sofia wanted to scream her frustration, to cry and sob for the injustice of the predicament he'd put her in, and most of all, the threat to her family and friends.

Love was a liability, she realized.

Maybe that was why the Kra-ell tried to eradicate it from their vocabulary. Honor and duty were their mantras, but deep inside, they were not all that different from humans. They were very good at hiding their softer feelings, but they had them.

Except for Igor.

He was the poster child for what the pureblooded Kra-ell strived to be, but what they didn't realize was that if more of them became like him, their society would be doomed.

25

KIAN

*K*ian spread the satellite photos over the conference table. The coordinates in Jade's fable were not accurate enough to pinpoint a specific location, which made the task of finding where she was being held difficult.

Each degree of latitude equaled about sixty-nine miles, and each degree of longitude equaled about fifty-five miles. That meant searching an area of about 3,800 miles. It was nearly as big as Connecticut.

It wasn't as densely populated, but it was still a lot of ground to cover. Karelia was densely wooded, and the few villages that fell within the area he'd delineated were small and situated near a lake. Any of them could be where Jade was being held.

When the knock sounded on the door, he walked over and opened the way for Turner. "Good morning." He offered the guy his hand.

"Good morning." Turner shook it and walked over to the conference table. "I've been looking at these satellite photos all week." He pushed them aside. "I need more time and more money. I thought my Russian subcontractor would have something for me by now, but he says he needs to hire more men and bribe more officials."

The investigation was already costing a small fortune, which Kian wouldn't have minded spending if he thought that it was crucial to find Jade or her captors, but neither he nor Turner thought that it was.

After the initial excitement over the email had subsided, Kian had decided not to evacuate the immortals from Safe Haven. Eleanor had to stay because she was the director of the paranormal program, and she couldn't just get up and leave, and Marcel couldn't leave the team of bioinformaticians to idle while he returned to the village either.

Leon and his team of Guardians had the complex on high alert, but no visitors had arrived during the week following the email.

The attendees of the new paranormal retreat had been carefully screened, with Roni hacking into their medical histories and finding out whether they had been vaccinated and treated for diseases.

If the captors wanted to infiltrate Safe Haven, they would send a hybrid who could pass for a human, but since hybrid Kra-ell didn't get sick and didn't require vaccinations, they wouldn't have a medical record at all. Even Turner doubted that Jade's captors would have thought to fabricate that.

In fact, Kian had made a mental note to include a fake medical record for immortals who needed a human cover, starting with Onegus and the Guardians.

"What did your contractor do so far?"

Turner sat down and crossed his arms. "He covered most of the villages, but he still has a few that he needs to investigate, and then he needs to comb the area. Drones are useless there, and there are many trails aside from the few paved roads. It will take him weeks to cover the entire area. Are you sure that you want to continue spending money on that?"

Kian groaned. "I've already started, so I'd better finish. Tell your contractor that he has until the end of the week. I promised Emmett to give him an answer before Friday."

"About that." Turner uncrossed his arms. "You should tell him to go ahead and notify the winners, including Jade. I hope he used the time to come up with a clever way to hide a message for her inside the Safe Haven's virtual library. Maybe she will respond with more clues and save us the trouble of continuing the search."

"She might not have the exact coordinates." Kian pulled one of the photos closer to him. "Think about it. If you were held captive and no one told you your exact location, you might be able to figure out approximately where you were, but not the precise coordinates. I doubt Jade's captors gave her a cellular phone with location services."

"She must have access to the internet to stumble upon Emmett's promotional videos. By the way, did the Clan Mother or Syssi find more clues in the fable?"

Kian let out a breath. "Nothing concrete. There is a strong emphasis on children and their importance to the lioness, which they interpret as Jade warning us not to bomb the place when we find it. Syssi thinks that Jade wants Emmett to sneak her out by digging out an escape tunnel, but I doubt that part of the fable should be taken literally. My mother thinks that the rabbit's part was significant, and that Jade wants someone to know that she's still alive and trapped."

"That makes sense." Turner rubbed a hand over his jaw. "As far as she knows, Emmett is a solo operator who can't do anything to help her. She also probably assumes that Vrog is alive, but two hybrids don't make an army or even a rescue team. Her goal was to let someone know that she and the other females are still alive."

"To what end?" Kian asked. "She took a great risk by sending that email."

Turner pushed to his feet. "If I were in her situation, I

would want someone to know. Besides, she probably suspects that there are more survivors out there and that Emmett might someday find them. The Kra-ell are long-lived, so that day could be a year from now or a hundred. If nothing else, it gives her hope."

EMMETT

*W*hen Emmett's phone rang and Kian's number flashed on the screen, his heartbeat accelerated, and his robe suddenly felt too stifling.

"Good morning, Kian," he managed with a nonchalant tone. "How are things back in the village?"

He couldn't care less, but it was important not to sound anxious. Kian was a damn good negotiator, and he would pounce on the opportunity to get Emmett to make even more concessions in exchange for allowing him to communicate with Jade.

Hell, after ten days of waiting for a response, he was more than willing to give Kian anything he might ask for to get the green light to announce her as one of the winners.

"Everything is fine, but regrettably, the same cannot be said about our investigation in Karelia. Turner's guy is barely done with questioning people in the villages, and he will only start combing the wooded areas tomorrow. I told Turner to pull him out if he doesn't find anything by Friday."

Emmett's heart sank. "What am I supposed to do with the contest winners? I need to announce them the latest by Friday."

"Go ahead and announce them. I assume that you came up with a way to hide a message for Jade in Safe Haven's virtual library?"

"I wrote my own fable, and I asked the community members to each write one so mine wouldn't be the only one. So far, I collected twenty-seven of them, and more are coming in."

"Excellent. When you announce the winners, treat Jade exactly like the other two. Put the three names up and send her a template email congratulating her on the win. If you can, try to hint in your fable that we need more precise coordinates. Nearly 4,000 square miles is a lot of ground to cover. When you're done, send it to me. I want to read it and give it to Turner to read as well."

"What about the satellite photos?" Emmett asked.

"Useless. Our satellite is not equipped with thermal imaging, and even if it was, I doubt it would have done us any good. Thermal imaging is usually of much lower quality compared to visual wavelengths because of thermal noise being an issue. Drones are better for that, but deploying them in that area would alert Jade's captors. There are no military bases in the area, and no tourists with camera drones. It's hard to believe that places like Karelia still exist."

"Sounds like the perfect place for you to hide your clan in."

Kian chuckled. "No, thank you. I like to be close to civilization. I'm not a farmer."

"What about your sister's people? Isn't the castle located in a remote area?"

"I thought that it was, but compared to Karelia, it's not."

"St. Petersburg is nearby." Emmett swiveled his office chair around.

"The distance from St. Petersburg to the edge of the quadrant is four and a half hours by car. To get to the middle of it would take ten hours. Do you still think it's not a big deal?"

"It doesn't sound that bad. Driving from Los Angeles to San Francisco along the coast takes eight hours."

"Trust me, it is. Especially since it's so wooded. Turner's contractor operates a team of six men. They go in twos and try not to attract too much attention. It's going slow."

"I hope Jade can tell us more." Emmett leaned back in his chair. "When I send the reply email, I will word it the same to all three, but I'll do it in a way that will point her in the right direction."

"Don't be too obvious."

"I won't. I know how to play the game."

"I'm sure you do, but you are also anxious to establish a line of communication with her, and you might not be as cautious as you should be. Let Eleanor and Leon read the email before you send it."

"I'll do that. Can I tell Vrog and Aliyah now?"

"It's your prerogative. Just remember that the more people who know about it, the riskier it becomes for Jade. Tell them just the highlights and use the clan phone. I don't want Vrog rushing to Karelia and playing the hero. He's waited for Jade's return for over two decades. If he has to choose between her and the clan, I'm not sure who he will choose."

"The clan. He might feel loyalty to Jade, but he has a son who is a member of your clan. He will not betray him. Or you."

"I hope you're right."

VROG

"Vrog, my man." Anandur clapped him on the back before pulling a chair out and sitting down with his sandwich and his coffee. "When did you come back?"

"Last night. I thought that as a Guardian you would know that."

"Nah." Anandur unwrapped his sandwich. "You are a trusted honorary clan member now. We track you only for your own safety, and since you are not important, I don't follow your comings and goings." He took an enormous bite of the sandwich.

"I don't know whether I should be flattered or offended."

Anandur finished chewing the huge chunk he'd taken and followed it with a sip from his coffee. "How did the trip go?"

"I sold the school, but I agreed to remain available as an advisor for the next twelve months, so I'm not completely done with it."

On the one hand, his continued involvement with the school made the sale easier, but on the other hand, it wasn't a clean break, which could have been better.

"You are a rich man now. What are you going to do with all that money?"

Vrog shrugged. "I don't know. The clan is providing the funds for the school I'm planning to open here, so I don't need to use any of mine. I might invest it in the stock market."

Anandur nodded. "Ask Kian for help. The market is crap right now, but some stocks are still doing well."

"Which ones?"

The Guardian laughed. "No clue. I transfer most of my pay to Shai, and he invests my money in the stocks Kian tells him to get. I don't even know how much I've made. I might have lost money and not know it."

"If you put such trust in Kian and Shai, I might as well do it too and save myself the headache of figuring out what to do with the money."

Taking a look around, Anandur leaned closer and whispered conspiratorially. "You should also ask Kalugal's advice. His dealings might be a little shadier than Kian's, but he makes more money on them."

Vrog lifted his hands. "I'm not a big risk taker. I prefer the safer, aboveboard investments."

"Yeah, I'm with you on that. But I heard people talking about the killing they've made with Kalugal's help, so I thought I would mention it." Anandur turned and looked at Aliyah, who was delivering a tray to the next table over. "Hello, pretty lady. Are you happy to have your man back?"

"I'm very happy." She leaned over Vrog's shoulder and kissed his cheek. "I thought that the five days he was gone would not be a big deal, but it was difficult." She pulled out a chair and sat down. "Next time, I'm going with you."

"I offered." He took her hand and brought their joined hands to his lap. "You said that you couldn't leave Wonder alone in the café."

"I couldn't. With Callie gone and Wendy working only part-time, most of the time, it's just the two of us, and one person can't handle everything. We put an ad on the clan's virtual bulletin board, but so far there have been no takers. Vivian said that she was willing to help out from time to time, but just as a volunteer. She doesn't want to commit."

"That's a shame." Anandur put his paw on Aliyah's shoulder. "But I can't say that I'm sorry. Callie's semi-official opening night is this Saturday. I'm crossing my fingers for her restaurant to succeed. She's an awesome cook, but she doesn't have enough help either."

Leaning back, Aliyah pulled her hand out of Vrog's. "I wish we had more Odus. That would solve everyone's problems."

"Yeah, well." Anandur finished his coffee in one sip. "It is what it is." He pushed to his feet. "I need to get back. Have a great rest of your day, you two."

He turned around and strode toward the pavilion.

"What did I say to sour his mood?" Aliyah asked quietly. "Does he have something against the Odus?"

"Why would he? I think he just needed to get back to work."

"Speaking of work, did Vlad tell you that he quit his job at the bakery?"

Vrog nodded. "His graphic design business has taken off faster than he expected, and he can no longer juggle both jobs."

"I'm happy for him." Aliyah sighed. "He's doing what he loves, while I didn't even figure out what I want to do with the rest of my life yet."

"There is no rush. You are working at the café and taking online classes. Wait until something catches your interest."

She grimaced. "The classes I'm taking are just stopgaps for the holes in my general education, and they are boring. I need something I can get passionate about." She pushed to her feet. "I'd better get back." She leaned and kissed him on the lips. "I have plans for you tonight."

124

"Oh, yeah?"
"Yeah. We are going hunting."

DARLENE

*D*arlene flipped a page, read a few more paragraphs without actually absorbing the story, and closed the book with a groan.

It was a sweet romance, the kind she usually devoured in one go, but lately the overly flowery language and the instant love had been annoying her. Reading about romance while her partner was in a coma felt like a betrayal, but what else was there for her to do?

If she were a Catholic, she could have clutched a rosary and prayed, but she'd been an atheist before joining the clan, and now she was a pagan who believed in multiple gods and the Fates.

Darlene chuckled.

The gods were real, so it was not a question of believing in them or not. Only yesterday, Toven had given Eric one of his blessings, and Annani was scheduled to give him one at the end of the day.

No one knew what the gods were doing when they were alone in Eric's room, and the monitoring camera was always turned off for these visits. For some reason, they were both very secretive about the ritual they were performing.

She imagined them laying their hands on him while their glow intensified, encompassing Eric with their healing energy. Or maybe they were breathing into his mouth. Wasn't there something in the Bible about God's breath of life granting immortality? Or was it something in Egyptian mythology?

Whatever they were doing, it was helping, and she was grateful to them. Eric was stable, he wasn't dying, and that was all that mattered.

It would have been better if he'd woken up already, but she was counting her blessings—literally. He'd gotten eight so far, five from Toven and three from Annani.

Letting out a breath, Darlene put the book down on the cot, pushed to her feet, and walked over to the bed.

Maybe she should read to Eric?

Not the romance, but maybe the one that Max had been reading to him. It was so gruesome that she left the room whenever he was reading it. Men loved those kinds of stories and considered sweet romances beneath them.

Silly gooses.

Real life was difficult enough. Why make themselves even more miserable by reading about torture and murder?

"You know what?" She brushed her fingers over Eric's forehead. "I'm going to read to you my romance novel, and if you think it's silly, you can make fun of it after you wake up."

Darlene turned back, picked up the book from her cot, and returned to his bed.

Before Max had brought her a stepping stool, she'd had to hoist herself up to the bed, but now she could climb easily and prop her feet on the step while sitting.

"Here it goes." Darlene cleared her throat. "As Veronica's legs encircled Marco's hips, he started pounding into her in earnest. Her eyes fluttered closed, but he would have none of that. Look at me, he commanded, and she snapped her eyes open. He kissed her then, his tongue thrusting into her mouth as brutally as his shaft was thrusting below."

She was about to flip the page when she noticed that Eric's lips had curled up slightly, and when she turned around to watch him closer, his eyelids fluttered.

Her heart racing, she put her hand on his cheek. "Eric? Are you awake?"

His lips curved up a little more, and then his beautiful eyes opened, but when he tried to open his mouth, he only managed a weak groan.

"Hold on. I'll get Hildegard. I can't believe the romance novel did it. I should have read it to you every day."

The door opened, and the nurse came in. "I called Bridget. She's on her way." Hildegard walked over to the cabinet, pulled out a paper cup, and filled it with water.

"You can wet his lips, and if he's up to it, he can drink a little."

Darlene's hands shook so badly that the nurse ended up doing it for her, and then Bridget walked in and took over.

"Welcome back, Eric." She raised the back of the bed, so he was reclined, and held up the straw to his lips. "Take very small sips. You were unconscious for two weeks. If you drink too much at once, it will all come back up."

MARCEL

*M*arcel debated whether he should eat at the lodge or at the small dining room in the paranormal enclave he and his team were sharing.

He was eager to see Sofia again, but he'd told her that he would meet her outside the dining hall, not inside.

Why was he making such a big deal out of such a small decision?

He should get her a phone or just ask Eleanor to allow her to use hers. Emmett's excuse for not allowing the retreat attendees to have phones was that it forced them to socialize. If they wanted to spend the night with someone or just meet people, they had to get out of their rooms and find the person they were looking for at the common area of the lodge.

It made sense, but Marcel knew that in the past, Emmett hadn't allowed phones because he'd enjoyed the complete control he'd had over the community members and the retreat attendees.

Now the community members had personal phones, but they had agreed to limit their use so they would keep some of their former way of life, which was all about the community and togetherness.

To Marcel, it sounded like a description of hell. He never could have survived in a place like that and would have blown his brains out.

Those who claimed that hell was a custom-tailored experience were correct. What was a safe haven to some was hell to others and vice versa.

"Aren't you joining us for lunch?" Kylie asked when he passed the dining hall and kept walking.

"Not today. I need to discuss a few things with Emmett."

"I see." She gave him a smile. "Then I'll see you at the lab after lunch." She opened the door to the dining hall and walked inside.

Why had he felt the need to lie to her?

Well, firstly, because he'd told her that he had a girlfriend, so telling her about Sofia would have confirmed her suspicion that he'd lied before. And secondly, deep down, he was a nice guy, and he didn't want to hurt her feelings. But that was a mistake. If things went well with Sofia, Kylie would find out anyway, and her feelings would be doubly hurt when she figured out that he'd lied to her not just once but twice.

In the lodge, he walked into the packed dining hall and scanned it for Sofia. He found her sitting with Roxana and two other ladies and headed toward them.

Her hair was once again gathered in a large bun on top of her head, and he wondered how it looked when it was loose. It had to be very long to create such a large thing.

She wasn't wearing any makeup, not even the lipstick she'd had on the day before. She looked lovely, fresh, and delicate. A natural, effortless beauty. Still, he had enough experience with women to realize that the lack of effort meant that she didn't consider him worthy of it.

She'd known he would come, and she hadn't bothered to make herself pretty for him. But wasn't that ironic?

He didn't like that Kylie was working so hard to tempt him, and now he was upset that Sofia hadn't.

"Good afternoon, ladies. May I join you?"

"Of course," Roxana said. "But we are done." She looked at the two other women. "Aren't we, ladies?"

Their plates were still half full, and they didn't look happy to abandon them.

"Please." Sofia rose to her feet. "Don't leave because Roxie wants to give Marcel and me space. We will move to another table." She gave him a tight smile. "Have you eaten?"

"Not yet." He gave her a discreet once-over.

She wore slim jeans, a white T-shirt, and a pair of flat, black shoes. It was such a simple outfit, and yet she made it look stunning with her poise and her grace. Small earrings adorned her ears, and the same gaudy pendant she'd worn yesterday hung around her neck. He assumed it held sentimental value because it looked like a cheap trinket.

Sofia nodded as if she'd expected that to be his answer. "I'll accompany you to the buffet." She surprised him by threading her arm through his. "The chicken dish I chose was dry. I want to try something else."

As he turned to wave goodbye at Roxie, she winked and gave him the thumbs-up.

Had she convinced Sofia to give him a chance?

Sofia was definitely acting friendlier toward him today than she had the day before.

"How was your first day at the retreat?" he asked, to start a conversation.

"Interesting." She took a fresh plate and put a tiny portion of fish on it. "I'm fascinated by all the paranormal talents."

He loaded his plate with the fish as well, but a much bigger portion of it, and added a scoop of rice and another scoop of grilled vegetables.

Sofia didn't add anything else.

"Is that all you're eating?"

131

"I'm saving room for coffee and dessert. We were supposed to meet for coffee, right?" She turned to look at him. "I thought that you would wait for me outside the dining hall."

"I couldn't wait," he admitted.

She lowered her eyes, but her lips curved up in a small, shy smile.

Damn, that demure expression made his shaft harden in an instant, and as he sucked in a breath, she looked at him with surprise in her blue eyes. "Are you okay?" she asked.

"Perfect. I saw a vacant table. Let's grab it before someone else takes it."

She laughed. "If you want us to dine alone, you'll have to eliminate six of the eight chairs. Otherwise, we will have company."

SOFIA

*S*ofia was nervous, but so was Marcel, which made it a little easier for her to flirt with him.

Despite his good looks and his sophistication, he was awkward around her, as if he hadn't dated in a while and didn't know what to do.

Maybe he was recently divorced, and she was the first woman he was flirting with in years?

If only that was true, it would make her job so much easier. He wouldn't notice how inexperienced she was.

As she sat down, he put his plate on the table and then started tilting the other six chairs, so their backs were resting against the table.

"If anyone asks, we are saving these seats for our six imaginary friends." He lifted the one remaining chair and brought it closer to hers. "It is a paranormal retreat, right? Imaginary friends or ghosts shouldn't surprise anyone."

She couldn't help the giggle rising up in her throat. "It shouldn't. What're their names?"

He pointed at the first chair. "That's Albert. Next to him is his wife Josephine, and the other four are their children. Susie, Sarah, Stephan, and Sirius."

"Are they ghosts or imaginary friends?"

"They are not ghosts because that would make you sad. They are our friends."

He was right. It would have made her sad to think of a family that had died together.

"How did you know that it would make me sad?"

He shrugged. "It would make anyone sad, and especially a sensitive paranormal. I saw the tears you wiped from your eyes after Emmett's speech, and before you feel embarrassed about it, I can tell you that you weren't the only one. The guy has a knack for tugging on people's heartstrings."

How had he seen her tearing up? He'd sat all the way on the other side of the dining hall, which was at least fifty feet away from where she'd been sitting.

He either had very good eyesight, or he had a phone on him and had used the zoom feature on his camera to spy on her.

That would have been an ironic role reversal.

"I'm not embarrassed. Roxie was sobbing openly, and Lydia and Felicity were tearing up as well. We all feel oppressed in some way, even if it's only in our heads."

Her oppression was real, but everyone else listening to Emmett's speech could probably think of how and why they were oppressed as well.

Marcel tilted his head. "We are all prisoners of our own belief systems. We live in a democratic country, and as long as we don't break the law, we can say and do whatever we please. If we don't, it's because of fear. There is fear of ridicule, fear of rejection, fear of not fitting in with the crowd, and so on."

As Marcel cut a piece of his fish, Sofia did the same. "Fear is a powerful motivator or rather an inhibitor. It's a prison for the soul."

For the next few moments, they ate in silence, or rather

Marcel ate, and she nibbled. She wasn't hungry, and even if she were, she was too nervous to eat.

Besides, watching Marcel eat was a treat.

He had such perfect table manners. She'd never seen anyone eat with such precision, and especially not any males. Usually, they shoved food into their mouths as if they were afraid someone was going to take it away from them.

When he was done, he patted his lips dry with a napkin and then glanced at her plate. "You haven't eaten your fish."

"I was already full." She pushed the plate away.

"Then I guess it is time for coffee and dessert." Marcel rose to his feet.

"Definitely." She followed him up and took the plate and the silverware.

After dropping the dishes in the wash bin, they headed to the other side of the dining hall, got their coffees and cakes, and returned to their table.

By now, most of the lunch crowd had dispersed, and only a few had stayed behind to sip on coffee or tea and chat with newfound friends.

It was only her second day in the retreat, and she'd already gained three new friends and one potential boyfriend. That was unprecedented for her, and she could only surmise that paranormals were special not just because of their abilities, real or imagined, but they were also nice people who were more open and inclusive than most.

"The coffee is not bad." Marcel put his mug down. "I hear that it's a big improvement over what they used to serve here, which was some sort of imitation coffee that was caffeine-free."

"That sounds nasty. Why would they serve such a thing?"

"The management hired a gourmet chef and tasked her with creating a healthy menu for the guests. You know, the healthy mind in a healthy body philosophy. But people complained about the food and the coffee and tea, and changes were made."

Perhaps that was her opening. "By management, do you mean Emmett Haderech?"

He shook his head. "This place is Emmett's baby, but he made some mistakes and had to take on a partner who was more business savvy. The partner was the one who hired the chef."

"Interesting. Who's the partner? Is it anyone famous?"

"Not at all. In fact, the partner is an organization. Not just one person."

Sofia took a tiny bite of the cake and washed it down with the coffee. "Do they run other resorts like this one?"

"They run hotels and vacation resorts. This is a new type of venture for them."

That didn't sound like anything Igor would be interested in, and she decided to drop that line of questioning. "How well do you know Emmett Haderech?" she asked.

Marcel leaned back in his chair. "Emmett is an acquaintance, not a friend. I know him, but not that well."

MARCEL

*M*arcel was starting to get suspicious.

Sofia was asking a lot of questions, and she was anxious. Could she be an undercover reporter?

If she was, her cover story was perfect. As a Finnish citizen on a tourist visa, she was an unknown, and he doubted that Roni could find out much about her. But then, it didn't make much sense for anyone to go to such lengths for a story.

Maybe she was just fascinated with Emmett, as most of the retreat guests were, and she was curious about the enigmatic former cult leader. Not that Emmett had ever called himself that. He claimed to be just a spiritual leader, a shepherd, but even after the changes Kian had made, the community members still worshiped Emmett with blind devotion. At least he couldn't take advantage of them anymore.

Perhaps his past had made Marcel more suspicious and less trusting than most, but he wouldn't feel comfortable with Sofia until he found out more about her and laid his suspicions to rest.

Leaning back, he smiled. "We've been talking about this and that, but you didn't tell me about your paranormal talent yet. Why are you here, Sofia? What do you hope to gain from participating in the retreat?"

She let out a breath. "My talent is very strange. It started as a party trick and grew into more." She seemed embarrassed to tell him about it.

"Come on, you can tell me. I promise not to make light of it."

She eyed him from under lowered lashes. "You are a computer engineer, the most pragmatic of professions. Do you even believe in paranormal abilities?"

"I've seen enough proof to make me a firm believer in paranormal phenomena." Marcel had no paranormal talent, but he was surrounded by people with a variety of them.

"My talent is catoptromancy. It's also called enoptromancy, and it is basically divination using a mirror."

He'd never heard of a talent like that. "Fascinating. What kind of fortunes do you see?"

"I don't see fortunes. I see people's true nature. You're a handsome man, but if you are rotten on the inside, your reflection will show the monster you are on the inside. It also works in reverse. An ugly or deformed person with a pure soul would appear beautiful in my mirror."

The mirror was probably just a focusing tool, and the real ability was inside of her, with or without it.

"What about you?" Marcel leaned closer to Sofia. "What do you see when you look in the mirror?"

She winced. "I just see my reflection. It only works on others."

For some reason, he had a feeling that she wasn't telling him the truth.

"Does your divination require a special kind of mirror, or will any mirror do?"

"It needs to be rounded. A mirror with corners doesn't work."

He crossed his arms over his chest. "That's a shame. I

wanted to stop by the lobby and have you look at my reflection in the mirror there, but it's not round."

She chuckled. "I know what I will see. You are the same on the inside as you are on the outside."

If her talent was real, she would be able to tell him things that he kept hidden, but if she thought that she needed the mirror for that, she would block the knowledge even from herself.

Marcel arched a brow. "And what am I like on the outside?"

"You are meticulous about your appearance, but you are not vain, which makes me think that you are a perfectionist. It means that you are never satisfied with what you do, and you always think that you can do better. You have a good heart, but you are afraid of getting hurt, so you keep it protected, and you are very careful about who you call a friend. How did I do so far?"

"Pretty good. You are very astute."

She shrugged. "It's a survival skill."

That was an odd answer. "What did you have to survive?"

She swallowed, suddenly looking even more anxious. Strangely, though, she emitted no emotional scents. Before, he'd thought that the scents of other humans were masking hers, but now that they were sitting alone and there wasn't anyone near them in a twenty-foot radius, he still couldn't scent anything other than pine and sunshine.

"My mother and I don't get along," she said after a long moment of silence. "She's very demanding, and I'm never good enough. I've learned to observe her moods."

"Did she abuse you?"

Marcel's fangs itched, but he forced them to stay dormant. Even if Sofia's mother abused her, she wasn't his enemy, and he would never use his fangs against a woman.

"No, she didn't. She just ignored me. She still does."

"What about your father?"

That brought a smile to her lips. "He's a good man, but he's powerless."

That was another odd thing to say. "Do you mean that he's powerless in the relationship?"

She tilted her head as if she didn't understand his question. "They are not together. Not anymore. He's just not very strong."

"Physically, mentally?" Marcel pressed, needing to get to the bottom of what she'd meant by powerless.

"He's not impaired in any way if that's what you're asking. He just could never stand up to her." Sofia chuckled nervously. "My meaning must have been lost in translation. As good as my English is, I still translate phrases and idioms from Finnish and get it wrong."

She was lying, and he didn't need to smell the lie to detect it.

But why? What was it about her parents that she was trying to hide?

Looking into her eyes, he sent a small thrall into her mind, but under the most recent memories of her interactions with Roxana and with him, he encountered a wall. It was as if her mind was locked up, or rather her memories were.

If Marcel hoped to get Sofia in his bed, he needed to find out whether she could be thralled to forget things, and he'd better do it now before she got to know him better.

"It's okay." He reached for her hand. "Men like to think that they are in charge, that they are strong, but most of us are putty in the hands of a strong woman. Your father is not the only one who ended up with the short end of the stick. I also allowed myself to get manipulated by a woman I cared about."

"Did she betray you?"

He nodded. "It was worse than that. She manipulated me into doing things for her that I shouldn't."

"Like what?"

Even though he was about to thrall it out of her memory, he wouldn't tell her the truth. He couldn't stand to even voice what he had done and why.

Instead, he told her the least of it. "She asked me to buy her a diamond necklace that cost me my entire savings. I could have bought a house with that money, but instead, I spent it on diamonds, and she walked away with them."

"That's terrible. She's a thief."

She'd been worse than a thief, but he pushed the ugly memories from his mind and reached into Sofia's, making her forget about the diamond necklace he'd given his evil paramour all those centuries ago.

SOFIA

*S*ofia couldn't imagine a woman being so manipulative and conniving unless it was revenge for serious wrongdoing on Marcel's part, like a betrayal of some sort.

The Kra-ell didn't believe in exclusivity, so the concept of cheating on one's partner was nonexistent. They practiced something that was very similar to Safe Haven's free-love attitude, but instead of calling it love, they called it survival of the fittest.

Heck, even Igor didn't demand exclusivity from Jade. If someone else could get her pregnant, that was fine with him. Since the male Kra-ell knew right away if their seed had implanted, there was no doubt about paternity.

Humans were different, and if Marcel had had sex with another woman, and his girlfriend or wife had found out, then she was entitled to revenge. The extravagant gift she'd demanded might have been her way of punishing him.

What had she asked for, though?

Why couldn't she remember what it was?

He'd just told her about it, but all she remembered was that it had been a very expensive gift.

Damn. Igor's repeated compulsion sessions must have messed with her brain, and she was starting to lose her short-term memory.

"What's the matter?" Marcel asked. "You seem troubled."

"I'm having issues with my memory. For some reason, I can't remember what you've just told me about that expensive thing that you got for your ex."

"I didn't tell you what it was. I only said that I spent a lot of money on it."

"Oh." She let out a breath. "That's a relief. Still, I should have remembered that you didn't specify what the gift was. I was panicking, thinking that I was starting to lose my memory at twenty-seven. That's too early for dementia."

"I'm sorry." He reached for her hand. "I didn't intend to cause you to panic."

"It's not your fault." She pulled her hand out of his grasp and looked at her wristwatch. "The lunch break is over, and I need to get going."

He rose to his feet. "I should get back as well. My team is waiting for me to open the lab for them."

She wanted to ask what they were working on, but she was out of time.

"Can I see you later in the evening? We can have dinner together and then go for a walk on the beach. Or, if you want, we can hang out in the common area of the lodge. There is some kind of social activity happening every night."

He shook his head. "I'm sorry, but I have plans. Maybe we can meet tomorrow."

It felt like a kick to the gut, and only sheer willpower prevented Sofia from wincing and clutching her middle.

He had plans? With whom?

And tomorrow was just a maybe?

What had she done to turn him off?

It didn't matter. She couldn't allow him to distance himself. She needed him.

"Tomorrow then." Sofia forced a smile. "Lunchtime?"

He nodded. "I'll try to make it."

That sounded like a no, and she felt like crying. Instead, she gave him a small wave and an even smaller smile and turned around.

The moment Sofia was out of the dining hall, she ran into the ladies' bathroom and locked herself in a stall.

Hyperventilating, she put her head between her knees and tried to regain control.

It wasn't about her stupid infatuation with Marcel. She would get over that. It was about losing her only thread and disappointing Igor. If she failed at her mission of collecting information, he would take it out on her family, probably her father and her aunts and cousins, and there was nothing she could do about it.

Perhaps she could lie?

She could make up stories about things that Marcel had supposedly told her. Valstar and Igor had no way of knowing. Not until she returned to the compound and Igor compelled her to tell him the truth. But then she would be there, and she could beg him to punish her and not her family.

Yeah, as if begging would help.

He would make an example out of her to put fear in the hearts of others.

But maybe she could lie and then kill herself so he wouldn't know that she'd lied. She could make it look as if she was murdered, and then her family would be rewarded instead of punished.

Sofia didn't want to die. But she would give her life to save the lives of those she loved.

33

MARCEL

*a*s Marcel headed toward the lab, he analyzed his interaction with Sofia and the oddities he'd noticed.

She had a block on her memories, but she hadn't been difficult to thrall. He'd erased the diamond necklace story with ease and precision and hadn't encountered any problems except her distress over forgetting what he'd told her.

So why were her other memories locked up tight?

If she'd been abused as a child, she could have suffered a trauma that had caused her to lock down the painful memories to shield herself from them.

Marcel didn't know much about human psychology, and no abuse took place in Annani's clan, but the Doomers were honed by it, and they were notoriously difficult to get information out of. But that was also because of Navuh's compulsion. Besides, abuse by a parent was much more emotionally damaging than the physical abuse Doomers went through in the training camp. There was no shame involved and no need to hide. All the boys were tormented the same way, even Navuh's own sons.

Perhaps if he pushed harder, he could've broken through Sophia's mental block, but could he justify the invasion?

The little test he'd conducted was allowed as a precaution to ensure that she could be thralled after they had sex. But to subject her to an intrusive thrall just to satisfy his curiosity was wrong, even if it was allowed, and it wasn't.

On the other hand, Safe Haven had become a strategic location for the clan, and anything suspicious happening there should be investigated, even if it was just a gut feeling or a hunch.

He couldn't just do it, though. He needed to call Onegus, explain about Sofia's peculiarities, and ask his permission to thrall her more intrusively.

Except, he didn't feel right about sharing what she'd told him with others. He had a feeling that she didn't give her trust easily and that not many knew about her family situation.

It was a conundrum, but when in doubt, the clan's security always came first.

He also wanted Roni to check her background and see if there were any shady holes in it. Until he sorted all of that out, he preferred not to engage with Sofia.

"It's about time." Corinne huffed when he reached the entrance to the building. "We've been waiting for you for nearly half an hour."

"I'm sorry. I lost track of time." He opened the door and led them inside.

"We don't have phones with us," Kylie said. "We can't even call you to remind you that you left us waiting for you in the heat. This whole thing sucks, and I want to go home. I'm so sick of seeing the same faces every day, eating the same food, and not getting laid. There, I said it. I'm not shy about it." She stomped after him into the lab.

"I'm sorry I kept you waiting," he repeated. "It's not going to happen again."

"Right." Kylie dropped into her chair. "This project is boring."

When he walked into his office, Corinne followed him inside. "When are Kaia and William coming back? They were supposed to be gone for a couple of weeks, but it has been much longer than that. Are they coming back at all?"

"I don't know. It depends on Kaia's mother and her health."

"How is she doing?" Corinne's tone softened.

"She's stable, but she's not out of the woods yet."

He hated to lie, but it was a necessity for immortals. Their survival depended on their ability to hide.

"If you speak with either of them, tell them that I wish Kaia's mother a full recovery."

"I will. I'm sure Kaia will appreciate it."

After Corinne left, he closed the door and called Roni.

"What's up, Marcel? Did you miss me?"

"Not really. Can you do me a favor, though? And by me, I mean the clan. I want you to do a thorough background check on one of the retreat attendees. You should have her on file. Her first name is Sofia, and she's a tourist from Finland. I didn't get her last name."

"I know who you're referring to. Did she do anything suspicious?"

"I befriended her and discovered that she has a block on her long-term memories. I thought it would be prudent to go over her file again and see if you could find more about her."

"No problem, but it might take me a day or two. I'm swamped."

That was regrettable, but he couldn't justify calling a hunch an urgent matter, and he knew that Roni wasn't exaggerating.

"Do it as soon as you can. It's not top priority as far as the clan security goes, but it's important to me."

34

ERIC

*A*fter showering, Eric felt like a new man.

He'd been in a coma for two weeks, and yet he didn't feel as feeble as he should have after such a long time without moving his muscles.

In fact, he felt pretty great, considering he'd woken up only a couple of hours ago.

The worst part had been when Hildegard removed the catheter, but other than that, he felt no pain. Wasn't he supposed to start growing fangs and venom glands?

Everyone had warned him that would be the worst part of the transition, but it seemed like it hadn't started yet.

Darlene had helped him get into the shower, and he'd only needed to lean on her lightly, and seated on a stool, he could have managed the rest on his own, but she'd refused to leave and had insisted on shampooing his hair.

Eric had been tempted to cut himself while shaving to test how quickly the wound would heal, but Darlene had taken the razor from him and shaved him so gently and lovingly that he didn't have the heart to take the disposable shaver from her.

"Look at you," she breathed. "You look ten years younger."

He grinned at her through the mirror. "Youth is in the eyes of the beholder. I still have wrinkles on my forehead and around my eyes."

"They are much less pronounced." She wrapped her arm around his middle and helped him back into the room. "Now I really look like your mother."

"Bullshit." He stopped and turned to her. "You are beautiful." He leaned and kissed her lips.

When he let go, she smiled. "Beauty is in the eyes of the beholder. I look my age, and you don't. Those are the facts."

"Screw the facts." He cupped her cheek. "You don't look a day over thirty-five."

"Right." She laughed. "Sit on the bed before you fall down on your handsome face."

He glanced at the cot that was tucked against the wall. "Did you sleep on that the entire time?"

"Most of it. I usually lay next to you until I was about to fall asleep, and then I moved to the cot."

"Thank you." He put his hand on her shoulder as he lowered himself to the bed. "I know that I couldn't have done it without you."

"I wish I could take credit for helping you through your transition, but that credit goes to Toven and Annani. They took turns giving you their blessings."

He hadn't known that. "I'm grateful."

Darlene nodded. "So am I." She pulled a duffle bag from under the bed and unzipped it. "You can get dressed if you want. I brought you a pair of track pants and a T-shirt."

It seemed like too much effort, and he was tempted to lie down with just the towel wrapped around his hips, but he didn't want Darlene to worry about him running out of steam all of a sudden.

She frowned. "What's the matter?"

"Nothing." He smiled. "I'm just not as strong as I thought I was. Do you mind if I lay down for a little bit?"

"Not at all." She dropped the duffel bag on the floor. "I'll help you." She lifted his legs up to the bed and pulled the sheet over him. "Rest for as long as you need to."

"My gums don't hurt." He patted them with his finger. "I was supposed to start growing fangs."

Suddenly, he was worried that he wasn't transitioning or that his transition was going to be a slow process like Kaia's. But they weren't related by blood, so why would they have similar experiences?

"Can you call Bridget? I want her to perform the test."

Darlene smiled knowingly. "Did you look at your face? I don't think there is any doubt that you are transitioning."

"I don't know. Maybe the long rest did that. Or maybe the gods' blessings had something to do with it."

She shook her head. "Don't be silly. If you weren't transitioning, you wouldn't have been in a coma after Toven bit you."

He couldn't argue with that, but he needed to know for sure. Except, his eyelids felt as if they weighed a ton, and he had to close his eyes. "Maybe I'll rest a little first."

35

VROG

The American Chinese couple who had bought Vrog's school had endless questions that he was more than happy to answer, but he would have preferred it if they made a list and sent them all at once instead of bombarding him with emails about every little thing.

Dr. Wang was more than capable of answering most of them, but for some reason, they preferred directing them to the former owner.

He was reading over his latest answer when his phone rang. Answering it without checking who the caller was, he was surprised to hear Emmett's voice.

"Good afternoon, Emmett. It is so nice to hear from you. How are things going in Safe Haven? I heard that the first paranormal retreat has started. Congratulations."

"Thank you. I have news that will make you very happy. Are you sitting down?"

The first thing that popped into his mind was that Eleanor and Emmett were expecting a child. That would indeed be good news.

Aliyah didn't want to have children yet, and the clan's doctor had given her medication that prevented pregnancies in humans. Vrog wasn't sure it would work on a Kra-ell hybrid, and secretly he hoped that it wouldn't.

"I am sitting down. What's the good news?"

"Jade contacted me."

Vrog felt the blood drain from his face, and dizziness assailed him. "When? How?"

"A little less than two weeks ago and very cleverly. She might have recognized me from the advertisements we ran, or maybe she stumbled upon Safe Haven's website. She sent in a fable for the competition we were running. She wrote it in a way that only I would know it was from her. I'll read it to you."

When Emmett was done reading it, Vrog had no doubt that the author was Jade. He still remembered the fables and stories she'd told him and the other children all those years ago, and the one she'd sent Emmett had been written in the same style.

"How did you know the fable was written by her? Did you hear her telling stories as a child?"

"Back then, she didn't spend time with the children, but she used my name." Emmett sighed. "My father wasn't happy about having a hybrid son, and he called me Veskar. Need I say more?"

Vrog frowned. "I don't understand."

"Maybe you are too young to know what it means, and no one mentioned it to you. Veskar is a small animal on the home planet that is very similar to a rat and is known for its craftiness and survival ability."

"I know what Veskar means. I just don't think it was meant as an insult. Your father must have seen in you the man you would become one day and gave you a fitting name. You are very crafty, and you have not just survived, you have thrived."

"It is nice of you to say so, but my father was not a good male, and his intention was to belittle me. The name he gave me made me the laughingstock of the pureblooded kids and the hybrids. I was bullied mercilessly."

That was regrettable, but at the moment, Vrog didn't care about Emmett's childhood torment. "Why did you wait so long to tell me?"

"Orders from Kian. He wants to keep it hush-hush, and he's right. Jade took a great risk by sending this email to me, and the fewer people who know about it, the less dangerous it is to her. Unknowingly, though, she also put the clan in danger. If her captors realize that her fable is more than a children's story entered into a competition, they might come to investigate. If it were only me, it wouldn't be so terrible, but there are many immortals at Safe Haven right now."

Worry churned in Vrog's stomach. "Then they should leave."

"It's not that simple, and so far, no one has come to investigate. Leon and his Guardians are on high alert."

"Hopefully, they have a good escape plan. I just don't understand what Jade thought to achieve by sending you this fable. How can we help her if we don't know where she is?"

"She opened a channel of communication. I will announce her as one of the three winners, which will give her access to Safe Haven's virtual library, and I will hide a message for her among a collection of fables written by the community members. I will also instruct her how to encode a message so only I will understand it."

"Do you need help writing it?"

"Thank you for the offer, but I've already figured it out." Emmett chuckled. "As my name suggests, I am crafty. After we hang up, I will send it to you. I'm curious to see whether you'll be able to decipher it."

"I'll gladly help in any way I can." Vrog closed his eyes for a moment. "If she sends you enough clues for us to be able to find her, do you think the clan will help us liberate her and the other females?"

"Frankly, I don't know, but I hope so. The three of us alone can't take on a group that overpowered the females and killed all the males of our tribe who were at the compound at the time."

"Maybe we can. The three of us can't launch an attack, but maybe we can help her and some of the others escape. Jade is pragmatic, and she wouldn't have risked communicating with you if she thought you couldn't help her. She must have a plan."

"Perhaps she does. I'll keep you informed."

"Can I tell Aliyah?"

"Of course. She's your mate. Just tell her not to mention it to anyone. You can also show her my email and see if she can decipher the hidden message. I'll give both of you access to the library so you can look for the clues."

"Sounds exciting. I'm looking forward to the challenge."

DARLENE

"*H*i," Eric murmured as he turned toward her. "Did I take a nap?"

"You slept for over twelve hours. I was afraid that you had slipped away again."

Darlene had kept a vigil all night, lying next to him and making sure that he hadn't slipped into a coma again. She was exhausted but also elated. Eric was alive, he was transitioning, and he was with her.

He smirked. "If I did, all you'd have to do would be to read me that smutty romance again." He lifted his head. "Where is it?" He glanced at the cot.

"I hid it when your family arrived at the clinic yesterday to congratulate you and witness the test. You couldn't keep your eyes open, so it was postponed to today."

He looked at her with a frown. "Was I awake anytime during their visit?"

"Don't you remember? They came in here, and you told Gilbert that it was his turn now."

"I must have been talking in my sleep."

"Maybe you were." She cupped his cheek. "How are you feeling? Are your gums hurting?"

"No. Maybe I should go back to sleep."

She frowned. "Do you still feel sleepy?"

"I'm fine." He leaned closer and pressed a soft kiss to her lips. "I dreamt that you were reading that steamy romance novel to me."

"So that's what woke you up this morning?" She laughed. "When it brought you out of your coma, I half expected your first reaction to be a hard-on, but I guess your blood flow was still so-so."

"My blood flow is just fine now." He pressed closer to her, his unmistakable length hard against her thigh.

"So it would seem." She reached with her hand and stroked him over the sheet. "Should I lock the door?"

He chuckled. "Right now, it's just bluster, but tonight I intend to compensate you for the two weeks you've had to do without."

With Leo, going for two weeks without sex had been nothing. Sometimes a month had gone by without him touching her, and she hadn't missed it. Darlene had had much more fun with a smutty book and her own fingers than she'd ever had with him. But she hadn't touched herself since Eric had lost consciousness. She had been too anxious to let herself enjoy anything. Besides, it would have felt wrong to pleasure herself while he was fighting for his life.

Now that he was awake, though, and the dark clouds of anxiety had lifted, she couldn't wait to reaffirm life with him.

As molten heat gathered at her core, she wrapped her arms around him and kissed him for all he was worth, which was everything. It took her a few seconds to realize that his arms were not as tight around her as they used to be, and it wasn't because of a lack of passion.

Eric was still recovering, and she shouldn't allow him to exert himself until Bridget gave them the green light.

With a sigh, she let go of his mouth. "I need to use the

bathroom." She really needed to pee, but it was also an excuse to stop what they were doing. It was robbing Eric of the little energy he'd managed to regain. "Do you need me to help you get there?"

"You go first."

"Are you sure? I can wait."

"Go."

"Okay." She slid off the bed and ran into the bathroom, barely making it on time.

When she was done, she opened the door to find Eric standing there naked, with his erection at full mast.

"Is that for me? Or do you need to use the bathroom?"

"Let's see what happens after I use it." He winked at her and swaggered inside.

For a moment, she watched his ass as he leaned over the toilet and braced his hand against the wall, but even though she'd helped him use the toilet yesterday, she figured he would prefer to have some privacy and ducked back into the room.

A few minutes later, she heard the shower going and went back inside.

Leaning against the vanity, she watched Eric soap up his muscular body. He hadn't been very hairy before the start of his transition, but she had a feeling that he'd lost some of his body hair when he'd showered yesterday, and as she lowered her eyes to the shower floor, her suspicion was confirmed. Small hairs were floating in the soapy water, and more were falling as Eric washed his legs.

"You are shedding hair." She pointed.

He lifted a hand to his head. "I am?"

"Not from your head. From your body. I guess immortal males have less body hair."

"Huh, interesting." He ran a hand over his chest and then lifted it to look at the hairs sticking to it. "I'll be damned.

You're right." He smiled at her. "Do you like the hairless look?"

"I like everything I'm looking at."

ERIC

"Who wants to hold the timer?" Bridget asked.

As Eric had expected, Gilbert raised his hand. "I'd be honored."

There was no doubt in anyone's mind that Eric was transitioning, but given that Kaia was still having her healing speed timed every couple of days, the cut test was more than ceremonial.

Making a one-time exception, Bridget allowed his and Darlene's family to gather around his bed, crowding the small room. Toven and Mia stayed outside together with Max and watched through the open door.

"Ready?" Bridget lifted her scalpel.

"I'm scared." He pretended to pout and held on to Darlene's hand.

Gilbert chuckled. "If you are a good boy and let the doctor cut you, I'll get you a lollipop."

"Okay." Eric extended his arm. "I'm ready."

Moving quickly, Bridget grabbed his hand, turned it palm side up, and made the cut.

Gilbert started the stopwatch at the same time.

It didn't even hurt, but a split second later, blood welled over the cut and it started to burn.

Still holding up his hand, Bridget reached for a square of gauze. "I'm going to wipe the blood off so we can watch the wound close."

As the cut was exposed, Eric watched it with bated breath, and it seemed to him that everyone else was holding their breath as well.

The bleeding stopped, which happened faster than it would have taken if he were still human, and then slowly, the skin started knitting itself back together.

When the wound disappeared, Gilbert stopped the timer. "One minute and nine seconds. That's not bad."

"Welcome to immortality, Eric." Bridget grinned. "I never get tired of saying that." She collected her tools. "You have ten minutes to be done with the congratulations, and then I want everyone out. I need to take measurements and blood samples."

Eric wanted to make a joke about losing too much blood already, but Darlene stopped him with a kiss.

He wrapped his arms around her. "I love you."

"I love you too." She smiled and backed away to let others come closer.

"You healed much faster than me," Kaia said as she hugged him lightly. "Congratulations."

Eric waited for Gilbert to approach the bed. "Now it's your turn, big brother. You have no more excuses for waiting."

"I know." Gilbert hugged him tightly. "For now, I'm just glad to have you back. Bridget kept reassuring us that you were doing fine, but you know me. Always the skeptic. I was worried."

Eric clapped him on the back. "Did you forget that my paranormal talent is staying alive? There was no way I wouldn't make it."

"I'm just happy that talent will no longer be tested."

Eric didn't want to correct Gilbert, but even immortals couldn't survive a plane crash, and he was a pilot. He had no doubt that his talent would be tested again, but it was good to know that he was more resilient now.

When everyone was done hugging and congratulating him, he cleared his throat. "Thank you all for praying for my successful transition. I'm sure your prayers, along with Toven and Annani's blessings, saved my life."

Karen wiped tears from her eyes. "When are you going home?"

"After Bridget is done with her testing."

"Do you need help getting there?" Gilbert asked.

"I can do that." Max walked into the room. "I'll get the golf cart. But if you want to take your brother home, it's fine with me. I don't want to butt in where I don't belong."

Eric hoped that Gilbert would accept Max's offer because he needed to talk to him. Darlene had told him about how supportive he had been over the past two weeks and also about his confession.

Evidently, friendship was important to the guy, and it was also important to Eric. Now that his move to the village had become permanent, he needed to start making friends.

Still, he didn't buy the story that Max's actions had been purely in the name of friendship. The guy had had his eye on Darlene, and he might have guessed Eric's intentions. Getting Darlene to like him and gaining her trust would go a long way toward making Eric's threesome plan work.

"You can help Eric." Gilbert clapped Max on the back and turned to Darlene. "Just let me know when you are heading home. I'll bring you dinner." He winked at Darlene.

Knowing his brother, Gilbert was planning some sort of celebration, and as usual he wanted it to be a surprise, but he was as subtle with hints as a bull in a china shop.

When everyone other than Darlene had cleared the room,

the doctor returned. "Let's start with measuring you to see if you've grown."

When Eric's eyes drifted down to his groin, Bridget and Darlene laughed.

"Men." Bridget shook her head. "That's the first thing they all check."

"What do women check?" Eric asked.

"Their faces to see if their skin looks better."

Eric lifted a brow. "Not the boobs?"

The doctor smiled. "Some check that as well."

"I knew that. What about my fangs? Why are they not starting to grow yet?"

Frowning, she pulled out a penlight. "Open wide and say ahh."

"Ahh."

She looked down his throat. "Your throat is a little swollen where the venom glands will eventually grow." She flicked the pen closed, put it in her pocket, and pulled out a pair of latex gloves. "You might be just going slow." She motioned for him to open his mouth and patted his gums. "Nothing here yet." She snapped the gloves off and threw them into the disposal container. "When they start growing, you will know, and you will want medication for the pain. It's not pleasant."

He didn't mind the pain. He would have gladly welcomed it to have everything progressing at the proper pace.

38

DARLENE

*a*s Bridget took Eric's measurements, Darlene read the message that Gilbert had sent her earlier.

Karen and I are organizing a Welcome to Immortality party for Eric at your place, and we need time to put up tables, chairs, and decorations and to prepare food. If you can ask Bridget to keep Eric in the clinic for a few hours, preferably until after five in the afternoon, that would give us enough time to get everything done without a mad rush to the finish line.

She typed up an answer. *I'll talk to her after she's done with Eric and let you know.*

She waited patiently as the doctor measured Eric's weight and checked his eyesight, his hearing, and his muscle strength.

He'd gained only a quarter of an inch in height, had lost nearly twenty pounds, and his eyesight and hearing had improved dramatically.

"So what's next?" Eric asked when the doctor pulled a tablet out of her pocket.

"The blood samples you've been dreading." She noted the last measurement on her tablet. "I'll send Hildegard to take your blood." She turned toward the door.

"I'll look for a lollipop." Darlene hurried after her. "I've seen some in your office."

When Bridget lifted a brow, Darlene put her finger over her lips, winked, and tilted her head in the direction of Bridget's office.

When they got inside, she closed the door behind them. "I'm sorry about that, but with Eric's improved hearing, I didn't know if it was safe to talk in the waiting room. Gilbert and Karen are preparing a party for him at our place, and they need as much time as you can give them. Can you come up with an excuse to keep Eric here until after five?"

Bridget glanced at the clock hanging on the wall. It was ten minutes to twelve. "I don't need to keep him here for five hours." When Darlene steepled her fingers and gave her a pleading look, Bridget relented. "Fine. I can tell him that I need the results from the blood test before I can release him, but since I didn't keep any of the other transitioning Dormants here until I got the results, including Kaia, he might get suspicious."

Darlene lifted a hand. "I'll handle it. You can go home, so he won't be able to ask you anything, and Hildegard will make herself scarce as well. I can tell him that you are concerned about his fangs not starting to grow, and that's why you are waiting for the test results."

Bridget shook her head. "Make some other excuse. I don't want to be in the position of having to lie."

"Please?"

Bridget rolled her eyes. "I was debating whether to put him through an MRI scan to check whether his fangs have started growing, and you've just helped me decide to do it. The technician who operates it works in the city, and she won't be back until after five, so that works out perfectly."

"Why MRI?"

"It provides a better image."

"Gotcha." Darlene gave her the thumbs up.

164

She waited until Hildegard was done taking blood samples before telling Eric about the MRI.

"First of all, where is my lollipop?"

She'd forgotten about it. "Bridget didn't have any."

Mirth dancing in his eyes, he pulled her into his arms. "I can return for the MRI later. I want to go home and get you in bed."

"You're not allowed strenuous activities. When Bridget tested your muscle strength, you got dizzy from lifting a kettlebell."

"Bummer." He pursed his lips. "Then again, I can think of a few activities that are not strenuous and yet very pleasurable."

"So can I." She pulled out of his arms. "But we can explore those activities after you are done here. It's better to complete the battery of tests and know that you don't have to come back to the clinic for anything other than pain meds."

"True." He sat on the bed. "Perhaps you can read that naughty romance to me."

If that would keep him in the clinic, she would, but after they'd had lunch.

"First order of business is to get you fed. I'll get us lunch from the café, and after we are done, I can read to you."

He lay back and pulled up his legs on the bed. "Can I read it while you are getting us food?"

"Sure." She pulled the book out of her purse and handed it to him. "Have fun."

ERIC

*E*ric's face was stuck in a smile as he read Darlene's romance. He could understand the allure now. No one died, the bad guy was not scary, and there was plenty of humor mixed in with the steam. It was pure enjoyment.

"Can I come in?" Max asked from the doorway.

"Sure." Eric put the book down open on his chest and raised the back of the hospital bed with the remote.

"What are you reading?" Max eyed the cover. "That's not the book I was reading to you."

"You were reading to me?"

"Bridget said that it was good for you. Some people are aware of their environment when they are in a coma, and keeping them engaged helps bring them back." He lifted the chair, brought it closer to the bed, and sat down.

"Thanks for reading to me, but I had no idea that you did that. Darlene didn't tell me."

"You're welcome. Where is she?"

"She went to the café to get us lunch." Eric glanced at the door and then at the camera mounted near the ceiling.

Could Bridget hear what was being said in the room?

Darlene had said that the doctor had gone to her office

next door, so only Hildegard was left to look over him, and she was chill. He would have preferred if she didn't hear the conversation he was about to have with Max, but if she did, it wasn't a big deal.

If Max agreed to his proposition to help activate Darlene's dormant genes, they wouldn't be able to keep it a secret anyway. Everyone knew that Eric's fangs and venom glands were not active yet, so he could not activate his mate.

"I need to talk to you," he said quietly. "And I'd appreciate it if you keep what I'm about to ask you confidential."

"Of course." Max put a hand on his chest. "No one will get it out of me. Not even with torture."

Eric smiled. "Dramatic much? If you are ever tortured to reveal my secret, you have my permission to spill the beans."

"Noted."

Eric scooted aside and patted the spot next to him on the bed. "Come closer. I don't want anyone to overhear me."

"There is no one out there." Max pushed to his feet and sat on the bed. "Bridget is gone, and Hildegard told me that she'd be in the back, filling up the supply cabinet, but if you needed her, you could press the button, and she'd come running."

"That's good to know." Eric took a deep breath. "So, you know that my venom glands and fangs won't come online until six months from now."

Max nodded.

"And it might take even longer than that because they didn't start growing yet. Bridget saw some swelling in the area where the glands are supposed to grow, but I can't feel anything, and since my transition started two weeks ago, they should have been well on their way by now."

"They'll come. Everyone experiences transition differently."

"Yeah, you're probably right. The problem is that Darlene doesn't have six or eight months."

"I know. But what can be done about it? She's your

truelove mate. She can't choose another male to activate her genes."

Eric swallowed the bile that had risen up his throat at the mere thought of what he was about to suggest. He couldn't allow his possessiveness to stop him, though. Darlene's very life was on the line.

"I love Darlene, and I want to spend the rest of my very long life with her, but to do that, she needs to transition, and she's not getting any younger. It's extremely difficult for me to suggest what I'm about to, but I have to do it for Darlene." He swallowed again. "Have you ever taken part in a threesome?"

As understanding dawned, Max's eyes widened. "Was that what you wanted to ask me? If I was willing to be the salami in your sandwich?"

Eric winced. "Technically, Darlene will be the salami, but yes. I can't think of anyone else I can tolerate touching her."

Max shook his head. "If you can tolerate the thought of me touching her, you are not her truelove mate. Fated mates are incapable of sharing their partners."

That was a surprise. Eric had been sure that Max had been hanging around Darlene because he'd guessed Eric's intentions. He'd told Darlene the sappy story about the best friend whose girl he'd seduced, and it might have even been true, but that was not why he'd been bringing her coffee and pastries each morning. Men were not that altruistic when it came to the women they desired.

It was also a huge relief.

If Max refused to do the deed, the threesome was not going to happen because Eric hadn't been lying when he'd said that there was no one else he could tolerate the thought of touching his mate.

Letting out a breath, he draped an arm over his eyes. "I'm such a jerk. I shouldn't feel so relieved. Darlene can't wait six months, and I need to beat my inner caveman into submission. Her life is more important than anything else."

Max rubbed a hand over the back of his neck. "Maybe we can do it in a way that I won't need to touch Darlene or even see her nude."

"How?"

"All I need to do is bite her, right? You can make love to her while I'm jerking off in the next room over, and when you are about to climax, I rush in, bite her, and leave as soon as I pump her with enough of my venom."

"Will that work? Don't the sperm and the venom have to come from the same male?"

Max shrugged. "That's a question for Bridget, but I doubt she would know the answer. I don't think anyone has ever attempted anything like that."

"There is a first time for everything," Eric murmured. "I need to run it by her. I mean Bridget. Darlene too."

Max shook his head. "First, let me explain how we will have to go about it. You will have to be shackled to the bed, or you'll attack me as soon as I enter the room. Darlene will have to ride you."

"Why would I attack you when I asked you to do that?"

Max smiled indulgently. "Your immortal hormones are not fully online yet. Wait a few days for them to kick in, and you'll know what I mean. You will become possessive and aggressive, and in the beginning, you won't be able to tamp down your urges. You will want to tear apart any male who even looks the wrong way at your mate."

"If that's so, time is of the essence. We need to do it before my immortal hormones kick in."

Max shook his head. "I won't do it unless you are shackled to the bed. I don't want to fight you. I'm a Guardian. It would look bad for me if I injure a civilian."

"Then shackled I shall be. I'll ask Bridget what she thinks when she comes in."

"Talk with Darlene first. There is no point in involving Bridget unless you get Darlene's consent."

"Good idea."

He'd already talked it over with Darlene, but that had been before he'd spent two weeks in a coma. She might have changed her mind.

40

DARLENE

*W*hen Darlene returned from the café, Max was there, looking as if he'd gotten some disturbing news. She didn't want to ask and spoil the elated mood she was in.

It was probably Guardian business, and she needed to take care of Eric, who looked so exhausted that she offered to feed him the soup she'd gotten him.

"I can manage." He took the spoon from her. "You can have my sandwich." He handed it to Max.

"Thanks, buddy. I'll eat it on the way. I'm needed at the office."

Darlene cast him a smile. "Are you still taking Eric home when he's done with the MRI?"

"Yeah. Call me when he's ready to go."

"Thanks." She turned to Eric.

The poor guy had fallen asleep while still sitting and holding the spoon.

Sighing, she took the spoon from his hand, wiped his mouth with a napkin, and lowered the bed so he could sleep comfortably.

The funny thing was that she shouldn't have bothered

Bridget with an excuse to keep Eric in the clinic. He'd supplied the excuse himself by falling asleep.

Nevertheless, she was glad that he was getting the fangs situation checked. It worried him, and hopefully the MRI would show that they'd started to grow.

A little after five, a knock sounded on the door and Hildegard rolled a wheelchair into Eric's room. "The MRI operator is here." She winked at Darlene. "Let's go, big boy." She patted the seat.

"I can walk," Eric murmured as he got off the bed and pushed his feet into a pair of flip-flops.

"I know you can, but this is the procedure. I don't want you swaying on your feet and bumping your head into something."

"You don't have to deal with lawsuits here," he grumbled as he sat down in the chair. "So, you don't have to follow silly hospital procedures."

"They are not silly." Hildegard motioned for him to lift his feet and put them on the footrests.

"Can I come?" Darlene asked.

"No, sweetheart." Hildegard winked again. "You'll have to wait here. It will only take a few minutes."

"Okay." Darlene leaned and kissed Eric's cheek. "I'll let Max know that you are ready to go. Do you want him to bring the golf cart, or do you want to take a ride in the wheelchair?"

"The wheelchair. I need fresh air."

"No problem. I'll let him know."

She was surprised that Eric didn't insist on walking home. It meant that despite his bluster, he still felt weak as a kitten.

When the door closed behind the nurse, Darlene whipped out her phone and dialed Karen. "Our ETA is about half an hour. Is everything ready?"

172

"We are almost done. We will be ready by the time you arrive."

"Don't hide and jump out from behind furniture. I know that he's supposed to be immortal now, but he's still very weak, and I don't want him getting a fright. He fell asleep after eating one small cup of soup."

"Don't worry," Karen said. "He'll be back on his feet in no time. Eric was resilient as a human, and he's an immortal now."

"I know, but I still don't want him to get scared."

Karen chuckled. "We can't hide even if we wanted to. Idina is waiting for Eric on the front porch with a bunch of balloons in her hand that say congratulations and you are number one. She refuses to come in until her favorite uncle arrives."

"Does she have any other uncles?"

"Nope. That's why Eric is her favorite."

Darlene smiled. "Now she has many honorary uncles. Eric will have to work hard to keep his favorite status."

"I'm not worried," Karen said. "He has a way with kids."

Darlene had a feeling that Karen wanted to add something about her and Eric having children in the future, but it was premature. Unless she transitioned and her biological clock was reversed, children were not an option.

"I'll let you go back to the preparations. I'll see you in a bit."

After ending the call, Darlene made another one to Max. "Eric will be ready to head out in about fifteen minutes. Can you come? You don't have to. I can push him myself."

"I'll be there. We are just finishing a briefing. Onegus is heading out to the surprise party."

"Awesome. Remember not to say anything to Eric."

"I won't."

When ten minutes later the door opened, and Hildegard pushed the wheelchair through, the smile on Eric's face was enough for Darlene to guess the results. "Did the MRI show your fangs?"

He nodded. "They are tiny, but they are there. I just need to wait patiently for them to push my canines out." He took her hand and pulled her onto his lap. "Where is Max? He said that he was going to wheel me home."

"He's on his way." Darlene pushed out of his hold. "I need to collect our things." She turned to Hildegard. "Should I take the bedding down?"

The nurse waved her hand. "That's my job, sweetie, but thanks for offering. I think you are the first one who's done that. All the others just assume that the cleaning happens by magic."

"I know that you don't have anyone to help you do the cleaning here." She pulled the nurse into a quick hug. "Thank you for taking care of Eric."

"It was my pleasure. I'll see you guys later." Her eyes widened when she realized her slip-up. "I mean, I'll see you when you come back for the pain meds."

Bridget was probably already at their house, and Hildegard would follow a few minutes behind them. The party was supposed to be just for the family, but how could they celebrate Eric's successful transition without inviting the people who'd taken care of him?

41

ERIC

*E*ric hadn't missed Hildegard's winks and Darlene's excitement, which he guessed had to do with the surprise his brother was planning for him.

In fact, he could feel Darlene's emotions in a way that he couldn't before or rather smell them.

The scent was lovely.

There was a purity to Darlene that he'd sensed before, but he'd thought that he was seeing her through the rose-tinted lenses of a man in love. She had a core of goodness inside her that had been stifled for far too long and was just now beginning to blossom.

Was it because of him?

He wanted to believe that it was. She was loved by him and by her family, and she was safe, and in that cocoon, she was finally free to be herself.

"I see balloons," he said as Max turned the wheelchair around the corner. "Is it someone's birthday?" He pretended not to know that they were for him.

Only the tops were visible above the shrubs blocking his view, but there was a big bunch of them swaying in the breeze.

"Yeah, it is." Darlene put a hand on his shoulder. "Yours. Yesterday, you were reborn, and today, we are celebrating."

Max made another turn, and as their house was in full view, he saw who was holding the balloons, and a grin stretched his face.

"Uncle Eric!" Idina jumped up and down. "You're back."

"I am." He motioned for Max to stop pushing the wheelchair and got up. "I can walk from here."

He rushed toward his niece and lifted her into his arms. "I missed you, munchkin." He kissed her soft cheeks, two kisses on each side. "Are these balloons for me?"

"Yes." She handed him the bouquet. "They say you are number one, and congratulations. I can read the number one," she said proudly.

Congratulations was printed on a banner that had been hung from the porch railing, and more balloons were tied to the posts.

Eric climbed the steps with Idina in his arms but lowered her to her feet before entering through the open door.

"Oh, wow." He pretended surprise. "Thank you for throwing a party for me." He walked over to where the two gods sat and bowed. "Thank you for saving my life."

He hadn't seen the Clan Mother before, but there was no mistaking who she was, and it wasn't only the glow that gave her away.

"You are welcome," Toven said before rising to his feet. "You should sit down before you fall over and waste all those blessings I worked so hard on." He motioned for Eric to sit in the armchair he'd vacated.

"I can't take your seat." He glanced at Gilbert. "Can you get me a chair?"

"Coming up." His brother swung one of the dining room chairs around and shoved it behind Eric's butt.

"Congratulations, Eric." As the goddess smiled, her otherworldly beauty turned blinding. "Welcome to my clan."

176

"Thank you." He dipped his head again. "I promise that I will earn my keep."

"I can't thank you enough," Darlene said. "Thank you."

"You are most welcome," the goddess said.

Toven nodded.

Eric glanced at Kian, who was sitting with Syssi on the couch. "Do you need another pilot?"

"Always. I also need a ship's captain. Do you know one?"

"I know a few navy captains, but I doubt they can pilot a cruise ship." He'd heard about the ship Kian was renovating for Alena's wedding.

Kian grimaced. "That's what I thought. I have a ship, a crew, servers, cooks, maids and security people, all except for a captain. I didn't know they were in such short supply."

"Dinner is served in the backyard," Karen said.

Eric sniffed the air. "I smell steak."

"Roni barbecued a mountain of them," Darlene said. "That's how he shows love. He came over a few times and read to you."

"I wish I were aware of what was going on around me, but I was out. I didn't even dream. When I woke up, I had no idea that two weeks had gone by."

"Shall we?" Toven offered Annani a hand up. "The smell is making me hungry."

"Indeed." The goddess took his hand, but it didn't look as if he was pulling her. It looked more like she was floating up.

"Where is Mia?" Eric asked his brother as Toven and Annani walked outside.

"She's back there with Kaia, William, and the twins." Gilbert offered him a hand up. "Do you need the wheelchair?"

Eric shook his head. "Not anymore. This was the last time." He was still a little weak, but he could walk.

He waved a hand at Max. "Come on. Let's eat some steak. I need to start building back the muscle I've lost."

Max grinned. "As soon as you are up to it, I'll start you on a muscle-building routine in the gym."

ANNANI

"To Eric." Kian lifted his beer bottle. "And to the successful transition of the other members of his family."

Annani lifted her wine glass. "To Eric, Gilbert, Karen, Idina, and in a few years, Cheryl, and a few more, Evan and Ryan." She smiled at the little girl. "She is still young enough to benefit from spending time with me." She turned to look at the twins. "The boys will have to wait a little longer."

As she shifted her gaze to Eric, she noticed how pale and tired he looked, but he also looked happy, and he was having a good time. "How are you faring, Eric? Do you need to lie down?"

"Thank you for your concern, Clan Mother, but I'm fine. I'm a happy man."

She nodded. "Do not overdo it on your first day out of the sick bed. As joyous as the occasion is, I think we should end the festivities soon and let you rest."

"I can last a little longer." Eric wrapped his arm around Darlene's shoulders and turned to his brother. "Let's make plans for your induction ceremony."

"Not yet." Gilbert shifted in his chair. "I have many loose ends I need to tie up, and now that you are out of the woods, I need to attend to them. It will have to wait until I return."

"I'll induce you," Toven said. "It worked well for Eric, so it should work well for you."

Toven's offer created a moment of stunned silence around the table, but it did not surprise Annani. He had assured Karen and Gilbert that they had nothing to fear, and he intended to do his best to provide them with the outcome he had promised.

Toven had told her that he felt responsible for the family, and he wanted to give Gilbert the same help he had given his younger brother.

"Thank you. That is very generous of you." He shook his head. "Wow. I did not expect that." He took Karen's hand. "Now you have less reason to fret."

"I still do." She smiled at Toven. "I can't help it. But I'm so grateful to you for doing this for us."

Toven lifted his wine glass and saluted her. "Eric was the first male I've induced, and it was much easier than I expected. It was really no trouble at all."

Poor Eric looked like he had swallowed a lemon, but he wisely did not say anything. He was no match for a god, and there was no shame in his swift defeat.

"It's not fair that Idina gets to be immortal first," Cheryl grumbled. "I should be next."

"About that." Karen turned to Annani. "How does it work? How much time does Idina need to spend with you to transition? And is it dangerous?"

"It is not dangerous at all. Idina will not even feel the change until she notices that her hearing, eyesight, and strength have improved. She will also need less sleep. As for how much time, it varies, but daily visits for a couple of weeks should do it. I will ask Alena to contact you and arrange playdates at my house with Phoenix. The girls can play while I watch over them."

Annani was looking forward to spending time with the girls. It had been a long time since she had more than one toddler girl at the sanctuary, and she missed the lively sounds of children playing.

"Thank you, Clan Mother."

"You are most welcome." Annani smiled at Idina. "She reminds me of Amanda when she was a little girl. Smart, willful, and full of mischief."

She caught Kaia frowning at her from the corner of her eye. The girl was smart and suspicious of the blessings and about the way the Dormant girls transitioned. It was time to do something about that before she figured it out.

Kaia was under strong compulsion not to reveal any of the clan secrets, but as Kian had pointed out, if Kalugal could overpower Emmett and Eleanor's compulsion, so could someone else. It was not likely, but it was possible, and the secret of what a god's blood could do was too great to risk.

"I was not willful," Amanda said. "You always said that I was a sweet girl."

"You were a pleasure." Annani patted her hand. "You still are, and there is never a dull moment with you around."

As always, Amanda was easy to placate with a compliment.

She smiled. "Evie is also such a good baby. She eats well, she sleeps well, and she's not fussy at all. Allegra is also an easy child, but with the twins joining our little daycare, we will need to hire another nanny. Four babies are too much for one person to handle."

"Did you tell Eric the good news?" Syssi asked Karen.

"Not yet. I didn't get the chance." She turned to Eric. "I got a job at the university, and I'm starting in two months. Their sysadmin is going on maternity leave."

"Congratulations." Eric lifted his glass of water. "The Fates are smiling upon us."

"Indeed." Annani lifted her wine glass. "Let us make a toast to our good fortune."

KAIA

"*I* need a hug." Kaia wrapped her arms around Eric. "I'm so happy to have you back." As she held him to her tightly, her eyes misted with tears.

She'd kept her stress and her worry hidden inside, in part because Gilbert and Karen had been worried enough without her adding to their anxiety and in part because she'd been afraid to let go of the tight leash on her emotions.

So much was resting on her shoulders that she couldn't afford to fall apart.

William had gone back to managing the lab, so she was in charge of the deciphering project with only minimal help from him. They worked in the same room, which meant that they could consult with each other at all times, but mostly, they worked on different things.

The truth was that she hadn't made any breakthroughs during the two weeks Eric had been in a coma.

At the rate she was going, Marcel would need to sign the team of bioinformaticians up for another three-month term. They weren't good for any breakthroughs, but they were helping her chip away at the manuscripts one sentence at a time, and that was better than nothing.

To solve the puzzle of Okidu's journals, Kaia needed a calm mind and a positive attitude, and she hadn't managed either since Eric had started his transition. But her worry about him hadn't been the only reason for the turmoil in her head and her crappy mood. She was still dealing with Edgar.

Kaia had met with Annani twice since the first time the goddess had entered her mind and had done her version of psychoanalysis on Edgar. Even though the Clan Mother was a masterful thraller, and she was very gentle, frequent thralling was not recommended, and Annani refused to endanger Kaia's mind.

Edgar was still taking up a big chunk of her soul, and she was impatient to banish him and her memories of her life as a man completely.

Well, except for the mathematical knowledge and analytical ability she'd gotten to keep. Losing that would mean losing her edge and her so-called genius.

Perhaps that was the nature of gifts. They came with strings attached, and she needed to figure out if the one she'd been given was worth the baggage it had come with.

Without Edgar, Kaia was a nothing special, somewhat intelligent girl, but with him, she was a deviant. Was it worth it?

If she got to decipher Okidu's journals because of Edgar's contribution, then the answer was yes. They might hold the secret to immortality for everyone, and not just those who carried the godly genes.

The thing was, Kaia had a feeling that until Gilbert and her mother also transitioned successfully, she wouldn't be able to get into the zone needed for solving this most important puzzle.

"I'm happy to be back." Eric kissed her forehead. "You shouldn't have worried about your old uncle. I'm a survivor."

"I don't have an old uncle." Letting go of him, she clapped

his back. "I have a young, handsome, awesome uncle." She wiped her eyes with the back of her hands.

"That's right." Eric grinned.

"Who wants to join me for cigars?" Kian asked.

"I do." Eric turned around. "I'm immortal now. I can smoke as many as I want."

Darlene shook her head. "You are still as weak as a baby. You shouldn't smoke."

"Then come with me." He took her hand. "We can sit on the swing and smooch while Kian and Gilbert puff on cigars."

Darlene smiled. "That sounds like a much better idea."

"I am going inside," Annani announced.

"So am I." Syssi rose to her feet. "Whoever wants a cappuccino, follow me."

Kaia walked over to William. "Are you going to stay outside with the smokers?"

"If you don't mind." He cupped her cheek and kissed her lips lightly. "You can stay, you know. You are an immortal as well."

William didn't smoke, and he wasn't overly fond of alcohol either, but he enjoyed chatting with Kian and the other guys, and Kaia didn't want him to miss the fun because he didn't want her to feel left out.

The truth was that they both needed some time apart. It wasn't healthy for a couple to spend every minute of every day together.

"I'll join the Clan Mother and Syssi for cappuccinos." She gave him a peck on the lips. "Have fun with the guys."

44

ANNANI

"*I*'m scared for Gilbert," Karen said. "But not as much as I was before Toven said he was going to induce him. He's done exactly as he promised with Eric." She smiled at Annani. "I want to thank you again for helping Eric with your blessings."

"You are most welcome. I am glad that I was able to help."

The truth was that she had not. Annani had only pretended to *bless* Eric, spending twenty minutes or so in his room and telling him stories. But she had not given him her blood because Toven's had been sufficient. She and Toven had decided that it was better not to experiment on Eric.

Even Toven had not known whether any gods had attempted providing a human with a mixture of their blood or taking turns with their transfusions. The blood of two gods might be even more beneficial than the blood of one, but it could also be harmful.

Perhaps if Eric's situation had deteriorated to a critical point, Annani would have given him her blood as a last resort.

"I'm so curious about how it works," Kaia said. "I wonder

if the energy gods emit can be studied or measured. There must be something therapeutic in it."

"Some humans have healing energy as well." Syssi handed Annani a cappuccino cup with a heart shape, artfully created from the foam. "It makes sense that gods would have that ability in order of magnitude. After all, we came from them, even those of us who don't carry the immortal genes."

That was a very astute assumption, and Annani wished it was true, but it was not. Hopefully, though, it would be good enough to steer Kaia's curious mind in that direction and away from the truth.

The girl was smart, and she loved solving puzzles. As long as the *blessings* remained a mystery, she would keep trying to figure out how they worked.

Perhaps it would be better if Annani nipped it in the bud, as the saying went. Thanks to Kaia's past life memories and her wish to banish them, Annani had free access to the girl's mind. She could take a detour and plant a suggestion to stop her from thinking about the blessings and how they worked.

"Kian and Toven seem unconcerned about Gilbert's and my mother's transition," Kaia said. "They must have great faith in the blessings." She put her cappuccino cup down. "Maybe it's a male macho thing. The ladies, and especially Bridget, seem much more concerned."

"It's the motherly instinct," Amanda said. "Generally, women are more empathic and tend to worry more. Men are less so. Maybe that's why they make better soldiers."

Syssi shook her head. "That's because they are physically stronger, and until recently, it was a deciding factor. With modern weaponry, physical strength became less and less important, and that's why we see more and more women in the military."

"Brawn is not the only factor. Generally speaking, men are more ruthless and less emotional." Amanda lifted her hands in the air. "Don't shoot me for not being politically correct. Some women are ruthless too and they make exceptional soldiers, but generally speaking, men are better at warfare."

"We are still apes," Mia murmured. "Aggressive for no reason."

"The gods were not peaceful creatures either," Annani said. "They only pretended to be." She sighed. "I wish we were as benevolent as we wanted humans to believe we were. I am doing my best to uphold that ideal, but I am not an angel even though I glow." She smiled at Kaia. "We should have another meeting soon. Perhaps tomorrow?"

The sooner she dealt with the girl's suspicions, the better. She also needed to talk with Kian and Toven about keeping up better charades. They needed to pretend to be more concerned than they actually were for the transitioning Dormants.

Kaia perked up. "I would love to. What time is convenient for you?"

"Can you come to my house at noon? We can have lunch together."

"Thank you." Kaia dipped her head. "I'll be there at twelve."

45

ERIC

*B*y the time the last of their guests had departed, Eric could barely keep his eyes open, but he'd been waiting the entire afternoon to tell Darlene about his conversation with Max, and he didn't want to postpone it until tomorrow.

Besides, he was horny as hell and wanted to play.

He might not be good for much, but he at least needed to hold Darlene in his arms with nothing between them. He'd been craving the feel of her skin on his, her lips, the look in her eyes that was full of love and lust for him.

Sitting like a useless sack of potatoes on the couch, he watched her cleaning up after the party and felt like shit for not offering to help. If he didn't fear falling on his face the moment he tried to get off the damn couch, he would have helped, but if he fell, he would just be adding more work for her.

"I know you are busy, and I wish I could help clean, but I'm exhausted. Can I bother you for a cup of strong coffee?"

She stopped wiping the dining room table and turned to him. "You should be in bed. Do you need help getting undressed?"

"I don't want to go to bed yet. Well, I do, but I want to sit with you on the couch and talk for a little bit. We haven't had any alone time in hours, and I miss being with you."

Her lips curved up in a smile. "That's an invitation I can't refuse." She looked at the mostly clean table and shrugged. "It can wait for tomorrow. I'll make us coffee." She headed toward the kitchen.

He gave her a grateful smile. "You're the best."

A few minutes later, Darlene returned with two cups of coffee and two pieces of leftover cake. "Karen is a surprisingly good baker for a career woman. This cake is delicious."

She set the tray on the coffee table and sat next to him. "This is nice. Just the two of us." She handed him a cup, took one for herself, and leaned into him. "I missed cuddling on the couch with you."

Eric ran his hand over Darlene's bare arm. "I was asleep for the entire time, so I didn't get to miss you, but since I woke up, I missed us being home together."

She leaned her head on his shoulder. "How is it possible that we've known each other for such a short time, and I can't imagine life without you in it? I'm not immortal yet, and you are a baby immortal, so it can't be the truelove mates' bond."

"We were meant to be together." He kissed the top of her head. "The Fates planned our union even before we were born."

She lifted her eyes to him. "You really think so?"

"I know so. I can feel it in here." He patted his chest. "That being said, I still think that you should transition as soon as possible. The Fates brought us together, but they expect us to put in some work as well and not leave everything to them. That's not how it works."

Darlene grimaced. "Can we talk about that some other time? I don't want to ruin the moment with talk about threesomes."

"We have to talk about it, and we have to do it now. I told Max about my idea."

Her muscles stiffening, she pulled out of his arms. "When?"

"While you were getting us lunch. He had an interesting idea that I think you will like."

Darlene shook her head and put the coffee cup down on the table. "No wonder he was looking at me funny. What's his brilliant idea?"

"He thinks that it might work with him only biting you and doing nothing else. While we get going, he will work himself up in the next room, and when I'm about to climax, he will come in, bite you, and leave."

Pursing her lips, Darlene tilted her head. "That doesn't sound too awful. I can even stay partially dressed. But will it work with the venom and sperm not coming from the same male?"

"I don't know, and neither does Max, but it's worth a try. If it works, great, and if it doesn't, we try something else. I can ask Bridget's opinion, but I want to know your thoughts on the subject first."

"I can't have sex with Max. If that doesn't work, we will wait until your fangs and venom are functional."

On the one hand, he was glad to hear that, but on the other hand her declaration made him anxious. If Max's idea didn't work, Darlene would have no choice but to have sex with the guy. The problem was that Eric no longer believed that he could take part in it.

He would have to ask Bridget to knock him out.

He let out a breath. "Max said that I wouldn't be able to tolerate another male touching you and that I would probably attack him when he comes to bite you. He wants me to be tied down to the bed."

Darlene shook her head. "It gets kinkier and kinkier. What's next? Brundar's club?"

Eric lifted a brow. "Brundar has a club?"

46

DARLENE

"*Y*ou didn't know?"

Eric chuckled. "I don't know a lot of things about the clan. I might have been here for a couple of weeks, but I wasn't conscious for it. Brundar is the last person I would have ever suspected of owning a club. What kind of a club is it?"

"The kind that caters to various kinks."

Eric nodded. "That I can imagine. When does he have time for it, though? Isn't he Kian's personal bodyguard?"

"He is, but since Kian hardly ever leaves the village, Brundar has plenty of time on his hands. Anandur takes part in the rescue missions when Kian doesn't need him, but not Brundar."

"I can imagine why. They don't want to traumatize the victims even more. The dude scares me, and I'm a veteran."

"Brundar obviously has issues, but Callie seems happy with him, and from what I hear, she helps him run the club, so she must be into some kink herself."

"Now you've made me curious. Can we go there?"

Darlene swallowed. "You might be sexually adventurous, but I'm not, and I'm certainly not into exhibitionism, which I hear is a big part of it. I heard Callie talking about a bondage class and other live presentations. I blush just thinking about it."

Brundar and Callie were both beautiful and had perfect bodies. They might be comfortable performing in front of other people, but she wasn't. Heck, even if following her transition she had a bombshell figure, she would never strip in front of strangers, and definitely not have sex while people were watching.

Eric frowned. "How can Brundar and Callie tolerate other people seeing them having sex? According to Max, they should be so possessive of each other that they would attack anyone who touches their mate or looks at her with desire. Or him. Max said that immortal females are just as bad as the males."

"Or good." Darlene leaned against his arm. "I like exclusivity, and I don't get excited thinking about performing for strangers. That's not my thing."

Hooking a finger under her chin, he turned her to look at him. "What is your kink?"

She felt her cheeks heating up. "I used to read a lot of ménage romances, and then I switched to reverse harem romances, which is basically the same thing. But fantasy is not reality, and in reality, I'm a one-man woman."

He dipped his head. "And I'm a one-woman man. I'm Darlene's man." He kissed her softly.

When they came up for air, Darlene was panting. "Let's go to bed."

"What's wrong with the couch?" He snaked his hand under her shirt and cupped her breast over her bra.

"There is too much light in here, and I'm still not comfortable making love with the lights on." She pushed to her feet and offered him a hand up. "Besides, I haven't slept in a proper bed for two weeks. I want to be comfortable tonight."

"Yes, ma'am." He let her pull him up.

In their bedroom, she led him to the bed and gave him a light push. "Sit down."

When he tried to plop back and pull her on top of him, she shook her head. "Tonight, I'm going to take care of you, and you are going to lay back and enjoy. Is that clear?"

"Yes, ma'am." Eric smiled.

Dropping down to her knees, she lifted one of his feet and took the flip-flop off, then repeated with the other.

"You have very nice feet." She threaded her hands under his pants and massaged his calves. "Nice legs too."

"Keep going," Eric smirked.

She tugged on his pants. "You will need to help me a little."

"Of course." He lifted his butt and pushed his pants and underwear down, exposing his erect shaft.

"You have a very nice arousal too." She wrapped her palm around his smooth length and dipped her head to give it a kiss.

Eric groaned. "More. Take it into your mouth."

"Yes, sir." She licked around the head for a moment and then sucked it in without warning, taking it as deep as she could.

He groaned. "Fuck, Darlene. That's so good."

If she could smile around the length filling her throat, she would have. That was the idea. She was going to fuck him with her mouth.

When her gag reflex kicked in, she backed off and rolled her tongue around the tip while pumping the length with her hand. His shaft was slick from her saliva, and her palm glided over it with ease.

Should she tighten her hold on him?

She wasn't great at oral, as Leo had told her countless times, and she was still too embarrassed to ask Eric for directions.

Given his reaction, though, she was doing something right.

Breathing heavily, he threaded his fingers into her hair and pulled, holding her at his mercy, and thrust up.

When he hit the back of her throat, tears came to her eyes, but she wasn't going to back off, and she pushed past the gagging sensation to take him even deeper.

The loss of control was an illusion because she knew he would let go the moment she signaled any kind of distress, but it excited her nonetheless.

Forcing her throat muscles to relax, she took him as deep as she could and then backed off, only to slam down once more.

"That's it." Eric fisted her hair, pulling on the roots and causing pinpricks of pain that only added to her excitement. "Take it all!" He thrust up into her throat.

His encouraging words made her work harder, her head bobbing fast over his length, her hand pumping in tandem, and then he jerked, and a split second later, his seed filled her mouth.

After she swallowed it all and licked him clean, he cupped her cheeks, pulled her up, and kissed her deeply, passionately.

Letting go of her mouth, he didn't release her cheeks and looked into her eyes. "I love you so damn much."

She smiled. "Because I give great blowjobs?"

Say yes, she pleaded with him silently, needing the reassurance.

Eric chuckled. "You blew my mind, but you know what I love even more than your fabulous blowjobs?"

"What?"

"Returning the favor." In a move that was too fast to follow, he flipped her on her back and pulled down her pants. "My turn." He dove between her spread legs.

Evidently, he wasn't as weak as she'd thought.

4 7

JADE

*T*wo weeks had passed since Jade had submitted her fable to the contest. She didn't dare check the email account often because that would have made her seem eager, which would have made Igor suspicious. Instead, she acted blasé and checked no more than twice a week.

If confronted, her story would be that she'd entered the contest to get free access to the Safe Haven library, which was supposed to contain a lot of material she could use to teach the children.

She'd found two other contests which she'd entered as well, so her original submission to Veskar's contest would not look out of place, and she'd also subscribed to several others that offered a free trial. Her desk was stacked with printouts from those sites, and her notebook was filled with ideas that those articles and stories had inspired.

She left the notebook on her desk during lunch breaks and bathroom visits so Igor could take a look and see that she was utilizing the material he'd allowed her to collect.

So far it seemed to be working, and he hadn't confronted her about any of it, but if he did, she had plenty of material to defend herself. The only way he could guess what she was up

197

to was if he went on the Safe Haven site and recognized Emmett Haderech as a hybrid Kra-ell.

That wasn't likely.

Veskar had done a great job disguising himself and his inhumanly youthful appearance for someone his age. His long beard and hair looked like he was wearing a wig or extensions and coloring his hair, and the robes he favored hid his body shape. Only someone who knew him as well as Jade could recognize him in that disguise.

As she knocked on the door and entered Igor's office, he lifted his head and pinned her with a dark look. "You've got an email from one of those contests you entered. You won free access to their library."

Her heart threatened to break through her ribs and flop on the floor, but she forced herself to calm down and nodded. "Which one?"

Schooling her features, she sauntered over to her seat in the corner of his office and flipped the old laptop open.

"The one with all the free-love spiritual nonsense. I don't know what you hope to gain from winning it."

"They have a big library with many motivational stories," she said as nonchalantly as she could. "The contest winners get lifetime access, so anything they add over the years will be at my disposal. Not a bad deal for a silly little story that took me ten minutes to write."

She hoped he hadn't read it, and if he had, that he hadn't figured out the coordinates that she'd so cleverly weaved into the story.

The question was whether Veskar had guessed what those numbers were. She didn't have the precise coordinates, and the ones she'd found were from a globe she used to teach the children about Earth's geography. Karelia was not enormous, and she didn't know the exact location of the compound, so it was just a guesstimate.

Some of the young humans were allowed to study either

in Helsinki or St. Petersburg, and since they drove to and from their universities, they could tell her the exact coordinates, but asking them was out of the question.

They would have reported her to Igor even if they didn't want to. The compulsion would have forced them to do that.

Angling her screen so she could see Igor's reflection in it, she checked whether he was watching her, but he had gone back to what he'd been doing when she'd entered.

Jade stifled a relieved breath, turned the laptop on, and opened the email from Safe Haven.

Dear Ms. Solveika,

Congratulations.

You are one of the three contest finalists. You should be proud of yourself. Out of a hundred and thirteen submissions, yours and two others were chosen to enter the final round.
Only one entry will win a free ticket to one of our world-renowned retreats, and we wish you the best of luck in winning it.
As one of the three finalists, you've won lifetime access to our extended library of motivational and spiritual material. We encourage you to read through the other contest submissions, which you can find under
http://Safe.Haven.org/contest.
Your access code is Winners-Circle-3.
The winner of the final round will be announced at the end of the month.

Best of luck,
Riley Montgomery.
Executive Director, Safe Haven.

Leaning back, Jade folded her arms over her chest and turned to look at Igor. "I'm one of three finalists. After the final round, only one of us will be selected, winning a free ticket to one of their retreats. What if I win?"

She knew he'd read the email, but she had to keep up the pretense of no big deal.

He didn't even lift his head. "You will give it to the runner-up."

"I know that you won't let me attend one of those retreats, but maybe you can send someone else in my place. It would be a shame to waste the prize. Those retreats are costly."

"So is a plane ticket to Oregon, United States."

Jade's heart thundered in her chest. Igor had obviously checked out Safe Haven and its location, but hopefully, his disinterest was genuine and not faked.

Just to be safe, though, she didn't immediately log into the website and use her access code. She would do that in a day or two. In the meantime, she would check the other websites and download more material to throw Igor off.

48

SOFIA

"Why are you scowling at me?" Roxie put her plate down. "I'm not the one who stood you up."

Sofia let out a breath. "First of all, I wasn't scowling at you. I was just gazing into the distance. And secondly, he hasn't stood me up because we didn't make any plans. He just disengaged, which is his prerogative."

That was only partially true, but it sounded less humiliating. Marcel had told her that he would try to make it after lunch yesterday, but it had sounded like a brush-off. Sofia had hoped that she'd misinterpreted it and that he would be there, but when he hadn't shown up yesterday or today, that hope had been squashed.

"Maybe he had a work emergency." Roxie patted her shoulder. "You don't have a phone with you, so he couldn't let you know."

"Maybe you are right." Sofia cast her a smile and pretended to dig into her meal.

Roxie was wrong.

Even if Marcel had to leave on short notice, he could have

left her a note, or he could've stopped by the dining hall and told her that he was leaving.

The fact that he'd just disengaged meant that he wasn't interested and that he had no respect for her. Otherwise, he wouldn't have just ghosted her. As much as it hurt to accept it, that was the reality, and she had to move on.

Time was of the essence, and Sofia needed to find a different source of information.

Last night, she had lied to Valstar and said that she was meeting Marcel later, but she'd been smart enough not to mention his name, so Valstar didn't know who she was seeing, and she could find a substitute.

Maybe one of the instructors, or maybe she could pursue Emmett Haderech himself and tell Valstar that her previous source had turned out to be a dud.

Was Emmett Haderech married? He seemed very cozy with Dr. Takala, but since he'd created a community based on the philosophy of free love, he most likely practiced it himself.

Sofia's skin crawled just thinking about seducing someone other than Marcel, but what choice did she have? She had to get over it.

Maybe if she got drunk enough, she could tolerate some other male's hands on her.

Right.

To get invited to stay, she needed to make the guy fall in love with her, or at least in lust, and she wasn't going to achieve that objective by just faking it. She needed to put on the best performance of her life and convince him that he was a superb lover and she couldn't live without him and his amazing, magical wand.

Ugh.

She would have had no problem with any of it if Marcel was that guy. But if he walked into the dining hall right now, she would punch him in the face for ruining her plans and endangering her family. He didn't know what was at stake, but he'd been rude and heartless, and she was mad as hell at him.

She was the spy who was supposed to feign interest to lure him, but her interest had been genuine while his had been fake. Why had he put on such a great show of being interested in her if he wasn't?

He couldn't have possibly known why she was there, so he had no excuse for the way he behaved.

But what if he knew?

Marcel hadn't mentioned having a paranormal talent, but he might have lied by omission. What if he could read her thoughts?

Nah, that wasn't likely.

Dr. Eleanor Takala had said that it was one of the rarest talents and that she'd only met one person who could do that. Most telepaths could sense emotions, intentions, and the strong ones could see the visuals in someone's thoughts.

If Marcel was a level nine telepath or below, he couldn't have guessed her purpose from sensing her emotions or intentions. Sofia's emotions were all over the place because she was attracted to him, and it confused her, because she was scared for her family and because she was scared for herself. And as for her intentions, they weren't nefarious because she had no idea what Igor intended to do with the information she was supposed to gather.

Mother above, the guy was confusing and infuriating. She was usually a mellow person, agreeable and nonconfrontational, but Marcel evoked extreme emotions in her.

She didn't know what she wanted to do more, punch him in the face or jump his bones and have furious hate sex with him.

She'd never done either, but there was a first time for

everything. Sex sounded better than hitting, but it looked like she wouldn't get to do either because the damn male was a rude jerk who didn't have the guts to tell her to her face that he was no longer interested.

49

MARCEL

*M*arcel glanced at his phone, picked it up, and checked the incoming calls. Sometimes he didn't hear it ringing, not because there was anything wrong with his ears but because he was so immersed in solving a problem that he didn't pay attention to anything else.

As Roni used to say, when Marcel was on a mission, the sky could be falling, and he wouldn't notice. His ability to hyper-focus was useful for a scientist, but it had been a hindrance when he was a Guardian. A soldier had to be aware of his surroundings.

There had been no missed phone calls, but there was a message from Roni asking him to give him a call.

Good.

Marcel had been avoiding Sofia until Roni found out more about her background and whether there was anything suspicious in her past, and he felt bad about that.

Frankly, he needed to put some distance between them because she was threatening to ruin the calm and unemotional persona he'd worked so hard to build.

Marcel didn't want to go back to the way he'd been before.

He'd been too trusting, too quick to fall in love and too easily hurt. That guy was dead, and Marcel had no intentions of resurrecting him. Not for Sofia and not for anyone else.

That guy had been a liability. A Guardian with no teeth had no business on the force, and that was one of the reasons why he had never felt as if he belonged and had eventually left.

He wasn't an empath, just slightly on the sensitive side, and he couldn't understand how a powerful empath like Arwel had the strength to endure a bombardment of emotions without closing his heart and his mind to the suffering of others.

Marcel's only option had been to turn that part of himself off, and he preferred it to stay in the off position.

Leaning back in his chair, he placed the call to Roni. "Good afternoon. How are you doing?"

"Busy as usual. So here is what I found out about your lady. I confirmed that she's been a student at the University of Helsinki for the last seven years, just as she claimed. I checked her records, including her grades, teachers' comments, her employment record, the hours she logged teaching, and a lot of other information. There is too much of it to be fake. Even I wouldn't have gone to such lengths to create a fake identity, and I'm pretty thorough. She doesn't have social media, which is odd for a person her age but not odd enough to be suspicious. A lot of people shun social media. More so lately. It's too politicized and too intrusive."

"What about before she joined the university? Did you find any high-school records?"

"I did. But there wasn't much in there. Just the basics. I checked the medical records of everyone attending the retreat, and she's gotten all of her immunization shots. Other than that, she had one case of strep throat when she was thirteen, and that was it. She sees a dentist every six months and gets her teeth cleaned. Anything else?"

"What about her family? Does she have a birth record?"

"Yep. I can email you the details. Her parents have different last names, so they either weren't married, or her mother chose to retain her maiden name. Do you want me to run a background check on them as well?"

Roni sounded like that was the last thing he wanted to do, and Marcel couldn't blame him. Roni's time was too valuable to waste on a wild goose chase for something that wasn't there.

"Since everything she said checks out, I see no reason to keep digging."

"What made you suspicious of her in the first place?"

"Her mind is like a vault, but she's not immune. It's as if parts of her are locked down, and others are not. I was able to thrall her to forget a little snippet of information, but I wasn't able to see anything deeper."

"You are not supposed to."

"I know." Marcel sighed. "I asked Onegus for permission to use a stronger thrall to get into her mind, but he said that I needed probable cause to dig deeper. Since you didn't find any inconsistencies in her story, I don't have probable cause." He chuckled. "Aside from my gut feeling, that is."

"Then go for it. Onegus is a lawman, and he must follow the law. You are a civilian, and the rules are laxer for us."

"I used to be a Guardian."

"I didn't know that. Does it mean that you are still bound by the same rules as active Guardians?"

"No, but civilians are supposed to follow the same rules, and I'm not a lawbreaker."

"Suit yourself. If I were you, and I suspected something, I would have dug deeper, but then I can't thrall for crap, so it's a moot point."

KIAN

*K*ian was about to turn into the pathway leading to his front door when he saw Kaia leaving Annani's house.

"Good evening, Kian." She waved at him and turned toward William's place, or rather her and William's home.

He waved back. "Good evening, Kaia."

It seemed like she'd arrived at the village only a few days ago, which wasn't that far off, and already she was another permanent resident, adding to the rich tapestry of the village population.

Kaia was a valuable addition.

Wondering what she'd been doing at his mother's, he decided to pay her a visit. If his mother was agreeable, he could call Syssi and ask her to join them with Allegra.

Kian knocked on the door, and a moment later, Oridu opened up. "Good evening, master." He bowed.

"Hello." Kian walked in.

"What a lovely surprise." His mother opened her arms. "Come and give me a hug."

Sitting next to her on the couch, he wrapped his arm

around her slim shoulders and kissed her cheek. "I saw Kaia leaving here a moment ago. What was she doing here?"

Annani arched a brow. "She needed my help with a personal matter. It does not concern the clan or its security, so I am not going to share it with you." She sighed. "But while I was helping Kaia with what was bothering her, I also took care of a problem that did have to do with my security, so I should share that with you."

Kian's hackles rose. "Your security? What do you mean?"

His mother signaled Oridu to come over. "Could you please bring a cup of tea for my son?"

"Of course, Clan Mother." He bowed.

"Kaia is very smart, and she loves to solve puzzles." Annani took a sip of her tea. "She wondered why you and Toven seem less worried about transitioning Dormants than other members of the clan are, including Bridget, and she came to the conclusion that you two must know something that the others do not. Then she wondered about the so-called blessings, and she set out to find the truth."

That was a troubling development.

"How do you know that?"

"I stumbled upon those thoughts while I was helping her with her private issue. Anyway, I thralled her to stop thinking about it. From now on, every time she starts wondering about Toven and my blessings, she will not be able to hold on to the thought, and her mind will wander to a different topic."

Kian let out a breath. "I'm glad you nipped it in the bud."

"Here is your tea, master." Oridu put the teacup in front of Kian.

"Thank you." He took a couple of sips before putting it down.

"Kaia is not the only one with good observational skills," his mother said. "I have already spoken to Toven and advised him to act more concerned about transitioning Dormants. You should put up a better act as well."

"You are right. I've become overly complacent lately. Maybe it's because of Navuh's lack of interest in us over the last year or so. What's going on with him? Did you talk with Areana about him?"

"Of course." Annani smiled. "I love my sister, and I enjoy talking with her, but I also do it to keep tabs on her mate and his plans. He does not tell her much about his day-to-day activities, but he does tell her about his grand plans. Areana says that Navuh is becoming more and more obsessed with China. He realizes that he has been ignoring the rising star to the detriment of the Brotherhood's future, and he is adamant about rectifying his neglect. The West is no longer his main focus. His new mantra is that to take over the world, he has to gain control over China."

Kian snorted. "At this point, no one can control China. It is on its way to becoming the next superpower, and it is not open to foreign influence like the West was. He has no chance."

Annani tilted her head. "I would not be so sure about that. Navuh might be unhinged, but he is very smart. Lokan says that he started bringing smart Chinese male students to breed with his Dormants. Once he breeds a new crop of Dormant girls with Asian features, he will breed them again until he gets warriors who look fully Chinese, are smart, and can blend in. It might take him several decades, but Navuh is not in a hurry. He makes very long-term plans."

"I'm not worried. This time around, Navuh's plans are not going to succeed. He's too late to the game. But I'm glad that's where his focus is. As long as he's obsessing about China, he's not bothering us."

SOFIA

When the last class ended, Sofia pretended to organize her backpack as she waited for the other attendees to leave. Naturally, Roxie stayed behind, tapping her foot impatiently. "Are you coming?"

Sofia cast her a smile. "Go ahead. I'll catch up with you." She kept an eye on the instructor, hoping he wouldn't leave.

He was an average-looking guy, but he seemed kind, and he'd been smiling at her throughout the class. Not only that, but he was also fascinated by her mirror divination and wanted to see a demonstration.

It was a great excuse to get him alone so she could put the moves on him.

"I'll wait." Roxie pulled out a chair.

"Please, don't." Sofia signaled with her eyes, hoping Roxie would get the hint that she wanted to have a word with the teacher.

A grin spread over Roxie's face. "I'll save a seat for you." She was out of the chair in an instant and practically ran out of the classroom.

Sofia turned to the instructor and rolled her eyes. "I thought she would never leave." She sauntered toward him and affected a suggestive smile. "I thought that maybe we could meet up later tonight at the social. If you want me to demonstrate my mirror divination, you can come to my room. I brought my special mirror with me."

"I would be delighted."

"Wonderful." She let out a breath. "I was afraid that there were rules about instructors and attendees fraternizing."

"Not in Safe Haven, and not as long as the lady initiates."

"Awesome." She slung her backpack over her shoulder. "I'll look for you at the social." She gave him another smile and waved goodbye.

Her smile vanished as soon as she was out of the classroom.

She hated it, absolutely detested having to seduce a guy she felt nothing for. Igor and Valstar would pay for forcing her to do that. She didn't know how or when, but one day, she would have her revenge.

Walking down the hallway, she debated whether she should go on a run and report to Valstar before having dinner or do it after. On the one hand, getting it out of the way would be a relief, but on the other hand, she shouldn't talk to Valstar while consumed by rage.

Not that she had high hope for feeling any calmer about what she had to do after dinner, but she might.

As she neared the dining hall, a tall, elegant figure leaning against the wall made her heartbeat accelerate, but she commanded it and herself to remain unaffected.

If Marcel expected her to fall into his arms, grateful that he had finally shown up, he was gravely mistaken. She was tempted to ignore him and just walk past him into the dining room.

But that was a coward's move.

She was a coward at heart, but she refused to bow to her cowardice.

In the end, she gave him a slight nod as she passed and continued walking.

"Sofia, wait." He rushed after her. "I'm sorry for not being here yesterday."

"No biggie." She gave him a tight smile. "I didn't wait for you." She scanned the room for Roxie and waved at her. "See you around." She lengthened her stride.

Luckily, there was only one vacant chair at Roxie's table, so Marcel couldn't join them.

Nevertheless, he followed her and just looked at her as she sat down. "Can I get you a plate?"

"I don't need help." She ignored him and turned to Roxie. "I'm meeting Edward later today at the social. I told him that I would give him a demonstration of my divination. I hope it's okay with you if I invite him to our room."

"Sure." Roxie cooperated. "I'm not planning to make use of my bed tonight." Smiling suggestively, she shimmied on her chair.

That should have been enough to make Marcel leave, but the guy was more stubborn than she'd given him credit for and not as mellow as he appeared.

With a growl that sounded a lot like male Kra-ell on a hunt, he pulled a chair from a nearby table and put it behind hers. "I'm not going to move from here until you let me explain."

"I'm not interested in your explanation."

Everyone sitting at the table was watching the spectacle they were making, and even though Marcel deserved to be embarrassed, Sofia didn't enjoy performing for a crowd.

"The facts speak for themselves." She rose to her feet. "I'm getting food."

She knew he would follow, but that was okay. She would say her piece, get rid of him, and that would be it.

Except, a small voice at the back of her head was calling her a fool.

So what if he was a jerk?

She wasn't looking for a boyfriend, and he was a means to an end. In addition, she was still attracted to him despite his jerkiness, and hate-sex with him would be a million times better than pretending to enjoy Edward's touch.

On the other hand, Edward would be easier to manipulate. He wasn't as smart and as guarded as Marcel, and she knew he would be putty in her hands.

Succeeding in the mission was more important than any other consideration, and since Edward would be much easier to ply for information, he was the obvious choice. But what if he didn't know as much as Marcel did?

Maybe Marcel was the better choice after all?

MARCEL

*S*ofia was pissed, and she had every right to be. Marcel had some groveling to do, and he was happy to do it if it helped him win her back.

He liked it that she didn't forgive him right away and was trying her best to get rid of him. It was a good sign that she wasn't planning on manipulating him. It also indicated that she'd liked him enough to be upset with him for not showing up.

He took a plate and stood behind her in line for the buffet.

"I said that I would try to make it yesterday at lunch. I didn't promise that I'd be there. It didn't work out."

"You could've sent a note or stopped by for a moment to say that you had something that needed to be done." She looked at him over her shoulder. "Not showing up was a clear sign that you were uninterested, and it was also rude. It was disrespectful."

"You are right, and I apologize. I didn't realize how it would seem to you. Can I make it up to you?"

She shrugged. "I don't see how. The damage was done, and I moved on. There are plenty of nice single men here for me to choose from." She put a piece of chicken on her plate and added rice pilaf.

"I'm not ready to give up on you." He put the same things on his plate. "It has been years since I've felt so strongly about a woman." He got close behind her so he could whisper in her ear. "Frankly, it scared me, and I needed to get some distance to make sure that I wasn't making a mistake."

She turned a pair of incredulous eyes on him. "Seriously? We were supposed to meet for lunch, not at the altar. It wasn't a monumental decision that you needed to examine with care."

How the hell was he going to get through to her?

Should he thrall her to forgive him?

No, that wouldn't be right.

Maybe humor was the key. His social skills sucked, but he was a good observer and a quick study. As a last resort, he could channel Anandur, and, if that didn't work, Onegus.

The chief was in a league of his own in the diplomatic and charm departments, so he would be more difficult to emulate, but Anandur was easy.

"Let's sit down and talk like the adults we are and sort it out. If by the end of dinner you still feel like punching me in the face, I will stand still and take it."

That got half a smile out of Sofia. "How did you know that was what I wanted to do?"

"The talk or the punch to the face?"

"Obviously, the punch to the face. I've already told you that I'm not interested in hearing your excuses."

"You looked like that was what you wanted to do. You were radiating aggression. It's not good for you to carry such anger, and because I'm the cause of it, it is fitting that you use me to give your rage an outlet." He scanned the room for a vacant table and found one next to the back wall. "Is over there okay?" He pointed, hoping she wouldn't just walk back to her table.

Sofia shrugged. "It's fine." She strode toward the table he'd pointed to.

Marcel felt like pumping his fist in the air.

Despite her tough talk, she was going to listen to him.

He'd better make it quick and to the point, because she was angry and impatient.

Catching on to the vibe she was emitting, people got out of her way. For a willowy dancer type with a delicate face, she cut an imposing figure when riled. There was coiled energy in her, like in a tigress, and apparently he wasn't the only one who sensed it.

When they reached the table, he pulled out a chair for her, and as she sat down, a guy who'd been heading their way with a plate changed his mind at the last minute and turned to search for a spot at a different table.

It hadn't been Marcel who'd scared him away. It was the stormy cloud hovering over Sofia's lovely head.

When he sat down, she waved a hand. "I'm willing to listen to what you have to say, but I can already tell you that it probably will not make a difference. The only excuse I can accept is that you had a death in the family and were too overtaken with grief to remember that you made plans with me."

"Thankfully, no one has died, so I can't use that as an excuse. I can only use my ineptitude in courtship. As I said, it has been a very long time since I courted a lady, and I'm not very good at social interactions in general." He rubbed his hand over his beard. "I should have gotten you a phone or at least a walkie-talkie. I didn't think any of this through, and I apologize."

53

SOFIA

S ofia's resolve to stay angry was weakening, and she didn't like it. She wanted to be strong, to stay angry and adamant, but Marcel looked so apologetic, and his excuses were so pathetic that she knew he wasn't making them up.

He was an intelligent man, so if he wished to lie, he could've come up with a much more compelling story.

Besides, he looked so damn good and smelled divine, which couldn't be said for Edward. The guy hadn't stunk, but he hadn't emitted a pleasant odor either, and he couldn't hold a candle to Marcel in any department, looks, smarts, or even charm.

Given that Marcel wasn't particularly charming, that was saying a lot.

The question was how to make the transition from wanting to punch him in the face to jumping his bones.

"Your excuses are not good enough." She looked at his plate and the food he had barely touched. "I think that by the end of dinner, I will still feel like punching you in the face, and you will have to stand still and take it."

"Would that earn me your forgiveness?"

Her lips twitched with a suppressed smile. "It might."

"Then you're on. Tell me where and when."

Resting her chin on the knuckles of her left hand, she pretended to think it over. "I don't want to embarrass you, and I don't want security to come running to arrest me for assault, so it will have to be either my room or yours. Do you have a roommate?"

"I have my own bungalow, but guests are not allowed in there. It's a fenced-off area reserved for the project I'm working on."

Maybe Marcel's project was what Igor was interested in? It sounded like he was working on something top secret, and he'd mentioned working in a lab. Could he be developing a drug to enhance paranormal abilities?

Otherwise, why work on it at Safe Haven?

But he was a computer engineer, not a doctor or a scientist, so maybe his project was related to artificial intelligence.

Both of those subjects could interest Igor.

Leaning forward, she gave him a seductive smile, and this time, she didn't have to pretend. "I share a room with Roxie. I can ask her to stay away for a couple of hours, but the walls are thin, and I can hear our neighbors talking, which means they can hear everything that's going on in our room, and if I punch you, and you groan, they might come in to see if you need help. You'll have to sneak me into your bungalow."

The gleam in his eyes looked like they were glowing from the inside, but that couldn't be. Marcel wasn't Kra-ell. He was human. It must be a trick of the light.

Smiling, he leaned closer to her. "Are you planning on hitting me for two hours straight?"

Oops. She'd let her real plans slip.

"It depends. If you sneak me into your bungalow, I might consider going easy on you and punch you only a couple of times."

"I'm sorry, but I can't." He seemed genuinely upset about

it, but then his eyes gleamed again. "There is somewhere I can take you where no one will hear me scream when you punch me."

"And where is that?"

"I can't tell you. It's a secret, and you will have to wear a blindfold. But don't worry. I'll carry you so you won't stumble."

Was he taking her to his secret lab?

That would be perfect for what she needed from him, and it also sounded sexy as hell. The image of being carried by Marcel while blindfolded had her nipples harden in anticipation.

Mother of All Life, it had been so long since she'd last had sex, and she was overdue for some carnal fun. But did she trust Marcel enough to let him take her to a place where no one could hear her scream?

She could tell Roxie that she was going with him and if she didn't return in the morning, to alert security.

"Fine. But I'm going to tell Roxie, and if I'm not back in two hours, she'll call security."

He laughed. "That's fine with me, but I happen to be friends with everyone on the security detail. I don't think you'll get much help from them." His expression turning serious, he reached for her hand. "Nevertheless, you have nothing to fear from me. Even though I'm not officially affiliated with Safe Haven, the resort's rules apply to me too. Everything is your call, and I have to abide by your wishes, no objections and no questions asked."

"I like these rules," she whispered, her voice sounding husky to her own ears. "Wait here." She rose to her feet. "I need to find Roxie."

"Hurry back."

She still intended to punish him for making her miserable for two days straight, and the blindfold he insisted she wore would come in handy.

Roxie grinned like a fiend when Sofia got back to their table. "Did you kiss and make up?"

"Not yet, but we are working on it. I need you to do me a favor."

"Anything."

"I'm going on a date with Marcel, but I promised Edward to meet him at the social tonight. Can you find him and apologize for me? Tell him that I couldn't make it, but don't tell him why. I'll bring the mirror to class tomorrow and give him a demonstration then."

Roxie tilted her head. "He doesn't care about your divination. He was hoping to hook up with you."

"I know, and I feel bad about doing to him what Marcel did to me, but I didn't promise him a hookup, only implied it, and I can pretend that the mirror was the only reason I invited him."

"Don't worry about it." Roxie rose to her feet. "I'll fill in for you."

Sofia's eyes widened. "That's going above and beyond. I can't expect you to do that."

Roxie shrugged. "I like Edward, and I have no problem being his consolation prize." She winked and fluffed her crazy hair.

54

MARCEL

*W*hen Sofia had gone to talk to Roxana, Marcel pulled out his phone and called Leon.

"What's up, Marcel?"

"I have a favor to ask. Can I take a lady to Emmett's old bunker? I can't take her to my bungalow, and she shares a room with another lady."

"Marcel, you scoundrel. Since when did you become a player?"

"Since I met a lady who tugged at my heartstrings. Can I use the bunker or not?"

"Go ahead. I'll text you the code for the keypad. Who's the lady?"

"A retreat attendee from Finland. I asked Roni to check her background before going deeper into the relationship."

"What's her paranormal talent?"

"Mirror divining. Have you ever heard of that?"

"Nope. Sounds fake to me."

"It might be, but she's special regardless of her talent."

"What's her name?"

"Sofia."

There was a moment of silence and then a whistle. "She's

beautiful. A little too skinny for my taste, but she looks graceful and refined."

"She is. She's a linguist." Marcel couldn't help but boast a little. "She's fluent in several European languages, knows many others, and is a professor's assistant at the University of Helsinki."

"Quality lady. Enjoy your time with her."

"I intend to."

"I'll text you the code as soon as we hang up."

"Thank you."

When he ended the call, Sofia was already walking back toward him, her narrow hips swaying from side to side in an alluring way. She was so graceful it was hard to believe she wasn't a professional dancer.

She should have been, but then people's choice of path often wasn't solely based on their aptitudes and preferences.

He was a classic example of that.

He'd chosen to become a Guardian because two of his best buddies had joined the force, but it had never been a passion for him like it had been for them.

He'd found his passion centuries later when he'd discovered that he loved engineering. The occupation wasn't emotionally laden, but it was creative and useful and benefited others. He could do much more to improve the lives of immortals and humans alike as an engineer than as a Guardian.

"I'm ready." Sofia stood next to him. "Are you?"

"I am." He glanced at his phone. "I got the code for the door."

"How about the blindfold?"

He didn't have that, but a cloth napkin would do. He took a clean one from the table, folded it several times over, and tucked it in his pocket.

Sofia tsked. "I never would have suspected you of being capable of stealing. You are so straitlaced."

"Appearances can be misleading." He rose to his feet and wrapped his arm around her shockingly narrow waist. "I'm not as dorky as I look."

"Dorky? You don't look dorky at all."

He led her toward the door. "What do I look like to you?"

"An executive. Someone who has an important job. I bet you are in charge of that special project you are working on."

"I am, but only because my boss, who was running the project, had to leave and asked me to take over."

She eyed him from under lowered lashes. "Don't sell yourself short, Marcel. I'm sure you are a big shot in the organization you work for."

He stopped at the edge of the back courtyard and pulled out the napkin he'd pilfered from the dining hall. "This is where I need to blindfold you."

She looked at his hands as he folded the napkin into the proper shape for a blindfold. "Are you sure you want to carry me? My skinny looks are deceiving. I'm heavy."

He snorted. "How much do you weigh? A hundred pounds?"

For some reason, she looked offended. Had he overestimated her weight?

Women were touchy about those things.

"I weigh sixty kilos, and I worked hard on getting to that weight."

Sixty kilos was a little over one hundred and thirty pounds, which was adequate for her height and slim build, but she didn't look it.

"My apologies." He dipped his head. "I meant no offense."

"None taken."

He snapped the folded napkin between his hands. "Turn around."

"Yes, sir." She pivoted on her heel.

"You will need to let your hair down. The napkin is not long enough to tie around your hairdo."

"Okay." She took out several pins and then shook her hair out.

It was magnificent, long, thick, and glossy, with a small curl at the bottom. She looked absolutely stunning with it tumbling down her back and tickling the tops of her butt cheeks.

Sucking in a breath, he got behind her and tied the blindfold around her eyes. "Okay? Or is it too snug?"

"It's okay," she breathed. "You smell so good."

Unable to stop himself, he brushed her hair aside and kissed her silky soft neck. "So do you."

55

SOFIA

*M*arcel's arms came around Sofia's back and legs, and he lifted her with ease, not even huffing out a breath, and carried her as if she weighed no more than a pillow.

How was he so strong?

He walked with her for a few minutes, but even though it was still early in the evening and the retreat guests were milling around, she couldn't hear anyone. Marcel must have taken her to a secluded part of the resort where the guests were not allowed.

Maybe she could learn something that she could report to Valstar?

As they entered a structure, she asked, "Where are you taking me?"

He chuckled. "Now you're asking?"

"Yes." She tried to wiggle out of his arms when he loosened his hold to type in the code. "There is no one around."

It must be the lab. What other structure had a door with a key code?

"That was the idea, wasn't it? You needed a place where

you could hit me in the face, and no one would hear me scream."

"Yeah, but that means that no one would hear me scream either."

Suddenly, she felt nervous, and it wasn't only the excited butterflies about getting intimate with a new man. After Marcel's comment about the security team being his friends, Sofia hadn't asked Roxie to get them if she didn't return by morning.

Roxie would probably do that even without being asked, but if they were Marcel's buddies, would they help her?

As the door closed behind them, his arms tightened around her. "This used to be Emmett's old place before he met Eleanor. She wanted a fresh start with him, so they moved into one of the bungalows, and this place was turned into guest quarters but not for the retreat attendees. Emmett's partner and his wife sometimes stay down here."

Marcel started down a flight of stairs. He was incredibly strong for a human, and his arms felt like bands of steel around her.

"Did Emmett used to live in a basement?"

"Sort of. It's a very nice basement." Marcel sat down with her still in his arms and removed the blindfold. "Take a look."

It was indeed a very nicely appointed underground apartment. She slid off his lap and sat down beside him. "Don't think that you are getting off with just a scolding. I intend to punish you."

He didn't look scared. In fact, he looked excited. "I hoped that you had changed your mind about punching me in the face and decided to torture me sexually instead."

They hadn't even kissed yet, hadn't touched each other intimately, and hadn't even talked dirty to each other.

How was she going to do this?

Sofia was out of her element, and since the entire

encounter had been unplanned, she hadn't come up with a strategy.

"That's actually not a bad idea." She affected a grin that she hoped looked wicked. "Maybe I should put the blindfold on you, tie you down to the bed, and then pleasure you for hours, holding you on the brink but not letting you climax."

Marcel's eyes blazed with an inner light. "That sounds like the best kind of torture possible." He cupped the back of her neck. "But before I submit to your ministrations, I need a kiss."

She needed it too.

As he captured her lips, she moaned and wound her arms around his neck.

With a groan, he cupped her face and licked into her mouth, sweeping his tongue inside and sucking on her lower lip.

An electric current rushed through her body, igniting all those forgotten feminine parts of her that had been yearning for such a moment, but she wasn't going to succumb to her need or his.

Not yet.

Marcel expected a punishment, and she had to deliver what she'd promised or lose credibility.

Besides, delaying gratification heightened the pleasure.

Pushing on his chest, she leaned away and took the folded napkin that he'd dropped on the couch. "What should I do first? Blindfold you or tie you to a bed?"

He chuckled nervously. "Let's see what kinds of beds they have down here. Not every bed lends itself to bondage."

She lifted a brow. "How much experience do you have with that?"

"None, but I have a vivid imagination."

56

MARCEL

*M*arcel had never engaged in bondage, not as the one doing the tying or the one being tied up. He'd never been curious enough about kink to even visit Brundar's club.

But for some reason, being at Sofia's mercy excited him. Maybe it was just the scent of her arousal and the pheromones she was emitting, and he would have gotten excited by any kind of scene she suggested.

Well, except doing it in public. He was too reserved to enjoy exhibitionism.

Then again, he'd also thought that he was too traditional and naturally dominant to enjoy being at a female's mercy.

Not that he would really be helpless. Unless she used titanium alloy handcuffs, he could get free from any restraints, so fear was not part of the equation.

Pain wasn't either.

He wasn't a masochist.

It was the power exchange, and also the atonement. He wanted her to forgive him, and he was willing to go to great lengths to clean the slate between them.

Why?

Because Sofia had forced him to feel again, to desire and yearn for more than physical gratification, and he hadn't allowed himself to have those feelings for so long that he had believed he'd lost the ability.

At the time, toughening up seemed like the right thing to do, but he hadn't foreseen the cost. To protect himself from emotional pain, he'd given up on the exhilaration of falling in love, or even just in lust, and on forming meaningful connections not just with females but also with males.

Since anyone he cared about could potentially hurt him, he closed himself off and didn't allow anyone to get close enough for him to care for.

Basically, he'd given up on everything that had given him joy, trading it for professional satisfaction in the lab and a humdrum existence outside of it.

"How many bedrooms does this place have?" Sofia opened the first door in the hallway.

"I believe there are four bedrooms. Emmett used to host orgies down here, so I bet we can find some rope or handcuffs."

She looked at him over her shoulder. "Orgies? Are you serious?" She waved at the bedroom's decor. "This doesn't look like a setup for anything kinky. It's just a regular bedroom."

It was nicely furnished, but Sofia was right about it looking mundane.

"That's what I heard. Perhaps the decor got updated under the new management."

Talking about decor helped deflate his raging erection, not completely but enough for him to walk comfortably. He opened a door on the other side of the hallway. "This one is almost identical to the other one."

The third bedroom had a four-poster bed.

"This is the one." Sofia walked over to one of the nightstands and opened the top drawer. "Nothing in here." She opened the bottom one. "And nothing in here either." She looked at him over her shoulder and smiled. "I guess we will have to make do with pillowcases. I can twist them into ropes."

"Hmm." He ran his hand over the footboard that was at least a foot thick. "This looks like it has a hidden compartment." Marcel tried to flip the top open, but it didn't budge. "It's either stuck or locked."

"If it's locked, the key could be hidden somewhere in this room." Sofia walked over to the other nightstand, opened the top drawer, and then lay on the floor to look under it. "No key glued to the underside."

Marcel could've forced the top of the footboard open, but that would have betrayed his super-strength. Instead, he ran his fingers over the underside. "Bingo. There is a hidden latch."

To release it required some strength, probably because it hadn't been used in a while, but when he flipped the top open, he was glad that it hadn't been easy. Syssi had stayed down here, and if she found what he was looking at, she would have been shocked.

Kian's mate was such a pure, gentle soul. She had probably never heard about such kinks let alone seen any of the paraphernalia.

"What's in there?" Sofia walked over to join him in front of the footboard.

"Take a look." He took a step back, curious to see her reaction.

SOFIA

$\mathcal{A}$s Marcel took a step back, Sofia leaned over the footboard and looked inside the compartment.

At first, she couldn't see a thing in the dark cavity, but as her eyes adjusted to the dim interior, she saw a slim handle and pulled it out.

It was a riding crop, with a small leather flap at the end. She held it up to show to Marcel. "What do you think?"

"Doesn't look too scary. Check what else is in there."

Sofia hesitated.

When she'd conceived the game, she hadn't had instruments of torture in mind. The crop looked like it could be used lightly, and she was going to test it on herself before using it on Marcel, but if the next thing she pulled out was a whip, she would have a panic attack.

To her, it wasn't a theoretical thing that she'd read about in a book. She'd seen whipping and flogging, and it was horrendous.

Thankfully, it was never used on humans, or at least not since she was old enough to be aware of it, but purebloods and hybrids who displeased Igor were severely punished.

What would he do to her if she failed to deliver what he was looking for?

Did he kill humans who displeased him?

She jerked as Marcel put his hand on her shoulder. "What's the matter? Are you having second thoughts about our game?"

She forced a smile. "I didn't plan on using torture implements. That's too much."

He chuckled. "Those are just toys." He pulled out a pink flogger. "See? The strands are soft suede, and it's pink." He handed it to her. "Check it out."

The strands were indeed soft, and as she flicked it over her thigh, she could barely feel anything through her jeans.

"I'm sure it stings more on bare skin." She flicked it on her arm, and it stung a little, but it wasn't painful.

Feeling better about the game, she put the flogger on the bed and pulled out the next item, which was a set of leather restraints.

That was what she needed, and all the rest was superfluous. She wasn't going to flog Marcel or hit him with a crop. All she was going to do was keep him on the edge until he could take it no more.

Turning around she held out the restraints. "Are you ready for your torment?"

His expression was hard to read, but she was sure he wasn't afraid, not for himself, anyway. He must have sensed her surge of anxiety and wondered what had caused it.

Hopefully, he thought it was her inexperience. He couldn't possibly guess that she'd witnessed whipping and knew how horrific it really was.

"I am, but are you? You seem out of your element." He gave her a crooked smile. "We can go back to the punch in the face idea, and after you punish me, I can take over and show you why it was a smart move to give me another chance."

It was tempting, but she didn't want to punch him either.

"Are you stalling, Marcel?" She ran the leather restraints over her hand. "What are you afraid of?"

"Nothing." He toed off his shoes and pulled his turtleneck over his head. "Nothing that you can do to me with those implements. But I'm terrified of what you can do to my heart."

Sofia swallowed.

Marcel had been hurt before. He'd told her about the girl-friend who'd demanded expensive gifts and then left him. He must have loved her very much to fall victim to her manipulation, or maybe it had happened a long time ago when he was still very young and naive and hadn't known better.

As he turned his back to her and pulled his turtleneck off, Sofia's eyes roamed over his surprisingly defined back muscles. The guy must be spending serious time in the gym to have a body like that. His socks and pants were next, exposing nearly hairless smooth skin and powerful leg muscles, and when he hooked his thumbs in the elastic of his boxer shorts, Sofia held her breath.

He deprived her of the sight of his manhood, climbing on the bed and lying down on his stomach.

The view was magnificent, and she couldn't wait to have her hands all over those beautiful muscles, but what she planned to do required him to lie on his back.

The flogger and the crop were still on the bed where she'd left them. Marcel probably thought that she was going to use them on him, which was why he'd left them there.

She wasn't going to cause him physical pain, but regret-tably, hurting his feelings was inevitable. He might not realize that she'd seduced him for information, but at some point she would have to leave, and she would need to make a clean break, ensuring that he didn't even think to follow her.

It was going to be painful for both of them, and she cursed Igor and her fate for forcing her to hurt a good man, a man she would have loved to keep for longer than a few weeks and see where the relationship took them. But she wasn't free to choose her guy, and her days of freedom were numbered. Igor might send her on missions where her linguistic skills were needed, but he would demand that she return to the compound.

So far, she hadn't been asked to breed with any of the purebloods to produce a hybrid, and in a few years, she would be deemed too old to serve in that capacity, and then she would be free to choose a human partner to father her children.

But he would have to be from the compound.

Her future was not with Marcel even if they turned out to be perfect for each other.

He was right. The pain she could inflict with the flogger or the crop would be nothing compared to the pain of betrayal.

MARCEL

*M*arcel lay face down on the bed and waited for Sofia to make her move.

He could hear her breathing, and he could sense her nervousness. The arousal he'd scented before had diminished when she examined the sex toys, but when he'd gotten naked, it was back, but not to the same level it was when he'd kissed her.

Didn't his body look pleasing to her?

He was in good shape, but he wasn't as muscled as he used to be during his Guardian days. Still, he knew that females found him attractive, so that wasn't it.

She was way over her head with that idea of hers.

"If you want to stop, just say the word. I don't want you to do anything you're uncomfortable with."

"For what I have in mind, you need to turn around," she said quietly.

"Yes, ma'am. You're running the show." He turned to lie on his back.

As Sofia's eyes roamed over his nude body and stopped at his manhood, her cheeks flushed. "You are even better-looking naked," she murmured.

When she licked her lips, his shaft twitched. He fisted it, running his hand up and down lazily. "You can come closer and get a better look."

She smirked as she sauntered over to the side of the bed. "Enjoy it while you can. I'm going to restrain the other hand first."

He flopped his arm to the side, offering it to her. "What are you going to do when you have me at your mercy?"

"You'll find out." She attached one end of the strap to the left post of the headboard, put the wide leather cuff over his wrist, and threaded the end of the tongue through the buckle. "Is it okay?" She tugged on it lightly. "Or is it too tight?"

The scent of her arousal was intensifying by the moment, and his body was reacting predictably. It was good that he had such incredible control over his fangs, or he would be flashing them at her by now.

"It's fine." Marcel gave the strap a perfunctory yank. "Good job." If he yanked any harder, he would either snap the leather or tear down the post.

She smiled as she moved to his left ankle and anchored it the same way. "Too tight? Not tight enough?"

He pretended to yank again. "It's a bit loose, but that's okay. I'm not going anywhere. There is nowhere I'd rather be."

Sofia turned to look at his swelling shaft. "So it would seem. Or is your manhood reacting to your skillful hand?"

"It's all for you, Sofia. Please hurry up and punish me already so we can get to the fun part."

"Patience, big boy." She moved to his right ankle. "We are going to have a lot of fun but not in the way you imagine."

Should he be worried?

What did Sofia intend to do to him?

The crop and the ridiculous pink flogger were still on the bed next to his feet, but so far, she'd ignored them.

The question was what she would do after she had him all tied up.

After securing his right ankle, she walked to the right side of the bed. "Play time is over, lover boy. I need that hand."

As he let go of his shaft and plopped his arm sideways, she didn't grip it immediately. Instead, she seemed mesmerized by his bobbing erection.

He chuckled. "Like what you see?"

"Very much so." She gripped his wrist lightly and secured it to the right bedpost.

Spreadeagled, he looked at her with hooded eyes, waiting for her next move.

He'd expected her to lift one of the implements and strike him with it, but he didn't expect her to start stripping.

"Is that your idea of torture? Are you hoping to taunt me with your nude body and not let me touch you?"

"That's the general idea."

When she pulled her T-shirt over her head and tossed it aside, Marcel sucked in a breath. She was wearing one of those pushup bras that he usually found ridiculous, but it looked damn good on her.

She was very delicately built, so he knew she wouldn't be well-endowed, not naturally anyway, but that was okay. Size didn't matter, and he preferred her breasts to be tiny but natural and not surgically enlarged.

Holding his gaze with her blue eyes, she reached behind her, unhooked the bra, and let it fall down her arms.

She was exactly like he'd expected. With only a slight swell, she was nearly as flat-chested as a boy, but there was nothing boyish about her nipples. They were dark, turgid, and begging to be sucked.

"I want to put my mouth on those berries so badly that I'm salivating."

59

SOFIA

*M*arcel's eyes were glowing, Sofia was sure about that, but since he was obviously human, she glanced up at the light fixture hanging over the bed.

It was probably a reflection. With his blond hair and fair skin, he couldn't be a hybrid. The Kra-ell dark coloring was a dominant trait, and even hybrids who had blond human mothers were dark-haired and olive-skinned.

It didn't matter.

All that mattered was the way he was looking at her as if she was a goddess of feminine sexuality, and he couldn't wait to have her.

But he would have to because she was about to teach him a lesson about leaving a woman hanging.

After pulling down her jeans and panties, she sauntered naked over to the bed, climbed on top, and leaned over him. "Do you want to suck on my nipples?"

"Yes." He hissed.

She kissed him lightly on the lips and then brought a nipple to hover several inches over his mouth, almost within reach.

239

He arched up, pulling the restraints taut, and caught it between his lips, sucking on it greedily.

Her eyes rolling back in her head and moisture pooling between her legs, Sofia moaned. When it became too much, she pulled back and offered him her other nipple.

His neck must be killing him, but Marcel was oblivious to his discomfort as he sucked, nibbled, and nipped, eroding her resolve to keep him on the edge.

She was so turned on that prolonging his suffering meant suffering alongside him, but it was a sweet kind of torment, and she was adamant about stretching it out for as long as she could.

"That's enough," she commanded.

With a groan, he obeyed and let his head drop back on the pillow. "That wasn't nearly enough."

Smiling, she turned around and fisted his erection. He jerked up, thrusting it into her palm, and when she dipped her head and kissed the tip, he groaned.

"Straddle my face and let me taste you."

She wanted to reply that he wasn't in charge and that she would do what she pleased, but her needy core had other ideas, and apparently, she was the boss because Sofia did as he'd asked.

When he licked into her, she closed her eyes and took a third of his erection into her mouth. It was as much as she could comfortably fit, but then it swelled even more, and her mouth got stretched further.

Pushing back to get more of his tongue and lips on her, she tried to keep a steady rhythm, her hand and mouth working in tandem, but with the sensations bombarding her on the other end, it was becoming more and more difficult to concentrate.

In mere moments, they were both right on the edge of orgasming, and Sofia was so damn tempted to let it happen that she teared up as she pulled her bottom away from

Marcel's mouth and squeezed his erection tight to prevent him from coming.

Marcel groaned. "You're evil."

She turned her head to look at him over her shoulder. "That's your punishment. I'm going to keep you on the edge until you scream in frustration."

"Can't you just flog me instead?"

"That wouldn't be as satisfying." She loosened her hold on his erection and licked off the drop of pre cum that had accumulated there. "Hmm. You taste good."

"Not as good as you. Give me back that sweet pussy of yours."

"Gladly."

He attacked it with such fervor that Sofia orgasmed in less than thirty seconds, but she didn't let him finish, repeating what she'd done before.

The leathers straps securing his restraints to the bedposts groaned as he pulled on them, and she had a feeling that he could have snapped them if he really wished to get free, but he was either enjoying the torment she was inflicting on him or determined to let her get her revenge.

When he brought her to her third orgasm, she turned around and straddled his hips. "I'm going to fuck you now."

It had been a while for her, and he was a fairly large male, but she was so slick from climaxing three times that she didn't hesitate. Gripping his aroused member, she lowered her soaking core onto him and pushed down until he was fully seated inside her.

The feeling of being filled by him was so incredible that if not for the slight discomfort of her sheath stretching to accommodate him, she would have orgasmed again.

Marcel's eyes rolled back in their sockets, and the animalistic growl he emitted pulled a new gush of wetness from her that eliminated the discomfort, leaving only intense pleasure behind.

For a long moment, she didn't move, absorbing the feeling of being connected to Marcel in such a primal way. But then he arched up, getting impossibly deeper inside her, and his arm muscles contracted pulling the restraints taut.

They were about to give, and when they did, she had no doubt that he would flip her under him and take over.

Rising on her knees, she looked into his glowing eyes as she slammed down on his arousal, and when she pulled up and slammed down again, a loud crack sounded and then Marcel's arms closed around her.

"My turn." He hissed as he flipped her under him.

60

MARCEL

*A*s Marcel got Sofia under him, his fangs were already elongated. Reaching into her mind, he thralled her to keep her eyes closed, and as he licked the spot on her neck, he sent another thrall to make her ignore his bite, and bit down.

She cried out, her body tensing under him, and as the venom did its thing, she cried out again, this time in ecstasy, and climaxed along with him.

She'd kept him on the edge for so long that his self-control had eventually snapped, and he was going at her full power, pumping her with copious quantities of his essence.

Long moments passed before the crazed haze of sexual frenzy subsided and his mind came back online, and when it did, he retracted his fangs, licked the puncture wounds closed, and prayed to the Fates that she was on birth control.

Immortal males were nearly infertile, so usually he didn't worry about getting a woman pregnant, but there had been nothing usual about Sofia, and not just because she'd tormented him and hadn't allowed him to climax until she'd been good and ready.

He felt it in his bones, in his veins, in his entire being, but he didn't know what it was.

He wasn't in love with her. He barely knew her. The attraction was there, and it was strong, but that couldn't explain the way she'd made him lose himself in her.

Perhaps she was a Dormant?

He hadn't allowed himself to entertain that thought, but it had been lurking in the back of his mind.

Sofia's paranormal talent was strange and unheard of, but so were Mey's and Jin's, so there was that. There was also the immediate connection he felt with her, and given her response, she'd felt it too.

Sofia didn't strike him as the kind of woman who routinely hooked up with men she'd just met, and he had enough experience with women who did that to know that she wasn't like them. And yet she'd been the driving force of their encounter.

She had been in full control of it, so he hadn't stopped to think it was odd that she hadn't asked him to procure a condom or brought one herself. She must be on birth control, but still. Pregnancy wasn't the only thing a human female needed to worry about.

Lifting his head, he looked at her blissed-out face, soaking up her beauty for a long moment before dipping down and stealing a kiss from her parted lips.

When she sighed contentedly, he thought she would wake up, but when she didn't open her eyes, he remembered that he'd thralled her to keep them closed.

She shouldn't be awake so soon after a venom bite, especially given the quantity he'd pumped into her. If she were a male, she would be dead by now. Thankfully, the venom produced in response to sexual desire was not deadly. It didn't slow the heart, and the euphoric effect only lasted a few hours.

Naturally, he would stay awake and watch over her to make sure she was okay.

But first, he needed to get them both cleaned up and throw the ruined restraints into the trash. He should probably get new ones and put them in the hidden compartment.

Pulling out gently, he kissed Sofia's puffy lips again, and then padded to the bathroom to clean himself and bring washcloths for her.

When he returned, he found her on her side, which was not how he'd left her.

Normally women didn't move a muscle until the venom's effect was spent, but as he'd already realized, there was nothing usual about Sofia.

She'd blown his mind.

After cleaning her up, he dropped the washcloths on the nightstand, pulled the covers over them both, and wrapped her in his arms.

She was so slight, seemingly so fragile, but he knew it was an illusion. He'd felt how strong she was, which was why he'd unleashed on her the beast hidden inside of every immortal without fearing that she would break. It hadn't been a conscious decision, but his beast had known she could take it.

SOFIA

*S*ofia opened her eyes with effort. She'd had the most wonderful dreams of soaring above the clouds and looking at beautiful landscapes. She felt at peace, happy like she'd never been before, but an insistent buzzing in the back of her mind intruded on those contented feelings of wonderment, reminding her that there was something urgent she had to do.

Something unpleasant, by the feel of it. Something that would shatter the beautiful bubble she was floating in.

Her mind was still too scattered to focus on what that thing was, the strong arms wrapped around her and the warm chest she was pressed against making it even more difficult to concentrate on anything other than the happiness she felt.

It was naive and a little ridiculous to think that fabulous sex could have a healing effect on her, but that was how she felt.

The truth was that she hadn't thought of herself as sick, injured, or impaired before, but with how wonderful she felt now, it was obvious that she hadn't been well.

She'd lived in constant fear.

Oh, yeah. Now she remembered. She needed to contact Valstar.

"Hello, beautiful." Marcel dipped his head and kissed her lightly. "Did you have pleasant dreams?"

Had he fallen asleep too and had woken up at the same time as she had? Or had he been waiting for her to open her eyes?

"The best." She smiled up at him. "Did we both fall asleep?"

"Only you did." His hand smoothed over the curve of her ass. "I enjoyed lying awake and watching you." His hand traveled back up. "You looked so peaceful."

"Yeah. I had such beautiful dreams."

"Was I in them?"

"No, but I'm sure you inspired them." She shifted in his arms, getting more comfortable in his embrace. "How long did I sleep?"

"Nearly nine hours."

Alarm bells rang in her head. "It can't be. What time is it?"

"It's a little after five in the morning."

"I have to go." She pushed on his chest.

Damn, she'd fallen asleep without telling Valstar that she'd report later this morning. He was going to be furious.

Marcel's arms tightened around her. "Breakfast starts at seven. You have plenty of time."

"I didn't go jogging after dinner last night, so I have to do it before breakfast. I never miss a day."

"I'll come with you."

Damn. What was she going to do now? She couldn't let him accompany her, but after the night they'd spent together, Marcel would expect her to want to spend more time with him, and since she needed him to fall for her, she couldn't rudely refuse.

Smiling up at him, she ran her hands over his nearly hairless chest. "Don't take it the wrong way, but I jog to gather

247

my thoughts, and if you come with me, I won't be able to think about anything other than how wonderful last night was. In fact, I will probably think about it even if you don't come with me." She lowered her eyes demurely. "It was the best sex I've ever had." She chuckled. "By a wide margin."

Hooking a finger under her chin, he lifted her head so she had to look into his eyes. "It was the best for me as well." His lips lifted on one side only, giving him a roguish expression. "I've never let anyone tie me up and torment me with pleasure before. If I'd known how turned on it would make me, I might have tried it. Although I doubt it would have been that explosive with anyone but you. You are special, Sofia."

His words shouldn't have meant so much to her, but they did. She'd never been told that she was special, or that she was anyone's best.

"Thank you." She lifted her hand and cupped his cheek. "I've never done anything like that before, and I don't even know where the idea came from."

"That's easy to guess. You probably saw that movie everyone was talking about or read the books."

Sofia shook her head. "I know what movie and books you're talking about, but I didn't see or read any of them. Causing or receiving pain does not appeal to me." She shivered as memories of whipping flitted through her mind. "That's why I punished you with pleasure."

"I think it's called funishment, and you are welcome to funish me anytime you want." He pulled her on top of him. "Maybe instead of a morning run, you can have a morning ride." He moved his hips, rubbing his erection against her stomach.

"I can have both." She reached between their bodies and gripped his rigid length.

62

MARCEL

*T*his time, their lovemaking was sweet and unhurried, and when they both reached their climax, Marcel didn't have to work hard to force his fangs to retract without biting Sofia.

He'd pumped her with so much venom last night that it would take a long time before the urge to bite would become overwhelming again.

For a long moment, they lay entangled in each other, enjoying the feeling of connection, until Sofia sighed. "I hate to go, but I have to."

"Stay." He cupped her cheeks and kissed her. "I'll call in sick."

She laughed and pushed on his chest. "I need to go to the bathroom."

Reluctantly, he released her and turned on his back. He felt too good to ruin it by going back to the lab. Hell, he didn't feel like doing any work at all. Not today, and not tomorrow, and not for the next couple of months. He imagined spending long days walking on the beach with Sofia, taking her out to restaurants, going shopping, to movies, plays, even musicals.

He didn't like them, but it didn't matter. Everything would be pleasurable with Sofia by his side.

Somewhere in the back of his mind a voice of reason whispered that he was falling down the rabbit hole again, and that his tendency to fall fast and hard for a woman had nearly destroyed him before. But he'd been listening to that voice for so long that he was tired of hearing it.

A life full of feeling was too good to squander on fear.

Sofia opened the bathroom door and frowned at him. "Why are you still in bed? We need to go." She collected her clothes off the floor and started putting them on. "Unless you can let me out of here without blindfolding me again, you can't stay in bed."

She pulled her pendant out of the pocket of her jeans and draped it around her neck.

"I don't need to blindfold you." No guests were supposed to know about the bunker, but it wasn't a clan secret that he needed to protect. "You just have to promise not to tell anyone about Emmett's bunker." He got out of bed and reached for his pants. "The orgies I told you about were not public knowledge, and he would like to keep it that way. It would be embarrassing for him and hurt the resort if rumors of it leaked out."

Marcel didn't want to thrall Sofia again to make her forget where the bunker was, but he intended to do that before the retreat was over and she left.

When imagining her gone felt like a kick to the gut, he pushed those thoughts aside. There was time, and many things could happen between now and the end of the retreat.

Maybe he would find out that Sofia was a Dormant and they would live happily ever after.

Yeah, right.

Even a dreamer like him didn't believe that would happen. He wasn't that lucky, and the Fates had never been kind to him.

In fact, they'd been quite bitchy.

"I won't tell anyone." Sofia looked around, and when she didn't find what she was looking for, she opened the bedroom door and walked into the living room. He followed, tucking his turtleneck into his pants.

"Here it is." She lifted her backpack. "I had a moment of panic when I thought I'd lost it." She pulled out a comb and ran it through her magnificent hair. "Why did you blindfold me last night if it wasn't necessary?"

"I thought it was. But I realized that if I trusted you enough to let you tie me up, I can trust you to keep a secret." He pulled her into his arms and kissed her.

"You knew that you could get free, so I don't know how much trust was really involved." She untangled herself from his arms. "Let's get going. I need to change into exercise clothes, and there isn't much time left before breakfast."

He led her up the stairs, punched in the code to the door at the top, and walked her through the cottage to Emmett's small garden.

"How long is your usual run?" he asked as they entered the lodge.

"Half an hour to forty-five minutes."

He wrapped his arm around her tiny waist. "Can you make it to breakfast at seven-thirty?"

Sofia smiled. "I definitely can. Will you meet me for lunch and dinner as well?"

"I would love to, but I need to have at least one meal a day with my team. They are cranky enough as it is because I've been neglecting them."

She tilted her head. "Why can't we all eat at the same table? You can introduce me to your coworkers."

"We have our own dining room, and I'm supposed to be eating over there."

"I didn't know that there was another dining room in the lodge."

"It's not in the lodge." He could tell her about the government leasing part of Safe Haven. That wasn't a secret. Only what they were doing there was. "The government rents the area north of the resort, and they are running a secret project there. That's why guests are not allowed inside the enclave."

Sofia's back muscles tensed under his arm. "Do you work for the government?"

"I don't. My team and I work on our own project, but since we also require enhanced security, we share space with them."

When they reached her door, Sofia put her hand on his shoulder and kissed him on the lips. "I guess you can't talk about either of those projects, right?"

He nodded.

"Then I'm not going to ask." She smiled, kissed him again, and opened the door. "See you at breakfast," she whispered and ducked inside, closing the door quietly behind her.

For a long moment, he stood in front of that door, staring at it with a goofy smile on his face and feeling like a lovesick teenager.

Reminding himself that he still needed to go back to the bunker and launder the sheets and towels they had used, he shook his head and forced his feet to start walking.

He was well aware that he was setting himself up for heartache, but it was too late to stop now.

He was already falling in love with Sofia.

63

SOFIA

*S*ofia waved at the guard as she jogged past him. "Good morning."

It was the same guy she'd seen there when she jogged in the evenings. Did he work around the clock like Igor's guards?

He smiled at her. "You're early today."

"I missed my run yesterday."

"Busy night?" he called after her.

"Very." She cast him a smile over her shoulder.

Laughing, he waved her off.

It was good that he'd grown to expect her jogging along the coastline. Routine was the best antidote to suspicion.

When Sofia reached her usual spot, she took a few moments to even out her breathing before reaching under her shirt and pulling out the pendant.

Valstar would be furious, but he would calm down when she told him the good news that she'd seduced the man she'd said she would. She'd done it mostly for herself, but he didn't need to know that.

If not for the axe hanging over her loved ones' necks, she

would have taken her time and gotten to know Marcel better before tying him to a bed and having her way with him.

At the memory, a smile curved her lips and a blush crept up her cheeks. He'd brought her to orgasm so many times that she'd lost track, and he'd exhausted her so thoroughly that she'd fallen asleep before he'd even pulled out of her.

That had never happened to her before, and it was a little embarrassing, but Marcel had thought nothing of it. This morning, he'd made love to her so gently and sweetly that she felt like tearing up from how emotional it made her.

He was such an amazing man. What a shame that building a life with him couldn't even be a fantasy.

Sighing, she pulled out the tiny earpiece from the pendant, stuck it in her ear, and pressed on the picture.

"Are you okay?" her grandfather barked.

That hadn't been the question she'd expected from him. Did Valstar actually care about her?

"I'm fine. I didn't get a chance to contact you last night because I was busy working on my objective. I seduced the guy."

He let out a breath. "Good job, Sofia. Did you get more information out of him?"

"I did, but I don't know how relevant it is to Igor. Turns out that the American government is using a portion of Safe Haven for a secret project they are running. The guy I seduced also runs a secret project, but it's not connected to what the government is doing, or so he says. I find it odd that his lab is located within their secure area, but he doesn't work for them."

"That's interesting. Did he just volunteer the information, or did you get it out of him?"

"A combination of the two." Sofia leaned against the rock and looked at the shoreline to make sure no one was coming. "I try not to ask direct questions, so he doesn't get suspicious, but I steer the conversation in the right direction for him to tell me more about what he does here."

"That's good. Make him trust you."

Marcel had let her tie him up, so he must trust her. But then he'd somehow gotten free without her help, so he'd probably known all along that he wasn't really at her mercy.

"I'm doing my best."

"I'm going to tell Igor what you've just told me and get further instructions. Stay where you are."

"Yes, sir."

Several minutes passed before Valstar came back to her. "Igor wants to talk to your guy. What's his name?"

She would have preferred to keep it ambiguous, but at this point in the game, she doubted that Marcel would ghost her again.

"Marcel. Why does Igor want to talk to him and how?"

"Instead of you wasting days on getting small tidbits of information out of him, Igor can just compel him to talk and get it done. And as for how you're going to achieve that, I have a plan. You'll go to the office and say that you need to call home because your father wasn't feeling well when you left, and you worry about him. When you call the number I'll give you, make sure that you are heard. I'll pretend to be your father and ask you if you've met any nice young men. You will tell me about Marcel, and I will demand to speak to him to make sure that he's not taking advantage of my daughter. After I disconnect, you'll make a fuss about your unreasonable father and ask if you can keep the phone so your boyfriend could call him."

A shiver ran down Sofia's spine.

Marcel would know that he'd been compelled, and he would have her kicked out of the retreat, or worse, arrested. If what he was working on was for the government, or even if not, her part in getting him to reveal the project's secrets would be considered espionage.

"Marcel is not attending the retreat, and he has his own phone, but I don't think that's a good idea."

"Why not?"

She'd better do a fantastic job of explaining, or contradicting Valstar and Igor would cost her dearly.

"Marcel is a computer engineer, so what he's working on has to do with computers, and it's not affiliated with Safe Haven and its management. Even if Igor is curious about Marcel's project, I doubt it's worth blowing my cover for. Marcel will know that he was compelled, and he will get me kicked out at best or arrested for espionage at worst. In either case, I will lose access to any further information."

"Igor can compel him to tell no one about the compulsion and to keep pretending that he's your boyfriend."

That could solve that problem, but it would cost her Marcel and still not help Igor achieve his objectives. Even though it would be his doing, he would blame her and punish her for a failure that wasn't her fault.

"That's an option, but I still won't be any closer to achieving the objectives of this mission, whatever they are."

"I'll talk it over with Igor and contact you in a few minutes. Stay where you are."

"Yes, sir."

DARLENE

*A*s Darlene entered the lab, she was greeted with cheers and claps from her coworkers as if she'd been the one who had transitioned.

"Thank you, but I didn't do anything to deserve your cheers." She headed toward William's office.

The door was open, and as usual, William and Kaia were sharing William's enormous desk, which was also less cluttered than usual thanks to Kaia, and also as usual, the two stopped talking the moment she crossed the threshold.

Darlene knew that they were working on a secret project, but that was ridiculous. Her so-called office was inside William's, and she had no choice but to go through his to get to hers.

"What are you doing here?" William asked. "You should be home with your mate."

She waved a dismissive hand. "Eric is doing great, and I have work to do. I can just imagine the mess waiting for me to sort out."

"I organized it in stacks," Kaia said. "I hope that helps."

"You're an angel." Darlene blew her a kiss. "By the way, I was thinking. Maybe Kaia can have my office and you can find me somewhere else to work? I hate coming in here and the two of you stopping your conversation mid-sentence."

William shook his head. "We are maxed out on space. Kian has left a lot of room for home expansion, but he didn't expect us to be doing so much work in the lab."

"Maybe we can use one of the homes," Kaia suggested. "Toven is already turning two houses into a studio and a test lab for the Perfect Match machines."

William let out a sigh. "He's working with the completed product, so he can do it in a residential environment. We are building things here, and we need a lot of space to do that. It's also messy and noisy and no one wants it near their homes."

"I can work from home," Kaia said. "Maybe we both can."

"I can't. I need to be here. You see how many times a day people come to me with questions and I go to help them. We will just have to manage." He gave Darlene an apologetic look. "I'm sorry, but you are stuck with your tiny office and with us as your roommates."

"That's no biggie. I like my tiny office." She opened the door, walked in, and hung her purse on the back of the chair.

"Do you need me to close the door?" she asked.

It was stuffy in there, and the air circulation wasn't good, but Kaia and William needed privacy for their super-secretive project, and she didn't want to force them to whisper.

"Leave it open," William said. "We will talk quietly."

"Thanks." She turned on the desk fan and sat down to work.

There were orders to file and track, inventory lists to update, and expenses to enter into the ledger.

Fun stuff, and Darlene didn't mean it sarcastically. She was good at organizing things, and a job well done provided her with the calm and satisfaction that she desperately needed.

Her life was better than ever, but it was also more complicated and full of turmoil than it had ever been before.

Eric's transition and subsequent coma had taken a toll on her, making her feel older and more exhausted than she'd felt when she'd first moved into the village. Then there was the scandalous threesome idea that Eric was pushing her into, and that was stressing her out even in its modified and less scandalous version.

Ever since Eric had told her about Max's idea, she'd been thinking about the logistics of it a lot.

During Eric's coma, she and Max had gotten closer as friends, which made the threesome idea even more complicated. She didn't want Max to see her naked, let alone climaxing while Eric was inside of her.

Maybe she could buy one of those burka things in size extra-large and wear it like a tent to hide her body while she rode Eric. She could position them in such a way that Max would only see her back when he came in to deliver the bite.

Could he bite her through the fabric, though? Or would she have to expose her neck and shoulder?

Ugh. Why couldn't Bridget milk Max's fangs like a snake's and put his venom in a syringe.

That would have made things so much easier.

SOFIA

*S*ofia's heart was racing. Contradicting Valstar and Igor had been such a gutsy move that it bordered on suicidal, and she was still reeling from it.

Her primary instinct had been to protect Marcel and their relationship, but the more she thought about it, the more she realized that she'd been right. It all depended on what Igor was after, and since the whole thing had started because of Jade's interest in Safe Haven and its paranormal retreats, it couldn't be about Marcel's project.

She didn't know much about computers, but she knew enough that they were not the answer to Igor's compulsion. Machines were not susceptible to it, but they probably couldn't protect biological beings from it.

Even animals fell under the power of compulsion.

But what if Marcel's project was about some innovative brain implant that could shield people from mind manipulation?

Hopefully, that wouldn't occur to Igor, and in the meantime, she had to come up with an alternative to Marcel. Emmett Haderech would be the best source of information about everything that had to do with Safe Haven, but how could she pull it off with him? He wasn't her boyfriend, and he was taken, so Igor couldn't tell her to seduce him. It wasn't because he was concerned with morality, but because she wasn't likely to succeed.

What excuse could she give Emmett Haderech to convince him to call her so-called father?

Maybe something about the rumors of Safe Haven being a cult and Emmett Haderech swindling money out of people?

"I'm back," Valstar said in her earpiece. "Igor agrees with your assessment of the situation. But since your boyfriend is useless as a source of information, he wants you to shift your focus to someone in Safe Haven's management."

That was what she'd expected.

"While waiting, I was thinking, and I came to a similar conclusion. Who knows better about what's going on in Safe Haven than its founder? I can ask for an audience with Emmett Haderech, and when I'm alone with him, I can beg him to call my father."

"Why would he oblige you if you are not fucking him?"

Sofia flinched at the crude language. "Emmett Haderech likes attention and flattery, and he likes to talk about how great he is. I can butter him up, telling him how much I admire him and the wonderful community he built, and that he's nothing like what my father warned me about. I can say that my father read the rumors about Safe Haven being a cult and Emmett Haderech swindling money out of people, and he thinks that Emmett is a crook. My father tried to convince me not to attend the retreat and we had a huge fight over it. If the benevolent and charismatic leader could do me a big favor and talk to my father, he would vindicate me. I would love to prove my father wrong."

Valstar chuckled. "That's not bad, and since Emmett Haderech is most likely not harboring government secrets, you won't be accused of espionage. Depending on what Igor gets out of him, he might not even realize that he was under compulsion to talk. Good thinking on your feet, Sofia."

The relief that washed over her had her knees buckle, and she slid down the rock to sit on sand. She still needed an argument to keep Marcel. "Marcel knows Emmett Haderech. He can help me get an audience with Emmett sooner rather than later."

"Good. You don't have much time left, and if Emmett doesn't have the information Igor is seeking, you will need to keep digging."

Sofia closed her eyes. "It would be really helpful if I knew what he was looking for."

"I agree, but that's how Igor wants to play it, and what Igor wants, Igor gets. Do you catch my drift?"

She grimaced. "Loud and clear."

"Good day, Sofia. May the Mother keep you safe."

"Thanks."

Was it her imagination, or was her grandfather being nicer than usual to her? He sounded proud of her, and that just didn't happen between pureblooded Kra-ell and their half-human children or completely human grandchildren.

The purebloods only valued their pureblooded offspring, and they sneered at hybrids and humans. Heck, they barely acknowledged being their progenitors.

MARCEL

*M*arcel had gone back to the bunker with the intention of removing the sheets and towels he and Sofia had used, but then he thought that maybe they would spend another night there, so why bother. Maybe he should wait to see whether Sofia wanted a repeat of last night and this morning?

Nah. He should launder the bedding regardless so they would be fresh for tonight, and if Sofia changed her mind about him for some reason and refused to see him, he would at least leave the place as he'd found it.

The community cleaning crews who worked at the resort probably didn't bother with the bunker while no one was supposed to be staying there.

After loading the washing machine, Marcel checked the time. He should go back to his bungalow and change, but it wasn't urgent. One of the advantages of wearing a nearly identical outfit day in and day out was that no one would notice that he hadn't changed clothes this morning.

He could stay in the bunker until the washing cycle was done and load the bedding and towels into the dryer before heading to the dining hall.

In the kitchen he loaded the coffeemaker, and as he waited for the coffee to brew, he opened the refrigerator to check whether there was anything inside. Unsurprisingly, it was empty, and so was the freezer.

Still, the kitchen was fully equipped to handle meal preparation, and it occurred to him that he could prepare dinner in the bunker and treat Sofia to a proper romantic evening.

Fates knew that his courtship had been deplorable. She deserved so much more. One problem was getting groceries, and the other was his limited culinary abilities.

Perhaps he could pay the chef to prepare the meal? It would need to be reheated, but it would most likely taste better than anything he could make.

A quick search through the cabinets produced a white tablecloth, two candleholders, and several candles. The living room was well stocked with plenty of good wines to choose from.

He had everything needed for a wonderfully romantic evening.

He could meet Sofia at the dining hall, ask her to put on the blindfold, carry her to the bunker again, and surprise her with a beautifully set table for two.

After the washing cycle was done and the bedding transferred to the dryer, Marcel headed out.

When he got to the dining hall, he scanned the room for Sofia, and saw that she hadn't returned from her morning jog yet. However, he found her friend.

Roxana waved him over. "Sofia will be here in a few minutes. Come sit with us."

He smiled at her and the other two ladies, then leaned to whisper. "If you don't mind, I'd rather have Sofia all to myself this morning."

Roxana pouted. "I do mind. You stole my friend from me, but who am I to stand in the way of love?"

"Thank you, and I promise not to steal her at lunch. She'll be all yours."

"Yeah, yeah." Roxana waved him away. "Off you go, you scoundrel."

When he found a vacant table, Marcel repeated the trick of leaning the chairs against the table to make it seem as if he was saving them for his companions, sat down, and waited for Sofia to appear.

He saw her enter the dining hall and scan the breakfast crowd, her face brightening when she found him.

She was still wearing her exercise clothes, and she looked good enough to eat in the tight leggings and cropped top. She was very slim, but she wasn't bony, and her body was toned. Her long hair was gathered into a ponytail instead of her customary bun, the dark tresses glossy and thick.

The girl was the picture of health and vitality, and despite her delicate build, there was nothing fragile about her. And yet Marcel felt an overwhelming need to protect her.

From what or who? He had no idea.

It was instinctive—an immortal male's need to protect his mate.

But since immortals could only bond with other immortals or Dormants, did it mean that Sofia was a Dormant?

Hope surging in his chest, he pushed to his feet and waited for her to reach him. "Good morning, beautiful." He pulled her into his arms and kissed her cheek.

"I'm sweaty." She pushed on his chest. "I didn't have time to shower and change."

"You look and smell amazing." He inhaled. "Morning sunshine and pine. Two of my favorite scents."

67

SOFIA

*M*arcel's compliment was so sweet, so sincere, that if Sofia weren't so stressed, she would have turned into a pile of goo.

"Thank you. That's such a nice thing to say." She smiled at him. "I didn't want to keep you waiting."

He glanced at the buffet. "There is no line. Let's grab something to eat before it gets busy again."

"Let's. I'm famished."

"No wonder. You've been very active." Marcel wrapped his arm around her middle, his hand resting possessively over her thigh. "You need to replenish your energy stores."

"I certainly do." She leaned against him. "Especially since I plan on being very active later tonight again."

She liked that he was flaunting their relationship. After he'd stood her up, she'd thought that he didn't want to be seen with her, but apparently his explanation had been sincere, and he wasn't very adept at courtship, which she liked as well. It meant that he wasn't a player.

Not that it mattered. Their relationship couldn't last, but she was going to enjoy it to the fullest as long as it did.

As they took their loaded plates and coffee mugs back to

the table, she cast him a sidelong glance. "It just dawned on me that you didn't sleep at all last night. How are you so peppy?"

"Peppy?" He chuckled. "I haven't heard that expression in years."

"Oh." Her face fell. "That's why it is important to live in a country to learn its language properly. My English professors at the university must have not updated the textbooks they were using."

"Your English is perfect." He put his plate down and pulled out a chair for her. "It's easy to forget that you are not a native speaker."

"Thank you." She sat down. "I try my best. Being here and speaking only English helps. I pay attention to how people talk and the idioms they use."

"You said that you plan on touring the country after the retreat is over. Do you have any concrete plans? Do you have friends you can stay with?"

She shook her head. "Other than the people I've met here, I don't know anyone. Roxie is from Washington DC, and she invited me to stay with her for a few days. I heard that it's a very interesting city."

She held her breath, waiting for him to suggest that she stay with him after the retreat was over.

Regrettably, she couldn't just enjoy Marcel's company. She had a mission to accomplish, and the timer was ticking.

He took her hand. "I wish you could stay longer. How about staying for the next retreat? I heard Emmett offering a fifty percent discount, and I might be able to convince him to allow you to attend for free."

That wasn't the same as Marcel asking her to stay with him, but it was a move in the right direction. It also opened the way for what she needed to ask of him.

"Speaking of Emmett Haderech, on the way here, I stopped by the office, and I've put in a request for a private audience with him." She scooped up scrambled eggs with her fork.

Marcel grinned. "You were going to ask him for a discount on the next retreat?"

"Frankly, it didn't occur to me to ask." She cast him a shy smile. "I didn't know that you wanted me to stay."

"Isn't it obvious?"

She shook her head.

"Then why did you ask for an audience with him?"

She shrugged. "While I was jogging, I remembered Roxie telling me about Lydia requesting an audience with Emmett, and I thought to myself, why not? He's a fascinating character, and I didn't think that I was going to attend another retreat. I'm still not sure that I will. But if I want to meet him face to face and get some words of wisdom from him, I'd better do it now."

Marcel regarded her with suspicion in his eyes. "Why was it urgent to put in the request this morning when you were pressed for time?"

She shrugged, pretending indifference. "He might take his time to answer, and I thought there might be a long list of requests ahead of mine. I wanted to make sure that I get to see him before the retreat ends." She took a sip from her coffee and put the mug down. "If you were serious about asking Emmett to give me an additional discount on the next retreat, maybe you could also ask him to meet me sooner rather than later?"

68

MARCEL

*M*arcel's suspicion kicked in.

Sofia's sudden interest in Emmett coincided too closely with their night of passion. Had she used him to get closer to Emmett?

Groupies did all kinds of crazy things to get to their idols, including hooking up with those surrounding the star.

She didn't look like the type, but he had a proven record of being a bad judge of character when it came to women.

It was still too easy to get him to fall head over heels and make him believe that the object of his desire was the epitome of goodness and perfection.

"You haven't expressed a desire to meet Emmett before. What has changed your mind?"

"I wasn't aware that he was granting private audiences until Roxie told me about it. He's a fascinating character, who has been the spiritual leader of a free-love community for over two decades. It would be an honor to meet him face to face."

She talked too fast, sounding nervous, even breathless. Where was the confident woman who had rocked his world last night? Had it been an act?

He narrowed his eyes at her. "Are you attracted to him? Is that what this is all about? He's taken, you know. He and Eleanor are together."

Unexpectedly, Sofia laughed. "Are you jealous? That's so cute."

"I am not." He crossed his arms over his chest. "It's just that none of this computes. You haven't breathed a word about him until this morning, and suddenly, right after we spent the night together, he's all you can talk about. I find it odd."

"Okay." She let out a breath. "I'll fess up. The truth is that I'm doing it because of my father. He read about Emmett Haderech and his cult of free love, and the rumors of him swindling his followers out of their money. My father didn't want me to attend the retreat, and we had a huge fight over it. He said that I was being naive and that I was spending my hard-earned money on a scam. Now that I'm here and I see how thriving the community is, and I'm learning so much about paranormal abilities, I know that Emmett Haderech is not a crook. He might have a penchant for theatrics, and he looks ridiculous with those wigs and robes he wears, but when he speaks, all of that is forgotten. His message is valuable, and he is very charismatic. I think that if Emmett spoke to my father, he could convince him that he was wrong." She sighed. "I don't want this argument to hang over my father and me. I want it settled so when I return home, he will treat me with respect and not look down his nose at me."

She sounded sincere, but he doubted a call from Emmett could convince her father one way or another. The truth was that Emmett was a crook, and the only reason he was no longer swindling his community was that Kian had taken over and was forcing him to pay them decent wages and share the retreat's profits with them.

"I can get Emmett to see you, but I don't know whether

he'll be willing to talk to your father. Does your dad even speak English?"

Her whole body language perked up. "He does, and that would be awesome. I can't thank you enough." She leaned to kiss him on the lips. "But I'll think of ways to express my gratitude later tonight."

Marcel leaned away. "I think you're deluding yourself that a talk with Emmett will change your father's mind about him. The guy can sell ice to Eskimos, and he might charm your father during their talk, but if your dad is a smart guy, and he has to be to have such a smart daughter, he won't be fooled by Emmett's gift of gab."

"Maybe he will, and maybe he won't, but it's worth a try. My father thinks that I'm naive and easy to manipulate, so he won't take anything I say seriously."

"Do you want me to talk to him?"

Her eyes widened in alarm. "No. He's also very strict and thinks that I'm still a virgin. I never brought any of my boyfriends home because of that."

"How many boyfriends have you had?"

She smiled and lifted her hand to look at her watch. "Oh, look at the time. My first class of the day is about to begin."

"Nice try. How many?"

"Including you?"

"Yes."

"Three." She leaned and kissed his cheek. "See you at dinner."

69

ERIC

"Good morning." Gilbert walked in with two cups of coffee and a food container. "Karen made lunch for you and Darlene, and she's inviting you two to dinner."

"That's nice of her." Eric put the book he was reading on the coffee table. "I should learn how to cook. I'm out of a job for now, and Darlene went back to work, and Karen has enough on her plate without cooking for us as well."

Gilbert put the glass container on the kitchen counter and walked over to the couch with a paper cup in each hand. "She's just cooking larger quantities. It's not like she's cooking separately for you and Darlene." He handed Eric one of the cups and sat next to him. "How are you feeling?"

"Not bad given that I'm toothless." Eric smiled and pointed to his mouth where both his canines were missing. "The pain meds are a lifesaver, but they also make me drowsy, so there is that." He removed the lid and took a sip. "I'm not complaining, though. I was so happy to wake up two days ago with both canines wiggling. The sooner my fangs show up, the sooner I can pleasure my mate properly."

Gilbert arched a brow. "I thought that the pain meds were making you drowsy."

"Not that drowsy." Eric chuckled. "I thought that I was a horny bastard before, but that was nothing compared to now, and Max says that my immortal hormones didn't kick in full force yet. Once they do, I'll turn into a rabbit." He leaned back, taking the cup with him. "Thankfully, Darlene is not complaining even though she's not immortal yet and doesn't have the stamina to match." He took another sip. "So, Gilbert, when are you taking the plunge?"

"Soon, but not yet. Now that you are okay, I can finally leave and take care of business. We left our house in the Bay Area as if we were just going for the weekend. I need to pack everyone's things and ship them to the clan's warehouse downtown, I need to put the house up for rent, and I need to visit my job sites and make sure that everything is running as it should. Once I'm back, I'll take Toven up on his offer."

"How long will all that take?"

Gilbert winced. "Too long. I don't want to be away from Karen and the kids for longer than I have to. I will have to hire someone to prep the house so it's presentable for rental."

"A week then?"

"Maybe two. Trust me, I won't stay a minute longer than I have to. I want to get going on the immortality thing before I lose my nerve again." He smiled. "Thanks for taking the plunge first and proving to me that it can be done."

"I was in a coma for two weeks, but Bridget said that I was never in danger and that I remained stable the entire time." Eric leaned back with the cup in his hand. "I want Darlene to start her transition as soon as possible too. She's about your age, and she shouldn't wait any longer."

Gilbert's brows dipped low. "Are you suggesting that she sleep with another male?"

"No. I don't think I can handle that. But I can handle another male biting her." He grimaced. "I hope. I asked Max if he was willing to help us out, and he said that he wasn't going to do it unless I was chained to the bed. He says that even though I want it done, I will attack him if I'm not restrained."

Gilbert put his cup down and leaned forward. "I can't even think of another man in the room with me and Karen when we are making love. I don't want another man's eyes on her. How the hell am I going to manage that?"

Eric chuckled. "You are already talking like an immortal, all possessive alpha-hole."

"Alpha-hole?"

"Yeah, the macho guy who needs to be in charge and beats his chest like a gorilla to scare other males away."

Gilbert pursed his lips. "Yep, I guess that's me. Don't forget that Karen and I have been together for many years, and we have children together. She's everything to me, and it's going to kill me to let another male bite her. I know for sure that I would need to be restrained to allow that to happen. But even if I could force myself to do that, I don't think Karen would agree."

"I was afraid of that, and I've spent the last two days thinking about a solution, and I think I've found it. What if the male's arousal is not directed at Karen but at you? Would you be able to tolerate a gay guy biting her while the two of you were getting it on?"

The face Gilbert made was comical. "Why would he agree to do that? And where am I going to find a gay immortal male?"

"I'm sure the clan has a similar percentage of gays as humans do, and since Dormants are so important to the clan, it shouldn't be too difficult to find a volunteer or two."

"I don't know about that." Gilbert rubbed the back of his neck. "It would sure make it easier for Karen and me, but I doubt any gay man would find my hairy ass and the tire I

274

carry around the middle attractive." He slapped his rounded belly.

Eric laughed. "Don't sell yourself short. You are still an attractive dude. I see how women look at you."

"Women are much more forgiving than men, especially when the object of their attention has money or at least a decent job. Men are visual creatures, and I'm not a young stud anymore."

"If you are attractive to women, you are attractive to gay men as well. I don't think there is a difference. Not all gay men look like they stepped off the cover of *GQ*. Most are just ordinary dudes with hairy asses and pudgy middles and all that crap that you are worried about."

"Yeah, maybe for humans it's true, but did you look at these immortals? They all look like they could be on the cover of a men's fashion magazine."

Eric regarded his brother with a frown. "Since when did you develop confidence issues? You've always been the most confident guy I've known."

"Since I got here and saw all these perfect people."

"They are not all perfect. Did you know that William used to be fat?"

Gilbert waved a dismissive hand. "The guy is a little padded, but he's tall, so it's not a big deal. He looks good."

"He does now. Darlene told me that he used to be really fat, and that he lost a lot of weight by changing his eating habits and engaging in physical activity. That means that these immortals have to work at looking good, and they are not perfect by design."

Gilbert let out a breath. "First, let's see if it works for you and Darlene. Perhaps both venom and semen have to come from the same male to work, and I would hate to go to all that trouble for nothing."

MARCEL

"Nice of you to grace us with your presence." Kylie gave Marcel a withering look. "I thought that you forgot about us."

"I'm sorry, I'm late." He lifted his eye to the scanner and waited for the door to open.

Breakfast with Sofia had taken a little longer than it should have, and his team had been waiting for him outside the lab when he'd gotten there. But the reason Kylie was making a stink out of it was that she was angry at him for not eating dinner with them last night or breakfast this morning.

Safe Haven was like the village, and rumors spread fast. She must have heard about his involvement with Sofia, or maybe had just guessed the reason for his absence from meals as of late.

Good. Maybe now she would leave him alone.

After going over their assignments for the day, Marcel left the three bioinformaticians in the main lab, walked into his office, and closed the door.

Sitting at his desk, he pulled out his phone and called Emmett.

"Marcel, my friend. How can I help you?" Emmett sounded more cheerful than usual.

The guy thrived on attention and adoration from the retreat attendees.

"Did you give a presentation today?" Marcel asked.

"How did you know?"

"You sound energized. Extroverts like you absorb energy from others. Introverts like me expend energy when they interact with people."

"True. I love interacting with my fans, and the paranormals are even more fun than the spiritualists. They are so open and accepting that it's a joy to teach them."

"I'm glad you're enjoying yourself. I have two favors to ask of you, and both are for the same person."

"Let me guess. It's for the Finnish linguist you took to my bunker."

Talk about rumors spreading fast. Had Leon told him?

"I hope you don't mind."

"Not at all. I'm glad someone is making use of my former pad. So, what can I do for Miss Sofia Heikkinen?"

"I would like her to stay for the next retreat. I heard you offer everyone a half off, but is there a way you can let her participate for free?"

"For you, of course. I owe you for deciphering the coordinates in Jade's fable."

"You don't owe me a thing, but thanks. The other favor I want to ask is if you can grant her a private audience. She put in a request, but she asked me if I can expedite things for her. She's quite taken with you."

He debated whether to tell Emmett about what Sofia wanted him to do, but decided not to. His task was to get her the audience. She could take it from there.

"I've seen the request." Emmett sighed. "I used to love granting those audiences, especially to beautiful ladies, but

Eleanor is the jealous type, and she gets upset when I do them, so I try to limit the number of audiences I grant, and when it is with a lady, I make sure to have Eleanor there. But that's neither here nor there. I can see Sofia after lunch today."

That was a surprise. "Thank you. She will be over the moon."

"Naturally. Tell me a little bit about her, and by that, I mean things that were not included in the file Roni prepared on each of the attendees."

"She's who she claims to be. When I started seeing her, I sensed that she was hiding things about her past, and since I needed to check whether she can be thralled, I peeked into her mind and encountered a wall. I later thralled her to forget a detail I told her, so I knew she could be thralled, but that wall she'd erected about her past bothered me, so I asked Roni to double-check her information. Everything checked out. She's a student and a teacher at the University of Helsinki, and she'd been doing that for the past seven years. Her medical record is legit as well."

"Have you gotten her to tell you more about herself?"

"She doesn't get along with her mother, and she argues with her father, who is very strict. That's all I got so far."

"You should have brought her to me sooner. I would have gotten her to tell you any information you wanted." Emmett chuckled. "It's advantageous to have a strong compeller as a friend."

"I could have also pushed harder and gotten deeper into her mind with a thrall, but that's against the rules, and the same rules apply to compulsion. Unless clan security or lives are at risk, thralling and compelling is not allowed."

Emmett huffed. "Those rules are more like guidelines, and as such they are meant to be bent."

"Not for a former Guardian."

"You're a civilian now, but it's your choice of course. If you don't want me to compel Sofia, I won't."

"I would appreciate that."

"Do you want to be there to make sure that I behave?"

"I'm sure that you would, but I'll try to be there."

SOFIA

*T*he note with the invitation to meet Emmett Haderech arrived during the last class before lunch, which meant that Sofia couldn't eat a bite.

Roxie was sure that it was excitement over meeting the spiritual leader, but it was fear over what she was about to do.

Would he agree to call her fake father?

Would he realize that Igor was compelling him? And if he did, what would he do to her?

Would he kick her out of the retreat?

She might not even get a chance to say goodbye to Marcel.

"Eat something." Roxie pointed to her plate. "You'll be hungry later, and the kitchen will be closed. Ask me how I know."

"How?"

"Yesterday, I wanted a snack, so I went looking for something to buy. There was nothing. You know how they usually have a bowl of cookies next to the coffee and tea buffet that's served all day long? They were all gone. Not even a crumb was left."

Sofia tuned Roxie out.

She was still wearing the exercise clothes from before, and even though Marcel had said that she looked and smelled great, she didn't want to meet Emmett Haderech like that. Should she run to her room and get showered and changed?

She could do that in ten minutes if she hurried. But maybe it was better to show up with her midriff exposed? Perhaps it would distract Emmett from noticing that her father was asking him too many questions and that he was disclosing too much information that he shouldn't.

Marcel had told her that Emmett and Dr. Eleanor were a couple, but that didn't mean that Emmett didn't have eyes. He could still notice a woman and feel attraction to her.

It didn't mean that he wasn't loyal to his partner or that he intended to cheat on her, only that he was human.

Except, Sofia wasn't a great beauty, and most men found her too slim to be attractive. Then again, Dr. Takala was tall and very slim as well, so maybe she was Emmett's type.

"Sofia." Roxie waved a hand in front of her face. "You are such a space cadet. Lydia asked you if you are going to wear something nice to your audience with Emmett Haderech."

"I don't have time. I'll go like this."

Lydia pursed her lips. "That would be disrespectful."

Felicity gave her friend a disapproving look. "Don't be such a prude. Sofia is gorgeous, and she has a great body. Do you really think Emmett will notice what she's wearing?" She snorted. "He'll notice what she's not wearing. Just look at that six-pack."

Lydia shrugged. "Yeah. You are right."

"I'd better head out." Sofia pushed to her feet and slung her backpack over one shoulder. "I don't want to keep him waiting."

"Hold on." Roxie lifted her satchel off the floor and pulled out a tube of lipstick. "You need some color on your face."

"Thanks, but I'm too nervous to bother with it."

"I'll do it for you." Roxie gripped her chin and dabbed the lipstick on her lips. "Smack them like that." She demonstrated. "That's better." She patted Sofia's arm. "Remember. He's just a man, and you are a paying customer. There is no need to be so nervous."

"You're right." Sofia took a deep breath and leaned to kiss Roxie on the cheek. "Thanks for being such a good friend. You're a wonderful person, and I will never forget you."

Roxie frowned. "Why does it sound as if you are saying goodbye?"

Sofia fought the tears that were welling in her eyes. "I'm not saying goodbye." She was. If Emmett kicked her out, she might not have another chance. "I just wanted you to know that I don't take you for granted, and that I appreciate your friendship."

"Oh, sweetie." Roxie pulled her into a crushing hug. "I love you too, and I'm not letting you go. After the retreat is over, you are coming to stay with me for at least a couple of months. I'll be your personal tour guide in Washington, and if you want to stay, I'll help you find a job. The coffee shop I work for is always looking for new servers, and since it's a popular spot for the lobbyists, the tips are great."

Choking on tears, Sofia nodded, patted Roxie's arm, and rushed off.

She managed to hold out for long enough to get to the ladies' room outside the dining hall and lock herself inside a stall. She had a few minutes to spare, and she was going to use them to let it all out before heading to her ruin.

EMMETT

"*C*ome in." Eleanor opened the door for Sofia.

The young woman looked like she was going to keel over, but that was a common reaction of Emmett's fans when granted a face-to-face interview.

They worshiped him.

Pushing to his feet, he walked over to the girl and gave her a reassuring smile. "You are safe in here, Sofia. No harm will come to you between these walls."

She nodded. "I know. I'm just so excited. I didn't expect my request to be approved so quickly, so I didn't prepare." She waved a hand over her outfit. "I would have worn something more appropriate."

"You look fine." Eleanor clapped her on the back. "Take a seat, make yourself comfortable, and ask your questions. We all have things to do."

Emmett winced. Eleanor's bedside manner, so to speak, needed work. "We are not in a rush, Sofia. Take your time to collect your thoughts."

"Thank you." She sat down and then glanced at Eleanor who was leaning against his desk with her arms folded over her chest and looking intimidating. "I thought that the audience would be just with Mr. Emmett Haderech."

"Eleanor is here for your benefit." Emmett spread his arms. "You are a young, beautiful lady, and these days it is not acceptable for a gentleman to conduct a meeting with a lady without another female present."

In fact, it was to prevent Eleanor from getting unnecessarily jealous, and if he weren't a compeller, it would have also served to protect him from sexual harassment accusations.

Sofia gave Eleanor a tight smile. "I feel safe here." She shifted her eyes to the camera mounted in the corner. "The security in Safe Haven is top-notch. If you don't mind, I would feel more comfortable discussing personal matters with Mr. Emmett Haderech in private."

Emmett gave Eleanor a slight nod.

"Fine." She uncrossed her arms and pushed away from his desk. "I'll be in my office if you need me."

Eleanor's primary office was in the paranormal enclave, but she also used the one next to his from time to time.

"Thank you." Sofia put her backpack on the floor. "I promise not to take too much of Mr. Haderech's time."

When Eleanor left and closed the door behind her, he leaned forward. "Please, call me Emmett, Sofia."

"Thank you, but I don't think I can. I admire you too much to call you by your given name."

"I insist."

"Okay." She lowered her eyes.

"What can I help you with, Sofia?"

"I don't get along with my parents, and I hoped you could give me some guidance."

That was a common request from the younger guests. "What are the points of contention between you and your parents?"

"My mother does not approve of me. Nothing I do is good enough for her. She's disappointed in me."

Emmett frowned. "I've read your file, and you are a very impressive young lady. You are a gifted linguist, and you teach at the university. Your mother should be proud of you."

"She should be, but she isn't. Her expectations are unrealistic, and I gave up on pleasing her a long time ago. My relationship with my father is a little better, and he is proud of my accomplishments, but we argue a lot. He expects me to remain a virgin until I get married, which isn't realistic either. I just don't tell him about my boyfriends."

That was very uncommon in most Western societies, and he wasn't aware of the Finns being particularly traditional.

"Is it a religious thing for your father?"

She nodded. "It is, but that's not the only problem I have with him. He doesn't believe in paranormal phenomena, and he didn't approve of me coming here. He thinks that Safe Haven is a cult and that you are a con man who swindles people out of their money."

Emmett nodded sagely. "Those who donated funds to the cause did that out of their own free will, and they gave it to the community. Not to me personally. I've helped countless people over the years, and it pains me to hear those accusations, but it is what it is. The haters will keep on hating, while the lovers will spread the love."

She smiled. "I like the way you think. I wish my father shared your attitude."

"Your father sounds like a difficult man, but he obviously cares about you. You are no longer a child, and you can lead your life the way you want with or without his approval. He doesn't have to know what you don't tell him. On your end, you can choose to focus on the negatives or the positives. If you focus on his love for you instead of the worldview that he wants to impose on you, you might feel better about your relationship with him."

285

"You are so smart." She sighed. "Can you talk to him? I think that when he hears you, he will realize how wrong he was about you. I would hate to return home and pick up where we ended before I left for the retreat, which was in a huge fight."

Emmett had never been asked to do something like that before, and his first instinct was to refuse, but Sofia looked so desperate and so lost. He could do the girl a favor and compel her father to believe that he was a saint.

"What's your father's name?"

"Jarmo Heikkinen."

"Does he speak English?"

"Yes." He pushed the phone over to her. "Call him, tell him that you're with me in my office, and put the call on speaker so we can talk to him together."

"Thank you." Her hands trembled when she picked up the receiver. "I'll pay for the call charges of course."

MARCEL

*M*arcel's phone buzzed in his pocket as he
headed down the hallway to Emmett's office.
He had it silenced out of respect for the no-phones policy of
the resort, but since he was in the office wing, it was no
longer a problem.

Seeing Eleanor's number on the screen, he answered, "I'm
here."

"Don't go into Emmett's office. Go into the one before it. I
left the door open."

He saw the open door and entered. "What's going on?"

She pointed at the computer screen. "She's early, and she
didn't want me in there. She knows the office is monitored,
though. So don't give me that disapproving look."

"I'm not. But why are you watching the feed?" And listening, he realized as he said it.

He could hear Emmett talking about Sofia's father.

"It's not what you're thinking. I trust Emmett, and I'm not
jealous, although he likes to think that I am. It's for his
protection. In today's environment, a man risks his reputa-
tion and his livelihood every time he's alone in a room with a
female employee or a client. I don't want some greedy bitch

accusing him of sexual harassment to blackmail him for money."

Marcel nodded even though he hadn't bought Eleanor's explanation. With her and Emmett's compulsion ability, that wasn't a problem she should be worried about.

The woman was possessive, and if she wanted to guard her mate, that was her business. He'd come along to keep an eye on Sofia even though he knew Emmett wouldn't do anything inappropriate.

It was instinctive.

Pulling out a chair, he sat next to the computer screen to watch and listen to the show.

"What's your father's name?" Emmett asked.

"Jarmo Heikkinen."

"Does he speak English?"

"Yes."

Emmett pushed his desk phone toward her. "Call him and tell him that I wish to speak with him."

"Thank you." She reached for the receiver. "I'll pay for the call charges of course."

Marcel frowned.

Why was she anxious? Was it about the phone call she was about to make or Emmett's proximity?

"Your girlfriend's story doesn't add up. And she's acting strange." Eleanor sat on the desk and crossed her arms over her chest.

"She told me about her father. He's very traditional and strict. He expects her to remain a virgin until she marries. Who does that these days?"

"Hi, Daddy," Sofia said into the receiver. "I'm speaking in English because I'm with Emmett Haderech in his office. I asked him to talk to you, and he graciously agreed. Is it okay if I put the call on speaker?"

She must have gotten an okay from her father because

she nodded, pressed the speaker button, and put down the receiver. "Go ahead," she said.

"Good evening, Mr. Heikkinen," Emmett said. "My name is Emmett. Can I call you Jarmo?"

"Yes," came the gruff reply. "You must forgive my English. It's not very good. I'm very sorry that my daughter is bothering you."

"It's not a bother, and your English is very good. I can see where Sofia gets her talent for languages. You must be so proud of her accomplishments."

"I am. I'm just not happy about her spending all the money she saved on nonsense."

The guy's accent didn't sound like Sofia's. It was harsher. Perhaps Jarmo wasn't a native of Finland?

Emmett chuckled. "I assure you that it's money well spent. Sofia is learning a lot about paranormal talents, her own and others. She's also meeting interesting people from all over, which is very important for networking and future success, especially for a linguist who one day might seek a translator's job. On top of that, when I heard that she traveled all the way from Finland to attend the retreat, I offered her a free pass to the next one, which starts right on the heels of this one. That's an incredible bargain that I've never offered to anyone else."

"Thank you. That's unexpected generosity from a man like you. Is it true that you robbed your community members of all their possessions?"

Despite it being true, it was an incredibly rude thing to ask right after Emmett had told the guy about Sofia's free pass to the next retreat.

Emmett seemed to think the same, and for a moment, he gaped at Sofia as if he didn't know how to answer that.

She blushed and mouthed, "I'm sorry."

"A simple yes or no answer will do," her father said.

"Yes." Emmett's answer surprised Marcel, and given the wild look in Emmett's eyes, it surprised him as well.

"Something is not right." Eleanor jumped off the desk and ran out of the room.

"What is your real name, Mr. Emmett Haderech?" Sofia's father asked when Eleanor burst into the room.

She disconnected the call before Emmett could answer. "Explain," she barked at Sofia.

"I'm sorry," Sofia said. "I didn't expect him to be so rude."

Marcel rushed in. "What's going on?"

"That wasn't Sofia's father." Eleanor glared at the girl before shifting her eyes to Emmett. "That was an incredibly powerful compeller. You would not have admitted to swindling the community members under any other circumstances."

Emmett looked more shaken than Marcel had ever seen him. "Unbelievable. If you hadn't ended the call, he would have made me reveal my real name."

They all looked at Sofia, who started crying silently. "I'm sorry," she murmured. "I'm so sorry."

What the hell had just happened?

What had Sofia done? And why?

Who was the man on the other end of the line, and why was he after Emmett? Was that a reporter? Was Sofia an undercover journalist?

As the phone rang, they all looked at it, but no one answered, and then Eleanor tore the wire out of the wall. "We need to run all incoming phone calls through the voice changer to prevent him from compelling anyone else."

"I'll call Leon." Marcel pulled his phone out of his pocket, walked out into the hallway, and ducked into Eleanor's office to make the call out of Sofia's earshot.

"We might have a problem," he told the chief of security. "It might be as simple as an undercover journalist working for a powerful compeller, or as serious as Jade's captor sending over a spy. He almost got Emmett to reveal his real name over the phone. Eleanor saved the day by disconnecting the call, but he might call back and compel someone else. You need to divert all incoming calls through the voice changer."

"I'm on it," Leon said. "Call me if you need anything else."

SOFIA

*I*t was over.

They'd figured it out.

But how? How did they know about compulsion? They talked about it as if they'd lived in Igor's compound.

No one had mentioned the ability to compel as one of the paranormal talents, so that wasn't how they knew about it.

Maybe they were Kra-ell hybrids after all?

Was that what Igor had sent her to discover?

It must be.

But why hadn't he told her to look for hybrids?

If she'd paid more attention, she might have noticed things about Emmett and Eleanor that would have given them away.

She'd noticed Marcel's glowing eyes, but she'd dismissed it because she'd never seen a blond Kra-ell, but what if there were blond hybrids in other compounds?

And why was she still sitting there frozen like a dummy instead of running?

Because there was nowhere to run. Safe Haven was in the middle of nowhere and she would be caught in moments.

Would Igor punish her family for her failure?

But hadn't she given him the answer to his question?

He must have figured out why the call had been disconnected. Humans would not have realized so quickly that compulsion was at work.

Tears flowing down her cheeks, Sofia closed her eyes and did the only thing she could. She prayed.

Dear Mother of All Life. I'm lost. But please save my family.

The Goddess must have answered because suddenly it occurred to her that there was one more thing she could do that might save her family from Igor's wrath.

Clutching the locket, she pressed the tiny lever to open it, and then pushed her finger inside to press on the picture. Without the earpiece, she wouldn't be able to hear Valstar, but he would hear what was going on in the room, and he would get his answers.

When she opened her eyes, Marcel crouched in front of her. "Care to explain why you set Emmett up?"

"I can't."

"She's under compulsion," Eleanor said. "Let me talk to her. I might be able to do something about it."

Marcel lifted a hand to stop her. "We need to search her first. She might be wearing a wire." He regarded her with hard eyes. "Did you come here to get an exclusive story on Emmett? Is that what you were doing? Digging for dirt to besmirch his name?"

Sofia shook her head.

"Where would she hide a wire?" Eleanor looked her over. "She can't hide a pin in that outfit. Maybe it's in the shoes?"

"The pendant." He reached for it. "I've been wondering why you always wore this ugly thing. I thought that it had a sentimental value."

Sofia's hand tightened around it. "It does."

"Give it to me," Marcel commanded. "I can take it from you, but I don't want to hurt you."

Why was he still being nice to her?

"Please," she pleaded. "Don't take it away from me. It means so much to me."

If nothing else, Igor would be impressed with her acting and would know that she'd done her best.

Marcel smiled sadly. "You give me no choice." He pried her fingers open as if she was an infant and yanked the chain over her head.

As it snagged on her hair, she cried out.

"I'm sorry. I didn't mean to hurt you."

The locket was still open, and as he let it dangle from her fingers, the little door swung out, revealing the picture inside.

"Is that your family?" Marcel asked.

She nodded.

"Smash it," Eleanor suggested.

"It's just a locket." He turned to the woman and mouthed something that Sofia couldn't hear. "But just in case it's more than it appears, can you put it in the safe together with everyone's phones?"

"Of course." Eleanor snatched it from his hand and walked out of the room.

Hope surged in Sofia's heart. Marcel either didn't suspect that the locket had a transmitter inside, or he did and was trying to protect her.

Maybe her betrayal hadn't sunk in yet, and when it did, he would stop caring about her.

The good news was that they thought she was a journalist looking for a story, which was much better than the truth.

Could she use it to her advantage?

If she told them that she was a journalist, they would demand to know the name of the publication she worked for, and if she named some random gossip magazine, they would call to complain or just to verify her story and it wouldn't hold water.

She could claim to be a freelancer, but even a freelancer

had to have some connections to newspapers that she could prove.

Marcel gazed into her eyes, his expression more pitying than angry, and then he turned to Emmett. "Can you get her to talk?"

"Not yet," Emmett murmured. "I need a few more moments to collect myself. I'm still reeling from the shock of being spied on. Let Eleanor do it."

A moment later the woman walked back in. "It's done." She kicked at Sofia's left shoe. "Take them off and then stand up on your bare feet. I'm going to pat you down."

Marcel straightened. "You said that she couldn't hide anything in this outfit."

"When in doubt, it's always good to follow protocol." Eleanor patted him on the back.

"I don't have anything on me," Sofia said as she toed off her sneakers and removed her socks as well.

"I'll pat her down," Marcel told Eleanor and turned to Sofia. "If that's okay with you. Would you prefer Eleanor do it?"

He was still trying to protect her despite knowing that she'd used him.

"You can search me," she whispered as a new torrent of tears began.

"Oh, for heaven's sake." Eleanor walked out of the room, returning with a box of tissues while Marcel was conducting a very thorough pat down. It included releasing Sofia's hair from its ponytail and searching through it.

"She's clean," he said when he was done. "As far as I can tell, that is. The safest thing would be to run her through a bug detector."

"Leon has one," Eleanor said as she handed Sofia a wad of tissues. "What kind of a sorry excuse for an undercover spy are you?"

"I'm not a spy."

Eleanor huffed. "A journalist, paparazzo, it's all the same. They all spy on unsuspecting people."

"I'll check with Leon." Marcel stopped and whispered something in Eleanor's ear before walking out of the room again.

Sofia blew her nose into the tissues and wiped her eyes and her cheeks. "I'm so sorry." The tears kept flowing, and soon there wasn't a dry spot on the wad of tissues.

"Yeah, yeah." Eleanor handed her the box, walked up to a mini fridge, and pulled out a bottle of water. "Catch." She tossed it to Sofia.

Fumbling with the bottle, she eventually managed to prevent it from falling out of her hands.

"Crappy reflexes," Eleanor murmured. "You are a really lousy spy."

MARCEL

hen Leon arrived with another Guardian, Sofia's eyes turned panicked. "Are they here to arrest me?"

"Not yet." Leon motioned for her to stand up and ran the handheld bug detector over every inch of her body, including between her legs.

If the guy weren't happily mated, Marcel would have growled a warning.

Even though Sofia had orchestrated Emmett's attempted compulsion, he still felt protective of her. She'd been a pawn, used by the powerful compeller to get closer to Emmett.

Had the guy known that Emmett was a compeller himself?

But that was a less important question than the why and who.

Marcel didn't really believe it was about an undercover story. He'd pretended not to find the transmitter in the locket for the sake of those who were listening on the other side, and he'd made a scene about accusing Sofia of being an undercover journalist for the same reason. He'd told Eleanor to continue the pretense, and after Eleanor had put the locket in the safe, they continued the charade in case Sofia was carrying more hidden bugs on her.

The scariest option was that the compeller was Jade's captor. If Sofia weren't human, that would have been the leading theory, but since she was, other possibilities needed to be explored.

Given that a compeller was involved, it might be connected to the paranormal retreat. Did someone consider it a threat?

They needed to check whether Safe Haven was taking business away from a competitor who happened to be a powerful compeller. The questions the guy had directed at Emmett had been about information to destroy him with. If news got out that Safe Haven's leader had admitted to swindling his followers, the place would never recover from the stink. Even if they got rid of Emmett, it would destroy the community's only source of income, and they would have to close the place up.

"She's clean," Leon said. "I suggest that we put her in the bunker until we figure out what's going on."

The irony wasn't lost on Marcel. Instead of using the bunker to entertain a lover with a romantic dinner, he would be using it to keep her prisoner. "We will do that after we question Sofia. We waited with that to make sure she wasn't carrying bugs."

If anyone was listening, the types of questions they needed to ask would have given them away, and he'd been very careful with what he'd said around Sofia so far.

Apparently, he hadn't forgotten his Guardian training yet. There was a reason he'd saved the transmitter for later use instead of destroying it. If the compeller believed that they were clueless, they could later use the locket to feed him false information.

"Understood." Leon pulled a set of handcuffs out of his back pocket. "I assume that you know how to use them."

Marcel shook his head. "Those won't be necessary."

Eleanor snatched them from Leon's hand. "Just in case. We can handle it from here." She smiled. "Sofia is just an ordinary girl with crappy reflexes. We can lock her in my office, and she won't be able to do anything about it."

Meaning, she was human.

Leon nodded. "Call me if you need anything."

"Will do," Eleanor said. When the door closed behind Leon, she leaned against Emmett's desk and looked at Sofia. "Let's start."

Marcel lifted a brow. "Perhaps I should do the questioning?"

Eleanor looked down her nose at him. "You don't have my special talents."

He wasn't a compeller, but in this case, thralling might work better. "I have other talents."

"Let me start," Eleanor said. "If I don't get anywhere with her, you can take over."

Folding his arms over his chest, he nodded.

"Is your real name Sofia?" Eleanor asked.

"Yes."

"Is your last name Heikkinen?"

"Yes."

"Was the guy on the other line your father?"

Sofia shook her head.

"That's what I thought. Why did you want Emmett to talk to him?"

"I didn't."

"Did he make you do it?"

"I can't say."

Eleanor smiled. "You're a smart girl. You should have figured out by now that there are sneaky ways around compulsion. I'll rephrase the question to demonstrate. Would you have ever stepped into the dog poo if the bad man didn't push you?"

The question confused Marcel, but Sofia seemed to get it.

Her eyes peeling wide open, she shook her head. "Who wants to step into dog poo? Not me. But if I tried to walk around it, someone I care about might have stepped on the poo, and I couldn't let that happen."

Eleanor smiled. "Excellent answer. It could mean that if she didn't do as she was told, someone else would have been sent to do the job, someone she cared about, or that if she refused, someone close to her would have paid the price."

Sofia lifted two fingers.

"The second one then." Eleanor let out a breath. "I'll try to release you from the compulsion, but if it doesn't work, we can continue telling each other stories." She leaned closer. "You will speak freely and tell us only the truth. Who sent you?"

Sofia shook her head. "I still can't tell you."

Eleanor braced her hands on Emmett's desk. "That's not really surprising given how strong of a compeller the guy is." She turned to Emmett. "You need to give it a try."

"It's not going to work. He was stronger than me, which means that I can't override his compulsion. You need to get Kalugal to try, but he might not be strong enough either."

The guy still looked as if he'd been hit by lightning. Leaning back in his chair, his feet propped on his desk, and an arm draped over his eyes, he was the picture of despondency.

Eleanor eyed him with a frown. "Snap out of it, Emmett. Nothing happened. So, you admitted to swindling the community out of money. Big deal. Unofficially, everyone already knows that. Even if he'd gotten you on tape, you could still save the situation. You've turned a new page and all that crap."

Had she really believed that Sofia had been working on an undercover story?

Marcel had told Eleanor to pretend, but now that they

were positive Sofia was carrying no more transmitters, it was safe to talk freely around her. Well, to a certain extent. If they were going to use her as a double agent, they had to be very careful about what they said around her.

"That's not why I'm depressed." Emmett removed the arm from his eyes and turned to look at them. "I'm terrified for you know who. What if that's the one holding her? We assumed that only a powerful compeller could keep her captive, and I just spoke with one. Coincidence? I think not. Also, a large portion of the area we've been investigating is in Finland. Do I need to say more?"

Emmett had instinctively chosen to talk in hints, but even that could have clued Sofia in on who he was and who he'd been talking about. But Marcel had been watching her closely, and she hadn't responded to Emmett's words in any way. She was still crying, the tears spilling out of her eyes in a never-ending trickle, and the ball of tissues she was holding was growing in size.

Eleanor was right. The girl was not a trained spy. She'd probably been chosen for the mission precisely because she had no special training or abilities and could fly under the radar so to speak.

76

KIAN

*A*s Kian listened to Leon and Marcel's report, he was more and more convinced that Sofia had been sent by Jade's captor.

They made the video call from Leon's office, which meant that neither of them really believed that it was a simple case of a journalist looking for dirt on Emmett, and especially not Marcel, who looked like he'd been hit by a train.

He hadn't said much about his relationship with Sofia, but it was clear to Kian that she meant something to him and that her betrayal was costing him. Given her paranormal talent, he'd probably hoped that she was a Dormant.

Except, the talent was probably fake, and she was just a human who'd been recruited by the compeller for this mission and coached on pretending to have a paranormal ability.

For Marcel's sake, Kian hoped that the girl was just a pawn in the game and not an extraordinarily good player who was fooling even Leon into thinking that she'd been forced into becoming a spy against her will.

"That's bad," he said when they were done. "The compeller

knows that Jade contacted someone, and he suspects Emmett."

"I don't think he suspects that," Marcel said. "I think he was shooting in the dark. He probably thought that since Emmett is Safe Haven's leader, he would know everything that was going on there, and he hoped that Emmett would provide him with something useful. He started his questioning with the swindling, which has been rumored for years, and then Emmett's name, which is obviously not his real name. If he was sure that Emmett knew who Jade was, or that he'd figured it out from her fable, he would have started with that."

Marcel's argument was logical, and Kian took it from there.

"The compeller might have seen Jade's email, but since he didn't know about Emmett, he didn't know why she was showing interest in Safe Haven. If he'd known that she'd contacted a former member of her tribe, he would have sent warriors over, or at least someone more capable than Sofia. She's obviously out of her element."

Leon nodded. "He knew that she wouldn't be detected because she's human and because she has a solid background that would pass even the most rigorous scrutiny, and he was right about that. Marcel had a gut feeling about her and asked Roni to investigate her more thoroughly. Roni didn't find anything that raised a red flag."

Kian pushed his chair back. "Did you manage to get anything out of her at all?"

Marcel shook his head. "Eleanor showed Sofia how to get around the compulsion by talking in metaphors and similes, but she was so distraught that she couldn't come up with anything coherent. I told Eleanor to take her to the bunker so she could rest."

"Keep her locked up until we can get her to talk. Does she know who and what you are?"

"We didn't tell her anything," Marcel said. "I was afraid that she might have a tap on her, so I pretended to think that she was an undercover journalist for the sake of whoever was listening on the other side. That turned out to be a good move because she had a transmitter hidden in a locket. I asked Eleanor to put it in the safe. Once we get Sofia to talk and figure out what we are up against, we can use that pendant to feed the compeller misinformation."

Marcel was a smart guy, and his years on the force had taught him well.

"Good thinking," Kian complimented him. "But it's only going to work provided that Sofia cooperates. From what you've told me, the guy is holding someone dear to her, maybe her real father or other members of her family, so she might refuse to cooperate even when she's no longer under his compulsion."

Leon moved his chair to get in the webcam's view. "We shouldn't waste time. Let's get Kalugal on the line with her, or even better, fly him out here. Emmett and Eleanor both say that compulsion works better face to face, and we need our best ammunition to override this guy."

Kian agreed, but getting Kalugal to leave his house would be mission impossible.

"Let's try the phone first, or even better, a video call. If that doesn't work, I can ask him to fly out to you, but he will very likely refuse. Since little Darius was born, Kalugal is in complete freak-out mode, and he refuses to interact with humans or anyone who has contact with them, which means that he doesn't leave his house, and neither do Jacki nor the baby. If this continues for much longer, I will have no choice but to send a team of Guardians with earplugs to rescue the poor woman from her prison."

Kian was joking of course, but Kalugal had definitely lost his mind, which given his family's history was a worrisome sign.

"Maybe the Clan Mother could override the compulsion using the same remote methods?" Leon suggested. "If Kalugal fails, that is."

"I'm not risking her, not even on the phone. I don't want to sound paranoid, but what if Sofia is a Trojan horse? Perhaps she was sent to find out who we have on our side and do some damage."

Both Leon and Marcel looked doubtful, and they were probably right, but Annani's safety came before any other considerations.

"What about Toven?" Marcel asked. "Would he agree to give it a try?"

"I don't want to risk him either. I'll run it by Turner and see if we can come up with a safe way for Toven to do that, provided that he agrees."

Toven had proven to be a good sport and readily available to help when asked. Kian had no doubt he would do that if they needed him to.

Perhaps he could wear the translating earplugs when he talked to Sofia. That would prevent her from sending any dangerous sound waves his way. The good thing about Toven was that he would most likely listen to reason and agree to wear the earplugs. The same couldn't be said about Annani.

"What do we do about security?" Leon asked. "We are operating on high alert, and Safe Haven has incredible defenses in place, but just out of an abundance of caution, perhaps you should send reinforcements."

"That's a good idea. I'll have Onegus assemble a team. Perhaps I'll also manage to persuade Kalugal to hop on the plane with them." He chuckled. "I'll get him a hazmat suit. On a more serious note, though, we should consider the possibility that if there was one spy there could be more, and they might not even be aware of each other. Emmett falling victim to compulsion was a warning. Imagine what could have happened if the compeller got ahold of you, Marcel. You are sitting on top of a hub of top-secret information and the servers at the lab are connected to the servers in the village."

"There are safeguards in place," Marcel said. "I can't freely access anything I want from here, and we have a protocol that mandates someone on the other side approving the request. That being said, I think I'm going to disconnect the servers completely for the time being. I think we should also send the bioinformaticians home. They have limited access to information, but even the little they know could be a problem if it falls into the wrong hands."

"You are right." Kian leaned forward. "Can you thrall them to forget what they have been working on so far?"

Marcel nodded. "Should I send them on a vacation or dismiss them entirely?"

"For now, send them on a vacation. We will decide what to do with them after we get Sofia to tell us what she knows."

"It might not be much," Leon said. "The compeller might have picked a random person to serve his needs."

"Perhaps," Kian said. "But I doubt it."

77

SOFIA

"Get some rest." Eleanor pointed to the bed. "I'll get your things from the lodge."

The woman acted tough, but she wasn't mean. She hadn't put the handcuffs on Sofia, and only warned her against trying anything.

They hadn't even had to pass by the lodge to get to the bunker. There was a side door in Emmett's office that led straight to the garden surrounding it, and the place was fenced off from the rest of the resort.

Sofia let out a breath. "What are you going to do with me? I don't know anything. I don't even know what I was supposed to do here."

Eleanor regarded her with a hard look in her dark eyes. "We need to find someone who can override the compulsion you are under so you can tell us who sent you. After that, it's up to the boss."

"Emmett?"

"No, not Emmett." Eleanor opened the door. "Rest while you can." She walked out and closed it behind her.

A moment later, Sofia heard the lock engage.

Plopping down on the bed, she covered her eyes with her arm and sighed.

It could have been worse. She was lucky that Eleanor had realized right away that she was under compulsion and couldn't tell them anything. Otherwise, they might have tortured her for information.

Not that it was likely. She didn't know what to make of these people. In some ways they acted like a military organization, and in others, they didn't. The security officer had a bug detector and handcuffs. Why would he have such equipment in a community of do-gooders who believed in free love?

Perhaps because of the mysterious project the government was running on the premises?

That would be the rational explanation, but she had a feeling that things were not as they seemed.

Who were these people? Could they be hybrid Kra-ell?

She'd wanted to ask Marcel or Eleanor so badly, but she couldn't do even that. The compulsion prevented her from mentioning the Kra-ell and anything related to them.

Hopefully, Igor or Valstar had heard what had been going on during the few minutes the transmitter had been on, and they'd gotten from it what they'd been looking for.

Marcel, Emmett, and Eleanor had been careful about the things they'd said in front of her, but she wasn't blind or stupid, and they were not who they pretended to be.

They were very familiar with compulsion and how it worked, both Emmett and Eleanor had the ability to compel, just not as strongly as Igor, but Marcel didn't have it.

That reinforced her suspicion that Emmett and Eleanor were hybrids while Marcel wasn't. He was something else, though.

When she'd thought back to all the little things she'd noticed and dismissed, the clues had coalesced into a clearer picture. He was incredibly strong without looking like a bodybuilder, and his night vision was excellent. His eyes glowed from the inside like a Kra-ell's, but he didn't have fangs and he ate a variety of foods that a hybrid wouldn't have touched. She'd seen him eating vegetables, fruit, bread, pasta, but no red meat.

He was either a very unique kind of hybrid, or something entirely different.

Could there be other species of long-lived people living alongside humans other than the Kra-ell?

She'd never heard that mentioned in the compound, but then not much information was shared with the humans. They were regarded as inferior and treated as servants. They were told things on a need-to-know basis, and they didn't need to know much to perform their duties.

None of her hypotheses could be proven yet, but she summed up her suspicions. Emmett and Eleanor were hybrids, Jade knew them somehow, had recognized one or both from their pictures in Safe Haven's online brochure, and had communicated with them for some reason. She wasn't happy being Igor's breeder, but she didn't have to be. She could breed with one or more of the other purebloods. Igor would probably make her life a living hell if she refused him, though, so maybe that wasn't an option.

The female purebloods and the female hybrids were not allowed to leave the compound for any reason other than hunting, but that was done for their own protection. Very few female babies were born to the purebloods, and they needed to be protected. At least that was the official explanation. But what if that wasn't true and they were being held against their will?

If that was the case, they probably couldn't tell anyone because Igor compelled them not to.

Jade was subjected to the same compulsion as everyone else in the compound, so she couldn't have told Emmett and Eleanor anything useful. Heck, she probably couldn't even tell them who she was, let alone give them information they could use against Igor or to free her.

However, Jade could have hinted at it by using Eleanor's method to circumvent compulsion. If she pretended to talk about something else, like dog poo symbolizing her predicament, then she could have communicated what she wanted to say, but only to someone who could understand the references she was making.

Sofia doubted that Jade knew how to do that. Before Eleanor had shown her the example, Sofia had never heard of anyone trying to get around Igor's compulsion by using unrelated stories. It was difficult to come up with something that conveyed the right meaning, and unless she emptied her mind and focused on the story, the compulsion still prevented her from saying anything that Igor had compelled her not to reveal.

Maybe with practice she would get better at it.

What she could do, though, was tell Marcel how sorry she was about deceiving and using him and convince him to forgive her.

Did it matter in the grand scheme of things?

Probably not.

Sofia had a feeling that she was never going to leave this bunker, and she was certainly never going to see her family and friends again or go back to the university.

Her life as she knew it was over.

Or worse.

MARCEL

*A*fter the tele-meeting with Kian, Marcel had stopped by the lab to take care of his grumpy team. He'd called each one into his office, muddled their memories of what they'd been working on, and had given them a half-assed excuse for why they were being sent on a vacation.

He wasn't sorry to see them leave. By now, he was familiar with their methods and could continue working on the project by himself until Kian decided that it was safe to bring them back. The question was whether he was safe with the knowledge.

Perhaps he should start wearing earplugs from now on.

After he was done with the team, he accompanied them to the dining room and collected two takeout boxes to take with him to the bunker. It wasn't the romantic meal he'd had in mind this morning, but he needed to feed Sofia, and they needed to talk.

The problem was that she couldn't tell him anything about her past or what had brought her to Safe Haven, or whether she'd felt something for him or had just used him to get to Emmett.

It didn't make sense given how hard he'd had to work to

get her to forgive him and give him another chance, but he'd been manipulated by a woman before, so he didn't trust his judgment.

He sucked at social interactions, romantic and otherwise, and he didn't understand the dynamics, and that was why he was such an easy victim in the hands of a skillful manipulator.

Down in the bunker, he found the key to Sofia's room dangling from a string tied to the handle. Eleanor had checked on her about an hour ago and reported that Sofia had fallen asleep.

Was she still sleeping?

It was quiet on the other side of the door, but then why wouldn't it be? There was no television in the room, and Sofia had no one to talk to.

She probably missed her talkative roommate.

When Eleanor had collected Sofia's things from her room earlier, Roxana had looked suspicious and had asked her a lot of questions. The story Eleanor had come up with was that Sofia had been invited to participate in a secret project and might not be back before the end of the retreat.

Tucking the takeout boxes under his arm, Marcel untied the string from the handle, unlocked the door, and pushed it open.

It was dark in the room, but the light from the hallway was enough for him to see the outline of Sofia's body under the thin blanket, and the fetal position she'd fallen asleep in tugged on his heartstrings.

When he walked into the room, put the boxes on the coffee table, and closed the door behind him, Sofia didn't move, but he could hear the change in her breathing and her heartbeat, and both indicated that she was no longer asleep.

"I know that you're awake." He walked over to the bed and sat on it. "I brought dinner. Do you want to get up and eat with me?"

She turned her head and opened her eyes. "Do you still want to spend time with me after what I've done?"

"I don't know yet what exactly you've done and why, but until we can find someone strong enough to override the compulsion you're under, I'm willing to give you the benefit of the doubt."

She turned on her back and pushed up against the pillows. "How do you know about compulsion? And how come Emmett and Eleanor can do it? Most people are not aware that it exists. All they know about is hypnosis."

"I think you know the answer to that. Your compeller is not the only one of his kind."

He didn't know how much he should reveal to her. She seemed to be susceptible to thralling, but she could have faked that to throw him off.

"You are not like that." She seemed to be searching for words. "You are blond. Emmett and Eleanor are not."

The Kra-ell were dark haired, and their skin was olive-toned. Was that what she was trying to tell him?

"People come in many shades, and appearances can be misleading."

"My father is blond." Her eyes pled with him to understand.

"You real father, I assume."

She nodded.

"So, your mother is the one with the dark coloring."

She nodded again.

Was she trying to tell him that her father was human, and her mother was a Kra-ell hybrid?

Perhaps he could force a thrall past the compulsion and peek into her mind?

Did he dare to do that?

Not really. The wall in her mind was strong, and to push through that would require brute force. He might cause her irreparable damage, and still not break through. He cared too much about her to risk it.

Kian had texted Leon and him Kalugal's phone number, so he could call him when Sofia was awake. Perhaps that would unlock her mind, but Marcel doubted it would. Kalugal was a powerful compeller, but they were dealing with someone of Annani and Toven's caliber.

Could a god be the leader of the Kra-ell who were holding Jade?

That would be one hell of a surprise, but he doubted Sofia would know that even if they managed to override the compulsion she was under.

"I get it. You don't get along with your mother, who is the different one, but you have a good relationship with your father. You lied about his strictness and the fight you had with him before coming here to trick Emmett into calling the man who pretended to be your father."

She nodded.

Marcel sighed and pushed to his feet. "We can keep this up for hours, but you need to eat." He offered her a hand up.

As she took it, and the blanket fell off, his breath caught in his throat. Sofia was wearing a tiny T-shirt that was so worn out that he could see the color of her nipples, not only their outline, and the pair of simple white panties she had on made her rounded bottom and incredibly long legs look delectable.

Sofia smiled. "I'm glad that you still find me attractive. I thought that you had lost interest."

"I wish I had," he admitted. "But you are not an easy woman to get over. I might be a sucker for punishment, but I pray that once the compulsion is overridden, what I learn will vindicate you."

"It will." She put her hand on his chest and looked into his eyes. "I used you, and I'm so sorry for that, but I had no choice. I was used too. I want you to know that my feelings for you are real, and I hope against hope that this is not the end of us." She lowered her eyes. "Or me," she whispered.

Marcel wanted to believe her, he wanted that so much that he was suffocating with the need, but he'd been fooled before, and he would never allow himself to be fooled again.

"We shall see. What I can promise you is that you don't need to fear for your life, and that I will keep an open mind. But I can't promise you that we can pick up from where we left off."

She nodded. "Thank you. That's more than I hoped for."

COMING UP NEXT
The Children of the Gods Book 66
DARK GAMBIT
The Play

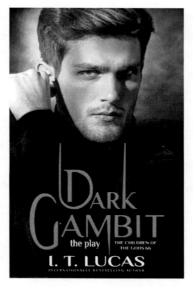

To read the first 3 chapters JOIN the VIP club at
ITLUCAS.COM —To find out what's included in your free
membership, click HERE or flip to the last page.

To get to Safe Haven's inner circle, the Kra-ell leader
sacrifices a pawn. He does not expect her to reach the final
rank and promote to a queen.

Dear reader,

Thank you for reading the ***Children of the Gods***.

As an independent author, I rely on your support to
spread the word. So if you enjoyed the story, please share

your experience with others, and if it isn't too much trouble, I would greatly appreciate a brief review on Amazon.

Love & happy reading,

Isabell

FOR EXCLUSIVE PEEKS AT UPCOMING RELEASES & A FREE COMPANION BOOK

J OIN MY *VIP C LUB* AND GAIN ACCESS TO THE VIP PORTAL AT
ITLUCAS.COM
CLICK HERE TO JOIN

I NCLUDED IN YOUR FREE MEMBERSHIP :

- FREE C HILDREN OF THE G ODS COMPANION BOOK 1
  (INCLUDES PART 1 OF GODDESS'S C HOICE)
- FREE NARRATION OF G ODDESS'S C HOICE —B OOK 1
  IN T HE C HILDREN OF THE G ODS O RIGINS SERIES .
- P REVIEW CHAPTERS OF UPCOMING RELEASES .
- A ND OTHER EXCLUSIVE CONTENT OFFERED ONLY TO
  MY VIP S .

If you're already a subscriber, you'll receive a download link for my next book's preview chapters in the new release announcement email. If you are not getting my emails, your provider is sending them to your junk folder, and you are missing out on **important updates, side characters' portraits, additional content, and other goodies.** To fix that, add isabell@itlucas.com to your email contacts or your email VIP list.

Made in United States
North Haven, CT
31 August 2023

40988456R00180